GW00818385

a spoke
in the
wheel

A Spoke in the Wheel

Kathleen Jowitt

2018

A Spoke In The Wheel

Published by Kathleen Jowitt

Copyright © 2018 Kathleen Jowitt

Cover design and photographs by Kathleen Jowitt.

All rights reserved. This book or any portion thereof may not be reproduced or used in any manner whatsoever without the express written permission of the author, except for the use of brief quotations in a book review or scholarly journal.

This book is a work of fiction and any resemblance to any real person living or dead, or any real organisation, is entirely coincidental.

First Printing: 2018

Printed in 11-point Palatino Linotype

ISBN 978-0-9935339-2-1

www.kathleenjowitt.com

Acknowledgements

I am, as ever, extremely grateful for the encouragement and enthusiasm of friends offline and online. I should particularly like to thank Katherine Last and Anne Norton for their expert advice, and Sam Hill, Nicola Janke and Kieran Pearson for their comments on the manuscript at various stages in its development. And, of course, all the cyclists and cycling fans in my life for their advice, support, and company. Particularly Tony Evershed. Any errors or infelicities that remain are attributable to my own stubbornness.

Chapter 1

The first thing I saw was the wheelchair.

The first thing she saw was the doper.

If you're thinking that I'm the one who comes off looking like a dick, I couldn't disagree with you. Not that this occurred to me at the time. I mean, I was regretting plastering on my shit-eating wheelchair-user-greeting grin, but that was only because I knew I'd been recognised. I might have got away with it otherwise.

If I hadn't caught her eye. If she hadn't been a cycling fan. If I hadn't gone onto autopilot and behaved as if I was doing some charity event for disabled kids.

I used to do a lot of that, having been a disabled kid myself once. There are still pictures floating around: seven year old Ben Goddard, with brave gap-toothed grin and gleaming wheelchair, next to Ben now – or, at least, Ben last month.

And the girl in the wheelchair in the café in this run-down seaside town was impressed by none of it. She met my eye, wearing a cold, blank expression that I supposed I'd have to get used to, exchanged a glance with her friend, and then looked down at a magazine on the table. I was pretty sure that it was *Cycling Monthly*, which was unfortunate if I was right. There was a five-page feature on great British hopes, and I was great British hope number seven.

Well, not any more, I wasn't. I'd dropped off the list, not just of great British hopes, but of ordinary decent people you'd want to pass the time of day with. My unfortunate little EPO habit had been exposed, and any self-respecting cycling fan would be perfectly entitled to give me the sort of look that I'd got from this girl.

And apparently I wasn't going to escape the cycling scene, however far I thought I was running away from it. Apparently I was always going to be Ben Goddard, doper, has-been, disgrace.

I thought about leaving. I told myself that it was very bad luck that the first place I'd walked into had contained someone who recognised me. After all, most people don't. Remove the Lycras, helmet and sunglasses, and a cyclist looks like anyone else. Joe Public could pick Bradley Wiggins and Mark Cavendish out of a line-up, but the rest of us are unrecognisable. I was just a white guy in his twenties, a bit skinnier than average, and I'd be safe in the next place, probably.

But I wanted coffee. And I wanted it now. That was one element of the cycling life that I didn't know how to give up. And why should I deprive myself of my recommended daily allowance of caffeine just because some opinionated bitch was glowering at me? I bought my coffee, and sat in the murkiest corner of the shop under a picture of a dilapidated Italian hill town in shades of cow-pat, and glowered back. Except I didn't glower at her; I just glowered at the world in general. She got in the way occasionally, that was all.

I couldn't hear what the two of them were talking about. I couldn't even be sure they knew who I was; but when the girl in the wheelchair went off to the toilet, her friend (who'd got up to hold the door open, but otherwise left her to it) came over to me.

'Excuse me,' she said, 'but you're Ben Goddard, aren't you?'

This woman seemed like she'd be more likely to approve of my being Ben Goddard, so I admitted to it. 'I am.'

'Would you – would you mind signing my magazine?'

This was really not how I'd imagined my new, non-cycling, life starting out, but a friendly face was a friendly face. And hers was friendly, and quite pretty, too, in a freckly, red-haired, snub-nosed kind of way. 'Sure,' I said. I scrawled my name on the front cover, right across the Union Jack held aloft by the women's pursuit team, who would no doubt be horrified to be associated with me like this. With that in mind, I added the date. 'There,' I said. 'It's a collector's item now.'

She looked quizzical. 'First thing you've signed since the news broke?'

'And the last,' I said firmly. 'Should I put your name on it?'

'Why not? Vicki. With a C K I.'

'And your friend?'

She laughed. 'Better not. Polly's got principles.'

Ouch, I thought.

Then Polly herself reappeared, giving me a dirty look in passing, and Vicki got up in a hurry, and didn't speak to me again. But she winked at me as they left.

I waited for the door to close behind them before sighing with relief and returning to my coffee. It was not amazing coffee, but I supposed that was something else I'd have to get used to. A discerning palate was a luxury that I could no longer afford. I considered the items I'd collected that morning. A copy of the local paper. The cheapest smartphone I'd been able to find. A pen; a notebook with some useful addresses – the Jobcentre, some lettings agents – copied into it. It didn't seem like much to show for this alleged new life of mine. I could barely feel the weight in my bag as I traipsed back to the dingy bed and breakfast I'd booked myself into yesterday. The icy January sea breeze should have refreshed me a bit, but it didn't; it blew straight into my face and just felt like yet another thing to make life difficult.

Still, it was warmer than my landlady's Arctic glare, the one she gave me when I slunk in. I muttered 'Good morning,' and then realised it wasn't morning any more. I'd have to get some lunch, but I couldn't face going out again, not just yet, so I trudged up the narrow stairs to my room, instead, and lay down on the bed without taking my trainers off. It couldn't make the covers any nastier than they already were, and anyway, what was the point?

I stared at the cracked plaster of the ceiling and thought about my options. Part of me wanted to pack up and leave. Meeting those two girls had to be a bad omen, that part of me said, and I should get out before worse happened. I'd been in town five minutes. I had nothing to keep me here. No home, no job, no friends. I'd only be throwing away the cost of a train ticket and two nights in this dive; it wasn't a high price to pay for another jab at the reboot button. I'd been unlucky, that was all it was.

But there was another voice that said: *you're going to have to get used to this, you know. If two people recognised you in this little town, what do you think it'll be like in a big city? Do you really want to quit so soon into this?*

Besides, it added, while I was thinking about the word "quit", *you don't believe in omens.*

Except of course I did. I was as superstitious as any man in the peloton. I used to throw spilt salt over my left shoulder, stroke black cats for luck, turn my race number upside down if I was allocated 13, just like anyone else. Look at how I'd ended up here, for God's sake. I'd stuck a literal pin in a literal map. (It had landed in the sea, but that was neither here nor there. This was the nearest bit of dry land.)

I was a quitter. Of course I was. If I weren't, I'd have taken whatever ban they handed out to me and badgered my team into keeping my contract open while I retreated to Majorca to keep up with my training and wait out the term in penitential fortitude. Instead, I'd flounced (there was no other word for it) into my team principal's black glass living room and announced that I was quitting the team, that I was quitting professional sport, and that I was quitting cycling altogether.

Henri had raised an eyebrow and carried on eating crisps. I suspect, with the benefit of hindsight and a cool head, that my act had solved more problems for him than it had caused. I'd only got in this mess because I was shit-scared he wouldn't renew me beyond next year. Now he had an excuse not to. At one stroke I'd turned myself from a liability into a scapegoat.

I'd like to say that at least I felt better for it, but actually I didn't. The hot mess of shame and anger was still boiling away inside me, and now there was the embarrassed consciousness of having behaved like an idiot. More of an idiot than I already was, I mean. It felt like I'd let him win.

For the thousandth time, I reconsidered my options – the options I'd had at the time, and the options I had now.

I could have dropped Henri in it. Or could I? It's difficult to work out the share of blame. I know that what I did was one hundred per cent wrong. And I knew that when I was doing it. But does that necessarily mean that everyone else was one hundred per cent right?

I called to mind those little hints that perhaps I should talk to Dr Wolfsen; that ultimatum, that if I didn't match Caprini's performance I didn't have a future in the team... But Henri had never said it in so many words: *There's always EPO, you know.* He'd left that kind of thing to Dr Wolfsen. So much for Henri: he could maintain plausible deniability, could claim he'd just been acting out of concern for my health, had no idea I'd take it *that* way. Dr Wolfsen: I could finger *him* – except somebody else would probably have done it by now, if it was possible. Mélanie, disposing of the evidence, and knowing what she was doing, and hating it. (Not as much as I did, I thought.) Caprini... (But perhaps he really was that much better than me...) I had no hard evidence. I'd just be another rumour on top of all the other rumours, and I couldn't afford to get sued by Henri, the way Leclos had.

OK, nobody could afford to get sued by Henri, but I couldn't afford much else, either. I wasn't quite stony broke, but I needed to get a job fast.

And that job wasn't going to be in cycling. I'd meant what I said to Henri. I was done with cycling forever. I'd left that world and I was going to start a new life doing something completely different. Where nobody knew me. Where nobody knew what I'd done.

Except for Vicki, with a C K I. And Polly, who had principles.

I didn't really care what job I got, so long as it wasn't in cycling. Chicken processing factory, sewage treatment plant: why not? And no, it didn't have to be here. I didn't have to worry about things like pins in maps any more.

Except... Say I went to Manchester, for example, started all this again. Or Leeds. Or Brighton, or Penzance. It didn't matter where: sooner or later there'd be a cycling fan. And it might not be on day one. It might be a month into a new job. It might be two years in. I might have met somebody. I might have got married, had kids, even, before somebody said, 'Excuse me – are you Ben Goddard?'

If that happened, would I up sticks and move on?

No. And even if that never happened, I'd always be waiting for the other shoe to drop. In fact, if I got a job – and I had to get a job – I'd have to drop it myself, or find some other way to explain a six year hole in my CV. I might as well wait for it here.

I sat up, reached for the newspaper and turned to the *Situations Vacant*.

Chapter 2

The next time I saw Vicki she was alone. It was Saturday morning again, and I'd allowed myself to go into town for a coffee to celebrate the fact that I'd got a job. Two jobs. Warehouse Operative at Benson's Foam Rubber, starting Monday morning; and waitering at the Grand Hotel on the seafront, starting Monday evening. Between the two of them, I figured, I could just about make ends meet, so long as I got enough shifts.

It was in the same café at the same time, and I suppose I should have avoided it if I hadn't wanted to run into one of the two women in the North West who knew who I was. But I had to admit that I was pleased to see Vicki, even if she did know of my shameful doping past. In fact, it was quite nice not to have to explain it to her, the way I'd had to explain it to two recruiting managers over the past two days.

'You're back!' she said, when she came in. It didn't seem like it was a horrible surprise to her, either.

'I am,' I admitted. 'Would you care to join me?'

She blushed and smiled. 'Why not?' She dumped a couple of empty pannier bags under the table at my feet and went off to buy her coffee.

'No Polly?' I said when she came back.

Vicki said, cautiously, 'Bad day. She's still in bed.'

'Oh,' I said. 'Is that... normal?'

Vicki raised her eyebrows. 'For her, yes. For me, sometimes, too.'

I smiled. I wasn't exactly a lark myself, not by nature, though years of dawn training rides had got me acquainted with the darker end of the morning. 'Now you come to mention it, it's fairly normal for me, these days. Whatever normal means.'

Vicki said, ironically, 'You sound like Prince Charles talking about Princess Diana.'

I laughed. 'What happened to her?'

She raised her eyebrows again. 'Princess Diana? The Queen arranged for her to be removed, obviously... Nah, it was just a car crash.'

'No, Polly.' It occurred to me that this perhaps wasn't the most polite question to have asked, but it was too late now.

Vicki frowned slightly. 'She got flu,' she said. 'She got flu over Christmas in her third year at uni, and she never got better.'

'Wow,' I said. 'But hasn't she...?' I realised as I spoke that I had no idea how to finish the sentence. I had no idea what might cure permanent flu. I just felt, extrapolating from my own experience of illness, that there should be something that would make her better, that somebody, somewhere, must be able to do something.

'She has,' Vicki said. 'Whatever you're about to say, it's either yes, she's tried it, and it didn't work, or no, because she can't afford it and also it's probably snake oil.'

'Oh,' I said. 'Fair enough, then.'

There was a little awkward pause before Vicki said, 'So how's life as a person who doesn't sign stuff any more?'

'Pretty good,' I said. 'I've found a job – well, two jobs – and I'm beginning to feel like there might be light at the end of the tunnel. I just need somewhere to live, now.'

'Hm.' Her eyes narrowed. 'Where are you living at the moment?'

'A grim B and B up beyond the golf course. I'd prefer to get out of there before my savings run out.'

'That seems reasonable enough.'

We were just about managing to drag this back to something resembling casual conversation. 'How about you? What are you doing in town this morning?'

Vicki was smiling with something that might have been relief. 'Much the same thing, actually. Going round the lettings agents looking for somewhere more manageable.' She paused for breath. 'I'd say you should come with me, except we'd waste so much time explaining that yes, we're looking for two properties, and no, we're not a couple, that I'm not sure it'd be worth it. Um. Because we'd be a woman and a man together, I mean. People are very ready to jump to the obvious conclusion. Not that it would be as obvious as all that, but if they didn't know who you were...'

If they did knew who I was, I thought, they probably wouldn't be very keen on renting a flat to me. 'Pity,' I said. 'I have no idea how to go about any of this real life stuff.' The fact that two separate people had been brave enough to give me a job – and hadn't rescinded the offer the moment I'd mentioned the whole doping thing – had seemed like a miracle. I didn't know how many more miracles I was due. 'So do you live with Polly? Why are you moving?'

'Yes, and our current flat is hopeless,' She shook her head. 'It has three steps to the front door, and it's the wrong side of the main road, which means that I have to cycle round this hideous roundabout every morning. And the blokes upstairs are racist arseholes, so I worry about Polly all day, and she worries about me.'

'That sounds less than ideal,' I said. 'Why on earth did you move in there in the first place?'

She chuckled grimly. 'It was cheap.'

'Ah.'

Vicki took a handful of sugar packets from the pot on the table and arranged them into a hexagon. 'I'm not hopeful of finding anything better, if I'm honest. If there were three of us, it'd be a different matter. The rent on a three-bedroom house divided by three works out a lot cheaper than a two-bedroom flat divided by two.'

'Oh?' I did my best to sound non-committal. I wasn't sure if the obvious answer had occurred to her in the same moment that it had occurred to me.

'I suppose I could pick up details on three-bedroom places and look for another lodger.' She looked hard at me, and she was blushing a bit. I reckoned she was definitely testing the water.

But if she was going to be vague then so was I. 'Wouldn't it be a bit weird, living with someone you'd met, like, twice?'

'I'd have to talk to Polly about that, obviously. She might not feel comfortable about... sharing with a guy, for example. But the advantage of living with strangers is that if it doesn't work out you never have to see them again.' She grinned. It was weird, I thought: she knew exactly who I was and what I'd done and yet she was treating me like a normal human being. I could get used to this. Which would probably be a bad idea.

I took a deep breath. 'In that case, do you mind if I follow you round the agents after all? I'll look for one bedroom places. Just in case, you understand.'

She smiled slowly. 'I think we understand each other very well.'

We finished our drinks and left. Vicki led the way to where she'd locked up her bike. 'I need to do some shopping, too,' she explained, 'and it's just occurred to me that it would be a good idea to have the bike outside the shop.' She clipped the pannier bags onto the rack.

It wasn't at all the sort of bike that I'd imagined she'd own: it was the sort of bulky steel-framed monster you see in the Netherlands, or Oxford and Cambridge, with a purple paint job, and a wicker basket on the front handlebars. I'd assumed, from Vicki's wiry build and her obvious interest in the professional sport, that she'd have a dainty carbon model.

As I followed her down the street, I said, 'You said you cycle to work? How far is that?'

'Fifteen miles each way, more or less. Don't worry: I don't do it on this.' She patted the saddle affectionately.

I laughed. 'I'd be in awe if you did.'

'It'd be nothing compared to what they did in the old days of the Tour de France.'

'Yes, well,' I said, 'that's the kind of bike you probably *could* weld together at a roadside blacksmith's.'

'And get disqualified for having a kid pump the bellows.' Clearly we both knew the story – but then is there a cycling fan anywhere in the world who doesn't? 'Anyway,' she said, 'I don't think we'll be seeing a Grand Départ round here so time soon after Yorkshire got it.'

'I wouldn't be here if I thought we were going to,' I said. 'Not worth the risk.'

She whistled lightly. 'You're serious about this disappearing thing, aren't you?'

'I can't go back, so it's better to get away from it completely,' I said, while she locked her bike up again outside the supermarket.

She darted a sharp glance at me. 'And we ruined your plans. I'm sorry.'

'Don't worry about it,' I said.

No, I couldn't go back.

People do. They sit out the twelve months or two years of their ban, and then they go back. Some are contrite, reclaiming their place in the peloton with vocal repentance and a reformer's zeal. Some act as if nothing ever happened, and seem to expect the rest of the world to pretend to have equally short memories. Some protest their innocence beyond all reason and keep up the act until they've lost all respect and credibility.

They're all of them braver than I am.

Disappearing, Vicki had called it. She wasn't far wrong. I couldn't face being Ben Goddard the cyclist, Ben Goddard the doper, any more, so he was just going to have to stop existing. Meanwhile, Ben Goddard – the who? – the what? – still needed money, still had to eat and sleep. Enter Ben Goddard the waiter, Ben Goddard the warehouse operative.

Could the new Ben Goddard live with people who knew about the old one? When we went into the estate agent's, I asked for details of one-bedroom properties, just in case it turned out that he couldn't. I was a stuttering wreck. I imagined that the friendly young blonde in the blue suit and the name badge saying *Rhiannon* could see through my garbled explanations to my ruined reputation; I blushed when I had to give my parents' home in Stourbridge as my address. Vicki, by comparison, was cool and confident, explaining that she was interested in both two- and three-bedroom properties (but they had to be south of the main road and wheelchair-accessible) as if it had never even occurred to her that Rhiannon might be speculating about our love lives. Was everyone like this in the real world? Or was it just Vicki?

'What *is* your job?' I asked, when we came out of the estate agent's.

Vicki tucked the papers into her handbag. 'I work for a homeless charity in Lingholme,' she said.

'And Polly?'

'Was going to be a doctor, before she got ill. I try to take it as an awful warning not to overdo things. But it's difficult.'

'I don't think she likes me much,' I said.

'She's never even spoken to you!' Vicki was indignant.

I nodded. 'That's why I don't think she likes me very much.'

'Well, I'll find out and let you know,' she promised. 'When do you start your new job? Jobs, rather?'

'Tomorrow.' It felt unreal, as if it was going to happen to somebody else.

She smiled. 'Good luck.'

'Thanks. So, you're going to talk to Polly about...'

'The housing situation. Yes. Let me have your phone number and I'll let you know.' She got her phone out. I got mine out, too, and read my new number out to her. I hadn't memorised it yet.

'So,' I said, when we'd double-checked and saved both of them. 'Let me know, whenever.'

'I will do. See you, then.' She turned away from me to go into the supermarket.

I didn't expect to see her again, or even hear from her. At most, I thought there'd be a text saying *Sorry, Polly isn't up for it.* The further I got through the week, the more sure I became that nothing was going to happen. And it wasn't as if I didn't have other things to think about, with two new jobs and two new teams to get to know, and two separate sets of tasks, health and safety procedures, and chains of command to memorise. I decided that I was on my own, and promised myself that I'd look at Gumtree and go through the small ads again.

But on the Thursday evening, just as I was changing out of my overalls before leaving the warehouse, Vicki rang me.

'Ben! Sorry I haven't called before.'

'Oh, don't worry,' I said. I didn't tell her that I was surprised she'd called at all. 'How's things?'

'Good, thanks. Good. Are you free tomorrow night?'

I ran through my shifts in my head. 'After about six thirty, yes.'

'Great. Still interested in a house-share?'

'Definitely,' I said, trying to keep it cool, and probably failing.

'OK. Polly wants to talk to you in person before she says yes or no.' Her tone was apologetic. 'If you can get to the Nag's Head on Berwick Street for about eight o'clock, we can, well, go through everything.'

'Hang on a moment.' I found a ballpoint pen in my pocket and wrote *Nags Hd Berwick St 8pm* on my left arm. I'd look up Berwick Street later. 'That's fine. Looking forward to it.' Though I wasn't entirely sure I was looking forward to *going through everything.*

'Great,' Vicki said again. 'See you there!'

I knew I'd made a bad impression on Polly before I'd even spoken to her. What was more, I could see her point, and I didn't want to admit it to myself. And I was beginning to get a little bit desperate. I'd looked at the listings for every single one-bedroom flat, studio apartment, and bedsit in the town, and I couldn't reliably afford any of them. Not for more than a couple of months of topping up my wages with my savings. I really wanted this to work, and I really didn't think it was going to.

What was the alternative? Going home. I couldn't do that. Home was full of people who knew me. Home was where my parents were, and, while they'd have to take me in, I didn't like the person I was when I was there. I wanted to get out. I wanted to rebuild my life – without using the designs from the old one. This seemed like the best shot I was going to get, and I had a horrible feeling that I'd already blown it.

The introductions were awkward, though Vicki performed them with a bullet-proof grace that suggested that *she* didn't much care whether we found them awkward or not. I couldn't think of anything to say to Polly, who wasn't any less intimidating seen up close than she'd been from a distance. She had a determined chin and heavy eyebrows. Her hair was clipped close to her head, and all in all she gave the impression of being someone you didn't want to mess with. And she was still wearing that expression that I supposed the whole world of cycling put on when it thought of me and my kind. Polly might not have looked much like the stereotypical cycling fan, but her look of disdain was definitely representative.

Nor did it help that the Nag's Head was very loud and very crowded. A band was doing its sound checks at the far end of the bar and around us the conversation was rising in pitch and volume to compensate. The rest of the clientèle averaged a good three decades older than any of us, and was divided almost equally between noisy fans of the band and regulars who resented, just as vocally, the presence of the interlopers. A game of darts was going on just behind Vicki, and people kept bashing into Polly's wheelchair on their way to the bar. I'd have suggested moving, but there was nowhere to move to. The girls had done well to bag this table.

'Vicki says you've given up cycling,' Polly said to me.

'Permanently,' I agreed, hoping that was the right answer.

'And you want to live with us.' Her expression didn't change.

I shrugged my shoulders. 'I've got to live with somebody.'

'So have we.' She didn't seem to like the idea much. 'So if you're stopping cycling permanently, what are you going to do instead?'

'Right now, or long-term?' I didn't wait for an answer. 'Right now, I'm waitering at the Grand, and throwing foam rubber around at Benson's warehouse on the industrial estate. Long-term, I'll see where that takes me. I just want a normal life, really.'

'Don't we all,' said Polly. The words *I want doesn't get* hovered in the air.

Vicki coughed. 'So how do we all feel about a normal life in the same house?'

Polly's face gave nothing away.

'It would work for me,' I said.

'I meant to ask,' Vicki said apologetically, 'what sort of contract you're on. It may make a difference.'

'Zero hours. I'm sorry.'

I must have looked worried, because Vicki laughed. 'I'll probably have to get my parents to stand guarantor, in that case.'

Polly looked as if she wanted to protest, but she didn't.

I asked, 'Will they mind?'

'Only if they end up having to pay. Which they won't. They did it before, for the last place. We didn't have much in the way of income at that point, but we had pride, and savings. And then Polly got her benefits sorted out. My dad's quite scary when he wants to be,' she added as an afterthought.

Rather than go into the scariness of Vicki's dad, I said, 'The last place?'

'Carlton Crescent. The other side of town.'

'How did you end up here?' I asked, curious. 'Why not Manchester, or Liverpool – one of the big cities? Wouldn't it be easier?'

'I was born here,' Vicki said, 'and moving back made sense at the time.' She grimaced. 'Now – not so much, but here we are, and I'm not sure I can face relocating.'

'You'd need a crowbar to prise me away from Dr Luchmun,' Polly agreed.

'OK,' I said.

We seemed to have reached an impasse, and I wasn't quite sure how. Nor could I see how to get out of it. We all sat there without speaking for several uncomfortable seconds.

'Excuse me a minute,' Polly said at last. She half-turned, reaching to get something out of the bag that was slung over the handles of her wheelchair. A folding walking stick.

And she got up out of her wheelchair. Then she saw me staring, and sat down again. 'What?'

I wasn't sure whether I felt more confused or more angry. 'I, er, I was surprised you were getting up.'

'Whoop-de-do, it's a miracle.' She smiled tightly. 'Actually, the vast majority of wheelchair users can walk, at least in theory. It's just bloody knackering, or painful, or both. However, in cases like the Nag's Head, where the only disabled toilet is down a frankly terrifying ramp the wrong side of the band it's marginally less knackering to walk to the ladies'. Which is just behind us.'

'Oh,' I said, feeling stupid.

Polly stomped off to the toilet and Vicki sniggered into the menu. I wondered to myself if Polly was entirely wise to get out of the wheelchair in public. Not everybody would have waited for the explanation. 'Why do you come here, then, if it's so inconvenient?' I asked Vicki.

She answered with a speed that suggested that she hadn't been all that interested in the food. 'Because everywhere else is either a very long way away, and we can't afford taxis that often, or is a place you wouldn't particularly want to be female.'

'Oh,' I said again. Put like that, it sounded pretty bleak.

'If we move, that might solve the first problem, and if you move in with us, that should sort out the second. Assuming you'd want to share your social life with us, that is.' It was impressive, the way she continued to imply that this was going to be in any way my decision. I knew, and Vicki must have known, that it was going to come down to Polly.

'I don't really have a social life to share,' I said. It was true, more or less. The lads at the warehouse had gone down the pub the day before, and I went with them, but I had been so terrified of giving myself away that I didn't dare drink. They probably thought I was a recovering alcoholic. It was a relief to go out with these two, who already knew the worst. Even if I couldn't stop offending Polly. 'I wouldn't mind sharing yours. If Polly can put up with me being an idiot.'

'Beggars can't be choosers,' Polly said over my shoulder. She flopped back into her wheelchair and I had to admit that yes, she did look a bit whacked.

But *beggars can't be choosers* went both ways, I thought. Was I prepared to face this kind of hostility every day? Then again, it was only what I deserved. I shrugged.

'You've made some fairly serious life changes,' Vicki remarked. 'Personally, I'm inclined to take it on trust.'

Polly frowned. 'We barely know you,' she said, looking at Vicki though she was talking to me. 'And what we *do* know of you isn't encouraging.'

Vicki glanced back at her, then turned to me. 'Could you give us a minute?'

'Sure,' I said. 'Can I get you two another drink while I'm at the bar?'

'Red wine, please,' Vicki said, just as Polly said, 'No, thank you.' I raised my eyebrows and she said, 'Well, a ginger beer, then.'

They started whispering as soon as they thought I was out of earshot. I looked back over my shoulder and called, 'I do know how to use a washing machine, by the way. Just in case you were worrying about that.'

'I should bloody well hope so,' Vicki called back. 'And we weren't.'

I got myself a pint of lager and sipped it thoughtfully while I waited. It was hardly the end of the world if the girls didn't want to live with me, I told myself. Something else would come up. There must be some other people looking for a house share. Or I'd make the sums add up and rent a place on my own. Of course it would be OK.

All the same, I was very relieved when Vicki called me over, and that she was smiling when she did.

Chapter 3

We fixed some basic principles. When to move. ('As soon as possible.') Where. (Within walking distance of the seafront, the industrial estate, and the railway station. Near a bus route. North of the main road. Still in Dr Luchmun's catchment area.) How we would split rent and bills. (So that mine worked out at approximately one third. 'Polly will make a spreadsheet,' Vicki said confidently.) What sort of layout we needed. (A bedroom for each of us, and somewhere to keep Vicki's bikes.) Who was going to be in charge. (Polly. But Vicki would do the legwork. I didn't object; it would save me a huge amount of trouble.) In fact, I just let the two of them get on with it. I was amazed at how easy this 'new leaf' thing was turning out to be.

I stopped thinking that once we got stuck into it. It became obvious very quickly that we would indeed need a guarantor. Viewings were tedious. Because Polly got tired so easily, and none of us had access to a car, we couldn't do more than one a day, and my shifts were so unpredictable that I wasn't always free when I'd thought I was going to be. Eventually, Vicki took a week's leave to sort it all out.

They ended up going for a house I hadn't been able to look at, though when we did move in – less than a fortnight later – I had no complaints. 14 Meadow Close was a three-bedroom semi-detached house on a cul-de-sac about half an hour's walk from the town centre. Upstairs there were two bedrooms and a bathroom; downstairs, the third bedroom, kitchen and living room. Out the back there was a square of muddy lawn, which Vicki said she'd mow, and a precarious shed. If you stood on tiptoe you could see over the back fence and down into the nature reserve behind. The décor was dated, and the whole house was a bit cramped – though I didn't mind that; it wasn't as if I'd got much stuff to put in it. Polly said, grudgingly, that it felt positively spacious compared to their previous flat, with the bikes banished to the shed and a clear run from the front path to her bedroom – she had claimed the one on the ground floor, for obvious reasons. 'Doors I can fit the chair through, too.'

I was less fussy. I had to be. I was just glad to be out of the Sea View. Things were looking up. I had a job – two jobs, in fact. I had a place to live. I just had to work out how to live with these two.

Polly hired a man with a van to move everything out of their flat and into our new house. In my case, it took approximately ten minutes to carry my two suitcases upstairs to my room and arrange their contents in logical heaps around the edge – so I spent most of the day helping to get the girls' furniture and belongings into the appropriate rooms. Vicki's law textbooks and Beryl Burton memorabilia, Polly's – well, Polly's *everything*; there was very little that she could carry herself.

'I'm not going to feel guilty about it,' she said defensively. 'I paid for the mover – and I'm getting the chips. What are you going to sleep on, Ben?'

'Um,' I said. The problem had occurred to me earlier, of course, when I'd claimed my room, but I'd filed it away to deal with later. 'The floor, tonight. I'll order a bed tomorrow, and get it delivered.'

'There's an airbed,' she said. 'Ask Vicki what's happened to it. You can't sleep on the floor.'

I was going to thank her, but she'd wheeled away to supervise proceedings in the kitchen.

'Getting the chips' turned out to mean 'giving Vicki a twenty-pound note and sending her off on the bike'. Which worked for me, and Vicki didn't seem to mind. She took the one I'd seen her with before, which left me free to take a professional – or ex-professional – interest in her road bike. For all that I'd sworn that I never wanted to look at another bicycle, some habitual curiosity lingered.

'Not at all what you're used to, I'm sure, Ben,' Vicki said as she chucked her handbag into the basket of the other one and turned her lights on. She pedalled off into the darkness before I could pass a verdict. It was a harmless enough machine, a mid-range carbon frame with decent wheels. It would have been too small for me, of course; Vicki was a good few inches shorter than I was, and I couldn't see her settling for a bike that didn't fit properly. I tried the brakes, which were firm and responsive, and the tyres, which were rock-hard. A discreet transfer on the down tube indicated that Vicki was a member of the Coastal Cycling Club. She evidently took it seriously. I suspected that she took most things seriously.

Me, I was seriously grateful to have a room to sleep in, even if it didn't have a bed in yet.

Chapter 4

I knew what the beeping meant: I had to move.

I had to move or I was going to die.

This had never happened to me before, but Dr Wolfsen had warned me often enough. My blood had thickened to a hyper-oxygenated gloop, my heart was slowing, and if I didn't get out of bed and onto a bike it would just *stop*.

I clutched at my chest, groping for the heart-rate monitor. I couldn't find it. It kept beeping. I didn't have *time*... I struggled out of bed, fighting the sheets, the mattress pitching and rolling beneath me. My bike would be there, ready on the rollers; I just had to get on and pedal until my blood thinned and my heart started working properly again.

The bike wasn't there. Surely I'd set it up last night.

I didn't know what to do. Had there been some mistake? Had Señora Garcia moved it for some obscure reason of her own? Was someone actually trying to kill me? I had to act fast.

It was then that I realised.

The beeping was my alarm.

I wasn't doped.

My heart was, if anything, beating rather faster than usual.

No wonder the bed felt weird. No wonder there wasn't a bike waiting for me.

Nothing was wrong. Nothing was wrong at all.

'Did you sleep OK?' Polly asked me when I saw her, later in the afternoon. She looked at me in a way that suggested she had a good reason for asking.

'I woke up with... a weird dream,' I admitted. 'I hope I didn't disturb you?'

She didn't answer that one. 'Were you *running*?'

'It was a very weird dream. I hope it won't happen again.'

That seemed to satisfy her: though who knows? Perhaps she was just glad to know that I found it difficult to sleep at night.

Even after that it took me ages to get round to actually buying a bed; I managed for the first few weeks with that airbed, and lived out of my suitcases like I had been before. I picked up the essentials bit by bit; but I really didn't see the point of fussing about objects. It wasn't as if I spent much time in the house.

My room at the bed and breakfast had always been too depressing for me to stay there for longer than it took me to sleep and dress, and once I found work I took on as many hours as I could. Nothing much changed when I moved in with Vicki and Polly. I didn't like admitting it to myself, but I was nervous around them. They were a unit; they'd worked out a way of living with each other. I felt like a spare part. I won't say that I treated the house like a hotel – I did my own cooking and cleaning, after all – but I spent very little waking time there.

My shifts were long; the work was hard – not difficult, once I'd got into the swing of it, but physically exhausting. I didn't complain. Work was what I needed. Both jobs kept me on my feet; both required me to keep my mind on the task in hand. I didn't want to dwell on the past; and these jobs wouldn't let me. Between the two of them, plus the walk home, I could wear myself out sufficiently to get to sleep without having to drink too much, or think too much.

Vicki's schedule was equally punishing. She'd told me about her commute, of course, but I hadn't realised what long hours she worked. Even when the warehouse had me on lates, I almost always beat her home. She spent her weekends on the bike – one or the other of them. The cycling club went out for a ride every Sunday; sometimes she did her own thing and headed inland until she found a climb with some teeth to it; and on Saturdays she pootled around town on her purple bike if she wasn't taking Polly somewhere.

Polly's illness kept her exhausted without any extra effort from her. She probably managed six hours more sleep every day than either Vicki or me, but it didn't seem to make much difference. She was always tired. She couldn't work, 'unless,' she said, 'you find an office without fluorescent lights that'll take me on for eight hours a week, no heavy lifting.'

Her social life, such as it was, centred around the church. I never quite worked out whether she was an actual believer or just went to get out of the house; either way, the church people were reasonably good at picking her up and driving her to the various events.

And that was where she'd met her boyfriend, too. I'd learned from Vicki that his name was Michael and that he did something in IT. Polly had yet to introduce him to me, but I was prepared to like him just from the simple fact that he got her out of the house and saved me from a few hours of her judgemental gaze.

Particularly on my birthday, which fell in the middle of February. Not that the girls knew that. So far as anyone here knew, this was just another day, and I wanted to keep it that way.

Of course, that didn't stop my parents calling. When I saw the landline number – I hadn't saved it as *home*, but of course it was burned into my own memory – flash up on the screen I almost regretted giving them my new mobile number.

As soon as I picked it up, I heard, 'Happy birthday, Ben!'

Well, I supposed that it was nice to hear it, really. Yes, I was glad that somebody had remembered. 'Hi, Mum,' I said. 'Thank you.'

'How are you? What are you planning to do to celebrate?'

'Oh, nothing special,' I said, keeping my voice down as I went to shut the door of my room. Vicki was still in the house, and I didn't want her to hear. I didn't see that there was much to celebrate. A quarter of a century gone, and what did I have to show for it?

'Nothing? Oh, that's a shame – you ought to do something to mark your twenty-fifth birthday! There were...' her voice became slightly muffled, '… there were moments when we didn't think... didn't think you'd get this far...'

'I know, Mum,' I muttered, embarrassed. 'I know.'

'Ben?' Dad must have taken the phone from her. 'Happy birthday!'

'Thanks,' I said. 'How are you?'

'Me? I'm fine. How are *you*? What's the news? Your mum's been worried, you know.'

'Yeah. Sorry. I'm OK. I've found some work and I'm sharing a house with a couple of girls.' Keep it vague, I thought.

'That sounds sensible. What's the job?'

'Jobs, plural.' I ran through a brief description of my duties for each of them.

'Hm.' He didn't sound thrilled. 'Well, that'll do to tide you over, I suppose. When are you going back to cycling?'

I clenched my fist; my fingernails dug into the palm of my hand. I'd known this was coming sooner or later. 'I'm not.'

'Well, I know you've got the ban and everything, but you should keep in touch with your team. You never know.'

If I never heard from anyone at Grande Fino again, that would be too soon. 'Dad,' I said, 'I'm not going to go back to cycling, ever.'

'Oh, come on, Ben, don't be ridiculous. You made some mistakes –'

'I cheated.'

'– you maybe weren't doing as well as we'd all hoped, but that's no reason to give it up now. You still have such a long way to go.'

In some other universe, maybe. 'A very long way to go,' I agreed. 'Too long.'

'Well, if you're going to take such a defeatist attitude then it's hardly surprising, is it?'

I didn't answer.

'Is it?'

I still didn't answer.

'Is it?'

I think Dad likes having a phone that he can slam down.

Mum phoned back half an hour later to apologise. I was in the corner shop by then, trying to decide between nasty wine and nastier lager. 'Your dad's quite upset, you see; he doesn't like the idea of your giving up.'

Well, nor did I, but it was a bit late now because I had. I didn't say that. 'Mum, I've just had enough of it all.' I slid my wallet out of the back pocket of my jeans, and picked up a bottle of nasty wine with the same hand.

'We just worry,' she said. 'You know.'

I did. 'Yeah,' I said, while at the same time engaging in a wordless conversation of raised eyebrows and waved debit cards with the shop assistant. 'Well.'

'Now,' she said, 'when can we come and see you?'

I made an excuse about not knowing what my shift patterns were going to be like, rang off without having reached any agreement, and went home to see my birthday out on my own.

Chapter 5

Was Mum justified in worrying? When I was cycling, I'd split my time between my parents' house, hotels, and a sort of cyclists' boarding house in Seville, where half my team lived between races. I had learned how to use a washing machine, because Señora Garcia drew the line at doing our laundry, but I came to understand that I'd had things pretty easy. I was aware that Vicki and Polly were doing a lot of the work behind the scenes, sorting out the utilities and so on, and I was pathetically grateful because it was all a closed book to me. Things like voter registration, council tax, broadband, that I'd either never thought about at all, or had assumed just *happened*, just, well, *happened*. Except I knew about them because Polly shoved things under my nose to sign, or Vicki told me to make sure I was up and dressed to let the internet man in.

I worked out how to feed myself. I'd followed enough nutrition plans in my time to know more or less what I was meant to eat, but converting that into a shopping list and then a recipe was beyond me. I started with things in plastic boxes that went in the microwave for as long as it said on the packaging. When nothing disastrous happened, I became more adventurous and moved on to things that went in the oven for as long as it said on the packaging.

Polly and I both paid rent to Vicki, who collated and handled the official payment to the lettings agent. An extra tenner per month went into a house fund for stuff like toilet roll and milk. We got through a lot of milk. This was because Vicki took her tea and coffee a very pale beige, I was slightly addicted to milkshakes, and Polly lived on breakfast cereal.

'Why cereal?' I asked once.

She looked at me with an expression of pity. 'Isn't it obvious? Quick, easy, claims to contain some vitamins, definitely contains some energy, doesn't go off before I get round to eating it, and at a pinch I can have it straight out of the box and don't even need to do any washing up.'

'But what about the sugar? And –' I vaguely remembered a school project – 'isn't it expensive?'

'There's more to expensiveness than money,' Polly said gnomically. I, guiltily aware that my own current diet would have given the team nutritionist kittens despite my best efforts, left it at that.

We'd been in the house about a fortnight before I met Michael. The first I knew of it was a lot of swearing from the kitchen – not from him, or from Polly, but from Vicki. Going down to investigate, I found her, still in her cycling gear, mopping up a flood of starchy, near-boiling water, complete with flotsam and jetsam in the form of wholewheat pasta strewn across the floor.

'Er... are you all right?' I asked.

'No damage to me,' she snapped, 'except I'm likely to become a homicidal maniac if I don't get my dinner soon.'

'That's why you're not showering first?' I found the dustpan and brush and started collecting pasta twirls.

She exhaled noisily. 'Thanks. No. That's because I want to be out of the way before Michael shows up.'

'Oh. He's that bad?'

'He's perfectly pleasant,' Vicki said. 'I just can't stand him.'

I was curious now. 'In that case... how about you go and have your shower, and I'll cook you some new pasta and finish mopping this up? I've got to meet the guy at some point.'

'Really?' She looked piercingly at me. 'That's very sweet of you.'

'No trouble,' I said. 'I've got to make my own, anyway.' And I was a bit worried that she'd set fire to something if she tried to repeat this performance.

'Well, thank you –' She darted to the stove, just saved herself from slipping in the spilt water, and turned the gas off underneath the sauce, which was beginning to smell scorched. 'Just scrape what you can out of this, OK? If you're sure you don't mind? I'm getting to the point where I'd eat my own bath flannel.'

'OK,' I said, 'that's fine. I'll leave your food outside your bedroom door. Don't tread in it.'

In actual fact, I had time to make both our dinners, and eat most of my own, before Michael arrived. When I took my dirty plate downstairs, I found him sprawled across the sofa. He looked, as Vicki had implied, pleasant enough: tall, but not intimidatingly so, with straw-like hair brushed down onto his forehead. His trainers were gleamingly white, suggesting a surplus of time, money, or both, but apart from that I couldn't find any reason on sight alone to dislike him as violently as Vicki did. Then again, she'd as good as admitted that her feeling wasn't entirely rational.

He was alone. Polly must have gone to the toilet or something. There were Indian takeaway boxes spread out on the coffee table, and a film flickered, frozen, on the TV screen.

'You must be Michael,' I said, before the silence could get awkward.

'You must be Ben,' he countered amiably.

I could only think in clichés. 'I would say that Polly's *told me so much about you*, but it wouldn't be true. She's been very discreet.' I wondered whether that had worked in both directions: had she been very discreet to him, about me?

'Ah!' He smiled as if he'd expected nothing else. 'So what do you do?'

Suspecting a trap, I told him, 'A bit of waitering. A bit of pallet-monkeying. What about you?'

'I work in IT,' he said.

'Oh, right, like fixing computers? Programming?' Not that I understood computers at all.

'Support. So mostly fixing, yeah, except ninety per cent of it is resetting people's passwords.'

I pictured him with one of those telephone headsets. 'People?'

'Two days at the hospital, three for the council. I'm on a bit of a weird contract.'

'Aren't we all,' I said. 'Polly said she knew you through church?'

'That's right.' His eyes darted left and right. 'She's been coming to my church... oh, a couple of years now, I suppose.'

'Sounds like you've been going there longer.' I was floundering here. I knew nothing about computers, and even less about church. Well, some of my team-mates had been religious, but I'd tended to think of it in the same way as salt and number thirteen; it couldn't hurt to ask the Madonna of Ghisallo to keep an eye on you – indeed, it probably helped, but I didn't exactly *believe* in it. I suspected that Michael thought of it differently.

'On and off,' he said. 'On and off.'

'I'm not religious myself,' I said, though he hadn't asked.

'It changes your life,' he said. 'It helps you achieve amazing things. All you have to do is believe.'

'Oh. Right,' I said, embarrassed.

He smiled self-consciously. 'Sorry. I don't like to preach. But really, everything's possible.'

'OK,' I said, wishing I hadn't brought it up. At that moment, fortunately, Polly came back. She didn't look very pleased to see me. I escaped to the kitchen to make my coffee, and did the washing up while I was there, to give them time to get well into the film. I wondered what on earth they saw in each other. Did he consider it his duty as a Christian to take care of her no matter how grumpy she got? Did she need all that unquestioning enthusiasm to balance out her own negativity? Giving the whole thing up as a mystery beyond my comprehension, I slunk back to my room.

Chapter 6

As winter wore itself out and we got to know each other better, I fathomed out what had happened. The girls had been at university, sharing a house with a couple of other people – a literal couple, in fact – when Polly became ill. She'd moved home to her parents' when it became obvious that this wasn't just a passing bug, but had found their well-meaning impatience with her slow recovery so aggravating that she'd simulated (consciously or otherwise) a quicker one and returned to her studies. This was a predictable disaster and she ended up worse than she'd begun; this time she didn't move home and Vicki became her de facto carer, in between finishing her own studies.

The other couple married each other and moved south. Vicki and Polly found a two-bedroom place: the beginning of their peaceful existence as a twosome, undisturbed until I rolled up.

As to *why here*, I eventually found out that Vicki's job had originally been based in the town, which was partly why she'd applied for it in the first place, but the charity had been restructured and all the office staff had been transferred to Lingholme. At that point she and Polly were two months into a twelve month contract on a flat, with no break clause. 'And by the end of that,' Vicki said, 'we were settled.'

They stayed another year in that flat, until their landlady decided to sell – or said she had. ('I knew I should have hidden the wheelchair,' Polly said.) After that, they'd moved into the alleged shithole of a place they'd been living in when I met them. That was a month-by-month contract, 'and really,' said Vicki, 'you wouldn't spend more than a month in there if you could help it.'

The wheelchair, which I'd naively assumed to have been a fixture since Polly's first diagnosis, turned out to have been a comparatively recent development. Polly seemed to have something of a love/hate relationship with it, though she dealt with that by transferring the hate to anyone who tut-tutted about it. I wasn't sure whether she felt resentful about needing it, or guilty about having it when she didn't need it as badly as all that, but either way it came out as defensiveness.

'Or paranoia,' she said, one evening when she was ten pages into a 52-page form. 'This bloody form! I keep having to remember only to say what I can do on a very bad day, and it's so depressing. I'm half-way to convincing myself that I can't do anything, ever. I can't cook for myself and I can't walk more than the length of a bus and I can't do my own shopping and I can't...'

I didn't get it. I'd seen her do at least some of that. 'Can't you tell them that you have good days and bad days?'

She scowled at me as if I'd designed the form myself. 'Not if I want them to give me anything, no. You write "good day" and they read "blissful existence of unalloyed delight".'

'And what do you get when you've filled all that in?' I asked.

'An appointment in an inaccessible office.'

'And after that?'

'Rather less than what *you* get for a thirty-seven hour work week,' she snapped.

'I can't afford to work less than forty-five hours at the bare minimum,' I said.

'That was my point.'

There wasn't much that I could say in reply to that, and from the little smirk she gave I could see that she knew it.

Michael came round a few days later and helped her finish the thing; they celebrated with pizza and board games. I knew this because they – well, Michael – dragged me in to finish the one and make up the numbers on the other.

'Ben will play. Won't you?' he called. 'All the two player stuff gets a bit old.'

I'd been in the living room, minding my own business, reading a circular about the Marsh Nature Reserve out of sheer boredom. I folded it up and went through to the kitchen. 'Yeah,' I said, 'I don't mind, if you want me to.'

Now that I was there, I wasn't at all sure that Polly did want me to, but for whatever reason she wasn't going to argue. 'I'll go and see if Vicki wants to play, too,' she said.

'Of course,' said Michael. 'That would be fine.'

I sat down and he and I smiled at each other politely across the table. Polly hauled herself out of her wheelchair and padded upstairs to find Vicki. We could hear her saying, 'Do you want to come down and play games?' Then, when Vicki's reply seemed to be unenthusiastic, 'Ben's playing too.'

Relieved, apparently, of the concern about being a third wheel, Vicki appeared, with Polly just behind her. 'Is it a four player game, or do you want me to make up a team?' she was asking.

'We haven't decided what we're playing yet,' Polly said.

'Articulate?' Michael rattled the box. It didn't make a very impressive rattle.

Polly looked at Vicki. 'What do you think?'

Vicki looked at me. 'Ben?'

'I don't mind, so long as somebody will tell me how to play.'

Vicki sat down next me. 'OK, so shall the two of us be a team? It's like charades, really, but with talking.'

Michael said, smiling, 'Perhaps if Polly and I go first, to demonstrate?'

'I suppose that makes sense.' Vicki sounded rather ungracious, but I thought it was quite a good idea.

It wasn't hard to pick up – but I wasn't very good at it. I was rubbish at describing stuff. 'It's, um, a river? In Hampshire? Or Dorset, maybe?' And by the time Vicki had guessed the Itchen, the Test, and, increasingly desperately, the Exe and the Thames, the time had run out; she looked at the card and told me the Solent wasn't a river at all.

'It *was*,' Michael said, 'in prehistoric times.'

Vicki glared at him, and took the timer back.

I thought that I'd do better at guessing. The clues that Polly gave were clear and easy to work out even when I didn't know what the answer actually referred to. 'It's... an abbreviation for a toilet. And, not meadow, not pastures...'

'W. C. Fields!' Michael announced triumphantly. He kept gazing into Polly's eyes as if he was transferring the answer from her head to his by sheer willpower. I thought that it really wasn't as impressive as all that.

But Vicki's clues made as little sense to me as mine had to her, and we got hopelessly tangled up with the moon landings and the Illuminati. The other two romped away, extending their lead in every round, and the only break that we got came in a free-for-all, when Polly said, 'It's a flower... *I'm half crazy, all for the love of you*,' and Vicki and I both yelled 'Daisy!'

But it was never going to put us back in contention.

'I'm sorry,' I said to Vicki, when the others had got all the way around the board and the pair of us were still only a measly fifteen spaces from the start.

'We should have played girls versus boys,' Polly said. 'We'd have slaughtered them.'

I thought that this was almost certainly true, but I didn't see that I needed to admit that. Vicki didn't say anything, and after a few seconds Polly laughed.

Chapter 7

February's *Cycling Monthly* had covered the news of my fall from grace with a hand-wringing half-column by a journalist called Suzie Balham with dark hints about "sources within the team". Nobody mentioned it. I only knew because I found it in the recycling bin, flicked through it, and wished I hadn't.

I wondered what would happen if I wrote everything down –

– Dr Wolfsen's little-by-little, drip-by-drip, "régime", starting small, the supplements and treatments that nobody could possibly object to, the 'Have you tried...? Well, what about...?' –

– the way that nothing felt wrong, the way that everything felt wrong, the information that went missing (or did it?) between him and our team doctor –

– if I wrote all that down, if I could ever get it straight in my own head, if I sent it off to *Cycling Monthly* or Suzie Balham...

I wondered if I'd ever stop hearing that knock on the door of my hotel room. If I'd ever forget that sudden moment of panic when I realised it was a test. Not knowing whether I'd fucked up or whether something had gone wrong in the lines of communication that Wolfsen swore he'd fixed. Not knowing what to do other than piss in a little tub while the testers watched. Knowing that it didn't really make any difference whose fault it was, because at that point I was comprehensively fucked.

Knowing that it had been coming for a long, long time.

No, I won't say that I missed the cycling lifestyle. I'd felt barely a pang looking over Vicki's road bike. I did miss the deliberate physical activity, though. Had I got addicted to exercise, I wondered?

Walking to work went a little way to address it. The physical nature of work helped, too, but it was still nothing compared to what I'd been used to. I found myself wanting to do more, to push myself harder. Once, I'd lived my life at the limits of my body, always fighting to go faster, further, longer; to endure more, to suffer more. The burden of competition had been lifted from me, and I was grateful for that, but there was something else that was missing, something that I missed. I might have no future as an athlete, but I hadn't yet worked out how to explain that to my body.

I started running almost by accident. From the moment I'd arrived in town, I'd got around it on foot. I hadn't worked out the bus routes and besides, the first bus of the day was far too late for me to get to a breakfast shift at the Grand. I couldn't afford to run a car, and, if I was honest, I was a bit scared of driving. I hadn't driven anything since passing my test when I was seventeen. And there was no way I was getting back on a bike. Walking it was, then. But it was too cold to walk, really, and my body wanted something more challenging. I started running.

I had no intention of becoming a serious runner. I didn't get any of that fancy tech to track distance or energy. I never even timed myself. Why would I? I knew how long it took me to walk to work, and it stood to reason that running would be quicker. On the other hand, it also meant that I had to shower when I got there, so I left the house ten minutes earlier, and very deliberately didn't look at the clock until I'd changed into my uniform. If I didn't know my own time, then I couldn't compare it to anyone else's.

Or, indeed, itself. I'd watched my own numbers too long, and for the wrong reasons. Power to weight, haematocrit, heartrate. I deliberately skewed my runs: I would take a longer route one day, loop around the wide tarmac paths in the public gardens, or down a different street; sometimes, if it had been dry, I made a diversion through the nature reserve; I might stop and sit down for a bit on one of the curlicued cast iron benches on the seafront; I walked bits. I didn't care about time or distance any more. At least, I told myself I didn't care. The truth was, I couldn't afford to think about the numbers.

Vicki cared about the numbers. She tracked her own. She followed everyone else's. She held the women's record over most of the climbs within fifty miles, and had a couple of them outright. She was always pleased to move up in the rankings, particularly when that put her ahead of a man named Paul Cunningham.

'The cycling club secretary,' she explained, 'and a total arse.'

When I asked what was wrong with him she muttered and shuffled a bit. 'He's got a reputation,' she said at last. 'If there's a trophy in the club cabinet that doesn't specifically say *Women* on it, it never goes to a woman. So I beat him over every segment that I can.'

Polly didn't like him, either. I assumed that was on Vicki's account. I couldn't know for sure, because Polly didn't talk about cycling with me.

She still talked about it with Vicki, though. I came in one Friday evening in March to find the two of them discussing it in a way that made me raise my eyebrows.

'The wonderful thing about cycling,' Polly was saying, 'is that no one can accuse you of watching it for the eye candy. Well, not for the human eye candy, anyway. The scenery is a different matter.'

'Really?' Vicki said. She waved at the TV, which was actually showing some panel show, so didn't help her case.

'OK, maybe Kristian House,' Polly said, as if I wasn't there. 'But on the whole, top-ranked cyclists are weird spidery alien beings with padded crotches, not attractive at all.'

Vicki nodded in my direction and said, 'You should say, *present company excepted.*'

'Should I?' She didn't.

Vicki said it for her. 'Present company excepted.'

'Er, thank you,' I said, embarrassed. I sat down on the sofa and tried to lighten the tone. 'What's Kristian House got that I haven't, then?'

'Nothing,' Vicki said, blushing.

Polly deigned to notice me. 'He's got that sort of piratey thing going on. Makes up for the general unsexiness of the helmet and skin-tight Lycras.'

'You can't see the pirateyness when he's racing,' Vicki objected.

'Which is handy, because the racing is what I want to watch,' Polly said triumphantly, though the logic seemed a bit circular to me. 'Not all of us are as shallow as you.'

Vicki looked sideways at me to see what I made of it all. 'Two words for you,' I said. 'Saddle sores.'

Vicki blushed even redder. 'I was thinking,' she said, changing the subject awkwardly. 'There's room in the shed for another bike.'

I tried to look interested. 'Are you upgrading the road bike? Or you could get one of those little folding ones, then you wouldn't have to leave it at the station on the days when you have to take the train to work.'

'I meant for you,' she said.

Polly snorted.

'Oh,' I said, shaken. 'I don't want to get a bike.'

'I wasn't going to get you to join the cycling club or anything.' Indeed, she looked horrified at the idea. 'But I thought you might like to come out with me sometimes, now the weather's getting nicer.'

'Oh,' I said again. 'No. Thank you for the thought. But I don't think... I mean, I've given up cycling. For good.' For the good of everyone.

She looked intensely embarrassed. 'Never mind, then.' Abruptly, she got up, went into the kitchen, and closed the door.

'Poor Vicki,' Polly said, her voice lower. 'She could do with someone to keep her company out on the road.'

'I think you understand why it's not a good idea for that person to be me,' I said.

48

She rolled her eyes, as if in her opinion that hadn't needed saying, and observed, 'If I had a million pounds I'd hire someone to drive me along behind her. Shout at her out of the sunroof. Sticky bottles. All that sort of thing.'

I'd been driven along race routes in the support car myself from time to time. The overwhelming memory was one of an intense desire to be out on the road. 'It wouldn't be the same, though, would it?'

'Well, no...' She looked at me as if I was stupid; then her face changed. 'Oh, you mean for me? No, but it would be close enough. Closer than I am at the moment.'

I was hopelessly confused. What on earth had she thought I'd meant? 'If that's what you say.'

'There's very little wrong about my life that a blank cheque wouldn't cure,' she said. 'Granted, I'd have to spend a lot of it on bribes, but – well, you'd be surprised. Of the hassle associated with my disability, only about twenty per cent is caused by the actual physical stuff. The rest is people not getting it, or things being set up badly. And you know, *things being set up badly* is a problem that can be solved by throwing money at it, if only you throw the money in the right direction.' She tapped the armrest of her wheelchair.

'People not getting it?' I repeated. I knew I wasn't, even though she was being a lot more forthcoming with me than usual.

She explained, 'If other people weren't bothered by the fact that I spent most of my time absolutely fucking knackered, I wouldn't mind quite so much myself.'

'Hang on, what? You're saying you don't want other people to care that you're disabled?'

She glared at me. 'That wasn't exactly what I said – though yeah, if my parents would stop treating it like the greatest tragedy since *Hamlet* it would save me a *lot* of emotional energy – but what I meant was that if society in general didn't expect everyone to be active, productive and cheerful twenty-four seven, I would spend less of my personal twenty-four seven feeling guilty about *not* being active, productive and cheerful.'

'But don't you want to be all that?' I said, shocked.

'Do you?'

'Of course I do,' I said.

Polly looked sideways at me. '*Really?*'

'Well... surely everybody does?'

'You *are* active and productive, certainly,' she allowed. 'It doesn't make you cheerful, that I've noticed.'

This was probably a fair assessment, but I protested anyway. 'Imagine what I'd be like if I didn't run.'

'Imagine what I'd be like if I *did*,' she retorted.

I couldn't resist saying, 'Cheerful?'

'No. I would cry. Then I would spend the next three days unable to get out of bed.'

Vicki was clattering around in the kitchen. I wondered if she could hear us over the TV. 'Oh,' I said.

'Granted, I spend a lot of time in bed anyway. But I wouldn't have the energy to read, or anything.'

'Is that what you do, then? Read?' I tried not to let my horror show. I'd only just stopped myself saying, *all* you do.

'Well, I listen. Actual reading makes my eyes go funny, but audiobooks are great.' She reached forward and picked up a mug from the coffee table, took a sip, and made a face. 'What do you think I do all day while you're out at work? I don't just sit around waiting to die.'

'Oh,' I said, discomfited. 'Well, I'm glad to hear that. Actually, I thought you were working on getting better.'

'I'm working on *not getting worse*. Better might never happen.' She said it like she actually believed that, and it wasn't a big deal.

'What will you do if it doesn't?' I couldn't imagine a future with no improvement.

'Get through the whole of *War and Peace*, I expect. Honestly, Ben, I like just being alive! This illness is a bloody nuisance, but it's a lot better than the alternative, and feeling sorry for myself gets boring. If you can meet with triumph and disaster, and so on...'

I knew it was a poem – I'd had a coach once who had quoted it at every opportunity – but I didn't see her point. I said so.

'The point is,' Polly said, 'I may never get better, and I'm not going to put off living my life while I wait for something that may never happen.'

It wasn't any less shocking the second time I heard it. 'You can't believe that,' I said, my head spinning.

'Believe what?'

'That you're not going to get better.' Unbidden, a memory surfaced from my childhood: Mum crying, Dad storming out.

'That I *might not* get better.' She was looking at me with a mixture of frustration and a kindness that I didn't deserve.

'Whatever. You can't just give up.' *Lose, and start again at your beginnings, and never breathe a word about your loss...* A tide of resentment swept over me. You couldn't give up, and if you did you couldn't be OK about it.

'Who said anything about *giving up*? I'm just trying to be realistic.'

'Yes, but...'

She glared at me. 'Look, you might have made a miraculous recovery and become a world-class athlete, but plenty didn't. *Don't*. And *giving up* has got fuck all to do with it.'

'You've got to keep a positive attitude,' I said helplessly.

'There's a difference between *keeping a positive attitude* and living in fucking Lalaland! I'm not going to get better by wishing. I've tried, believe me.'

'But...'

She sighed loudly. 'Look. I think we're talking at cross-purposes. Can we just change the subject?'

51

Vicki came back in then, so we did.

Chapter 8

I was enjoying a rare day off. No breakfast shift at the Grand. Nothing at the warehouse. No money, of course, but I'd been working so many hours for the last few weeks that I was OK for the moment. I'd woken early and then lain in bed for ages, watching the sunlight shining steadily more brightly through my curtains, hearing Vicki pottering around getting ready for work and the house settling back into silence after she left, enjoying the sheer luxury of not having to get up. I took a leisurely shower, then got dressed.

The thing that Vicki had been singing had got stuck in my head. 'Show me the doper,' I sang, 'show me the cheat, show me the wanker who claims he's an athlete...' *And I'll show you an idiot who had everything going for him and lost his sense of perspective and blew the whole lot.*

It didn't scan. It was probably just as well that the doorbell rang before I could get any further into it.

I went downstairs and opened the door to greet the postman. He looked confused by my appearance, but then I supposed he'd never seen me before; I'd always been at work. 'Parcel for Miss Victoria Whitaker.'

'She's at work,' I said. 'Do I need to sign anything?'

'What? Er –' He glanced at the box. 'No. Er. Is that the lady with the wheelchair, is it?'

'No,' I said, shortly. Since the parcel said *BIKE ESSENTIALS* in huge red letters across the top, it seemed a bit of a no-brainer. Although, I reproved myself, Vicki was always using bike tools to fix bits of Polly's wheelchair, and it wasn't beyond the bounds of possibility that they'd come up with some sort of crossover hack for it. And I knew for a fact that they'd discussed Polly's starting to cycle when she became a little better. It made sense; cycling a mile is far less tiring than walking a mile. Perhaps it wasn't such a stupid question.

'So she'll be Miss Polly Devine, then.' He handed me three envelopes and a Jiffy bag with a triumphant grin. 'There you go, sir. And you must be Ben Goddard. Letter for you.' I recognised the logo of the charity of which I was patron, and I knew it couldn't be good.

'Thank you very much,' I said, and shut the door with a faint sense of having said too much – though I couldn't see how I could have said *less*.

I took the post inside, put the box on the kitchen table where Vicki could see it when she came in, and opened my own letter. It had been forwarded from my parents'; I recognised Mum's fussy handwriting on the envelope. I drew out the single sheet of paper:

Dear Mr Goddard,
It is with regret...

I sighed. I supposed I should have seen this coming – before the post arrived, I mean. I supposed I should have resigned as patron myself and saved them the embarrassment of telling me that my services were no longer required. I supposed that they'd be able to find someone else to do what I used to do – shake hands, smile, wear the logo on my sleeve (which Henri grudgingly allowed because it made him look like a nice person) and get my photo taken with seriously ill or disabled children, who probably didn't have the foggiest idea who I was or what I did. All the Premiership footballers must have been too busy.

That all sounds cynical. I wasn't, at least at first. It was one of the few things about being a pro that I enjoyed wholeheartedly. I did seem to cheer the kids up when I visited hospitals. Maybe it was the fact that I'd been there and done that; maybe it was just that I made a change from their degrading, depressing routines. The parents definitely seemed to like me, to take comfort in my existence. I was a sort of talisman against their worst fears, proof that it was possible for someone to go through what their beloved children were going through and come out fitter and stronger. And even on a practical level, if I signed a jersey or a photo and gave it to the charity, they made a decent sum off that at auction. If I shared a link to someone's sponsored run, they probably raised a little bit more than they would have done otherwise, and the money could be part of a dialysis machine or a new MRI scanner, or whatever. It was all worth doing. I honestly did believe that. It was only when I started to disbelieve my own talk about *believing in getting better* that I lost motivation.

And the truth is, my own illness was so long ago that I can barely remember what it was like. I've been well for so long, I was a professional sportsman for so long, that those days of pain and frustration and having to get my mum to do every little thing for me seem like they belonged to a different person altogether.

I had a horrible feeling that this was why I'd blown up at Polly when she'd suggested that maybe getting better wasn't always an option.

'What was that?' Polly called, as if I'd woken her up by thinking about her.

'Mm? Oh, just the postman.'

She put her head around the door. 'Anything interesting?' she asked.

'Bike bits for Vicki. A couple of things for you.' I hid my own letter in my pocket. After yesterday's conversation, I didn't fancy bringing the subject up again.

'Cool. Thanks.' She smiled at me. Evidently we had a ceasefire. 'You doing anything interesting with your day off?'

'Just going out for a run,' I said. I hadn't come up with anything more exciting. 'Thought I'd go a bit further than usual, see what there is to see along the coast.'

'Sea, I should think.' It was a feeble pun, and she acknowledged that with a grin.

'What about you?' I asked.

'Going out with Michael this afternoon.'

'Oh, OK. Anywhere nice?'

'Cinema, probably.'

I nodded. 'Sounds good. Enjoy that.'

For all that it had been an unimaginative option, I enjoyed my run. I ended up going further than I'd meant: a long way north along the coast road. The tide was out, and the low sun gleamed on the miles of wet sand, a dazzling expanse in the corner of my eye. I went on and on. I could have kept going for hours, but I wasn't sure how much daylight I'd have left. When I got to a signboard explaining the coastal defences I made an arbitrary decision to turn back, and retraced my steps.

By the time I'd got home Vicki was back from work, and had opened her box of bike bits. She was cooing over a chain ring, but when she saw me she shut the lid of the box. 'Anyway, Polly,' she said, her voice unnaturally high and calm, 'you were saying about the film...?'

I raised my eyebrows and didn't comment. Polly noticed my not commenting, but heroically kept her mouth shut. Unfortunately, Vicki noticed the silent interplay and blushed furiously.

'New toy?' I said, attempting to make things less embarrassing. It didn't seem to work.

Vicki said, 'Nothing you'd be interested in. Bike stuff.'

I'd had no idea that this was going to be such a huge issue. I tried to change the subject back again. 'What did you see, Polly?'

'Oh, leave me out of this, you two,' she snapped.

'Polly,' Vicki said suddenly, 'did you take your meds today?'

She spun round. 'I... oh, shit, no.' She plodded off to her room and re-emerged with one of those plastic cases with compartments for each day of the week. She laid this on the table, then got herself a glass of water. 'Michael came earlier than I expected,' she explained between swallows.

'Oh, right?' Vicki said neutrally. There was the faintest suggestion of a frown. Then, as if determined not to make a big deal of anything at all, she turned to me and said, 'Ben, can you remember whether we have any rice left?'

Later, I asked Vicki, 'Can you *tell* when Polly's behind on her medication, then? Are there signs to watch out for?'

'Lucky guess,' Vicki said. 'That's all.' She wouldn't say any more. But she seemed to have got over the bike thing, so I supposed that was something to be grateful for.

Chapter 9

I'd kept in touch with my parents, of course, and we'd all continued to make virtuous noises about their maybe popping up to see me. It hadn't happened yet, and I was secretly relieved about that. I knew what a massive disappointment I'd become, and I wasn't sure that I could face seeing that written all over Mum's face.

As it happened, we had to deal with Polly's family long before mine came sniffing around. Her mother and stepfather swept up, together with her younger brother and his girlfriend, after some negotiation around the logistics of their travel and an appointment of Polly's that couldn't be moved.

'Which is a real bugger,' she confided, 'because it will mean that my health is the topic of choice, and I was really hoping we could talk about something else.'

'They fuss, do they?' It didn't seem like the moment to tell her that my mum had been just the same, long after I'd been pronounced fit and healthy.

'They hate my using the wheelchair,' Polly said. 'They think it's the last stop before turning my face to the wall and dying. I'm not going to stop using it in front of them, but I'll tell you for free that there'll be a lot of grief on both sides.'

'Sounds delightful,' I said.

Polly shrugged her shoulders. 'With any luck we won't have to talk about it too much,' she said. 'The great thing about living in a seaside town is that if the worst comes to the worst you can go to the beach and build sandcastles.'

I couldn't imagine her building a sandcastle; it seemed a bit beneath her dignity. 'What if it's raining?' I asked. It usually was.

'Then we'll go to the arcade. Play pinball.'

'Eat fish and chips?' I suggested. 'Ice cream?'
'Now you're getting the idea,' she said.

Polly had told me that her family was terminally disorganised, but they managed to arrive half an hour earlier than they'd said they would, which in the event turned out to be an hour before she got back from her appointment. I suppose that proved her point, though not the way that we had expected. Vicki was, of course, at work, so I was left to entertain the Devine family as best I could. Four people – five, counting myself – was a lot in our little living room. Polly's mother and stepfather shared the sofa. She had a smart green dress and an anxious air; he was tall and balding, and somehow managed to give the impression that none of this was anything to do with him despite keeping his arm permanently around his wife's shoulder. The brother's girlfriend sat on the very front edge of the armchair, visibly wishing she was somewhere else, while the brother himself perched on the arm. If either one of them had got up, the other would have landed in a heap on the floor.

I, meanwhile, hovered uncomfortably in the doorway, wondering whether I should bring in one of the kitchen chairs, but hoping I wasn't going to have to stay there long enough to make that worthwhile. It was all a bit awkward, making polite conversation while trying surreptitiously to find out whether they knew who I was; whether they knew that their daughter disapproved of me so mightily; and, if so, why. At the same time I had to play down my knowledge of Polly's condition.

They were disappointed that she wasn't there to welcome them, and it didn't help that I couldn't explain exactly – or at all – who her appointment was with or what it was about. Her mother kept saying, 'But didn't she tell you? You're sure it's nothing serious?' until the brother said, '*Mum*. He doesn't know. Shut up.'

'And is she eating properly? She needs to lose some weight.'

I said, 'We don't eat at the same time. I'm usually still at work.'

'And is she still taking the... which drug was it? And is it working?'

'I really don't know about her medication,' I said, uncomfortably. *And even if I had,* I added in my head, *I've lived with Polly long enough to know that discussing it with other people without her consent is not going to impress her.*

'But she's still using the wheelchair.' This time there wasn't room for me to confirm or deny it. 'She really needs to get out of that thing and start thinking positively, or she's never going to get better.'

'Well, she'll be back soon,' I said. It didn't leave us with much else to talk about, but, inspired by my conversation with Polly earlier in the week, I gave them a virtual tour of the attractions along the front, beginning with the pier and ending with the thing that looked a bit like a lighthouse and wasn't. I knew how to pick my fights, and I certainly wasn't going to pick one of Polly's. But I was beginning to understand, now, why she had so little patience with everyone else. Staying on speaking terms with her family must have used up most of her goodwill.

I was relieved when she got back from the clinic and could answer the questions herself. And they came fast.

'Polly! You didn't tell us you were going to the hospital! What did they say?'

She gave me a dirty look, and said, to them, 'I didn't want to worry you. It was only a check-up.'

'And?' The look on her mother's face was almost painful. 'Will you be able to stop using the wheelchair?'

'Same old, same old. I've told you about the wheelchair before.' Polly looked acutely embarrassed, having the family laundry washed in front of me. Rather than tell her I'd already seen it, I excused myself politely and went and hid in my room until they all went out. Actually, I got the impression that she couldn't answer the questions, not the way they wanted her to, but at least she didn't have to worry about

61

betraying her own confidences. Or did she? Whatever, it wasn't my problem now. I waited until they were all safely out of the house, then made myself a cheese sandwich and sat down in front of the TV for some drama that nobody could expect me to get involved in.

They dropped her off again four hours later, declined my offer of a cup of tea, and left. The day seemed to have been a comparative success, but Polly looked knackered.

'Phew,' she said. 'I'm glad that's over.'

I knew that I'd have said the same thing had it been my parents visiting. Even so, I was faintly shocked. 'You don't get on with them?'

'I love my parents dearly,' Polly said. It wasn't really an answer.

'And?'

She sighed. 'And they love me dearly.'

'But?'

'But *because* they love me dearly they want me to be well and happy, and they get upset if they think I am not well and happy. And because I love them I don't like them being upset, so we've been playing Let's Pretend all day, and now they've gone I've stopped.'

There was only one possible response to that. 'Would *you* like a cup of tea?'

'I'd *love* one. Sorry for being grumpy.' She wheeled into the kitchen after me, and kept talking. She didn't actually sound all that grumpy, just urgent, as if she'd been keeping a lid on herself all day and was only now releasing the pressure. 'It's always been like that. I couldn't ever tell them if coursework was getting to me or if my love life was a mess, or anything, because they'd just worry and worry and hassle me and then worry some more and meanwhile I'd resent them for hassling me and feel guilty about resenting it *and* for worrying them... Sorry, I'm babbling.'

'Babble away,' I said. 'So long as you don't want a solution, because I'm shit at dealing with my parents, too.'

'I think I saw your parents on telly once,' she said.

'Could be,' I said. 'They used to come to a lot of my races. My mum never really got out of the habit of fussing over me after *I* was sick.'

'I keep forgetting about that,' Polly said. 'I'm sorry. I really should remember.'

'It was a long time ago,' I said. But I couldn't resist adding, 'Not that Mum thinks of it that way.'

Chapter 10

We'd scarcely got over all that excitement when, on my next free morning, Polly said, 'Ben. I hate to ask –' and it was obvious that she actually did – 'but can you take me into town today? I really need to go to the bank.'

'Of course,' I said. 'No problem.'

'If it was just the bank,' she added hurriedly, 'I'd get a taxi, but I need to go to the library too: I've run out of renewals on a couple of books, and it's just too far to wheel myself and not far enough to get another cab...'

'No problem,' I said again.

We made it to the bus stop without anything going wrong, if you didn't count the fact that it was raining. That was about as good as it got.

The bus was twenty minutes late, for a start. When it finally arrived, we discovered that a folding bike, a lad with a huge rucksack, and three buggies were squashed into the wheelchair space. Two of the mothers saw what was going on, emptied the prams and folded them up. The cyclist, shamed into action, did the same with the bike, and the teenager helped them all to heave the apparatus into the luggage rack. Then he shuffled a little way up the aisle, and apologised to an old lady for bashing her in the face with his bag.

Which was all very well, but there still wasn't space for Polly.

She said to the third woman, who seemed to be pretending not to have seen her, 'Excuse me, please: could you fold up your pushchair so that I can get into the wheelchair space?'

'No,' the woman said to the empty air.

I cleared my throat and looked pointedly at a label on the window that said *Please fold pushchairs if a wheelchair user requires this space*. It made no difference whatsoever.

The woman glared at Polly. Polly glared back. Eventually, the woman snapped, 'I've *just* got him off to sleep.'

Polly was unmoved. 'I can't stay here. I'm blocking the gangway.'

I wondered whether it would be easier to fold the *wheelchair*; but there were no free seats, and I wasn't stupid enough to ask Polly to stand all the way into town.

The driver shouted over his shoulder, 'Can you sort yourselves out, please? You're holding us all up.'

One of the other babies started crying, which set off all of them, including the one in the buggy in the wheelchair space.

'Do we get off and walk?' I asked Polly.

'No,' she said flatly. 'Apart from anything else, the bank would be shut by the time we got there.'

The bus driver slammed his little door shut and threaded his way up the aisle.

'Madam,' he said very stiffly to the buggy woman, 'I need to ask you to fold up this pushchair, *as it says on this window here*.'

'Or what?'

'Or I must ask you to get off this bus.'

'But I got on first!' she protested over the baby's howls.

'Madam, under the terms and conditions of this bus company, a wheelchair has priority in a wheelchair space.' He managed to imply simultaneously that *these were the rules*, that *the rules were not to be challenged*, that *he didn't think much of them himself*, and that *logic was on his side*.

'And what if I don't leave the bus?' the woman said triumphantly.

'Then this bus doesn't leave this stop.'

The other passengers made their feelings known about this possibility. Allegiances seemed to be mixed; however, the depth of feeling revealed was enough to drive the mother to get the baby out and fold up the pushchair. Muttering defensively that it was disgusting, she balanced the baby on her hip and turned meaningfully to face away from Polly. Who wasn't looking, too busy manoeuvring her chair into the recommended position, facing backwards.

Satisfied at last, the driver returned to his seat and the bus moved off. Polly stared ahead, tight-lipped, all the way into town.

At the bus station we sat tight – well, Polly sat, and I tried to cram myself into the corner next to her as the other passengers barged past me – until everyone else had got off. I gave the bus driver my blandest smile as we alighted.

'I'm very sorry about all that fuss,' Polly said, in exactly the tone she'd have used if she was telling him she was sorry about all his possessions being destroyed in an earthquake.

'Not your fault,' he told her.

He couldn't possibly have said anything else. Not to Polly.

'What do you want to do first?' I asked when we were safely on the ground.

'Bank,' Polly said. 'It shuts first.'

'Right.'

It was a bloody mission to get to it. The pavement down one side of the street was blocked by scaffolding.

'We might be able to squeeze through,' Polly said doubtfully. But as we approached it became obvious that it came down the middle of the walkway, leaving insufficient room either inside or outside it.

'There's too much of it for us to go along the road, too,' I said.

Polly sighed. 'We'll have to cross. OK. Listen. The bastards have blocked the kerb drop. The easiest way to do this is for you to take me down backwards into the road, turn round, cross diagonally and get onto the pavement on the other side at *that* kerb drop.'

'Got it,' I said.

It mostly went to plan, except for the bit where I stopped to put two fingers up at the car driver who thought we should have used the zebra crossing.

'We can't *get* to the fucking zebra crossing, there's fucking scaffolding in the way,' I grumbled as he sped off.

'Welcome to my world,' Polly said, taking her brakes off. I was glad that her reflexes were good. 'OK – you're clear now.'

Apart from having to ask three tourists, a busker, and a balloon seller to move out of our path, we got to the bank without any further trouble.

We got *to* the bank. We couldn't get *into* the bank. The access ramp had black-and-yellow tape stretched across both ends.

'For fuck's sake!' I said. 'Why?'

Polly gave a derisive little laugh. 'Some knobhead's pulled the handrail half-way off the wall, look.'

'We don't need the fucking handrail!'

'Yes, but somebody else might.' She sighed again. 'OK. Two options here. I can get out and you can haul the chair up the steps. Or we can duck under the tape and have the argument if we have to.'

'I vote for option two,' I said. 'I'm in the mood for an argument.'

'Make the most of that mood,' Polly advised. 'It doesn't last forever.'

So we ducked under the tape. Polly had to lean all the way forward while I shoved her under the strip, then put her brakes on while I got myself under. It was slightly easier at the top, except we had to negotiate the second barrier without losing so much momentum that the chair would roll back down the ramp. But we did it.

The lad patrolling the floor did a double-take when he saw us. 'I, er, hope you didn't have any problems getting in,' he said to me.

'Oh, er...' I said.

'We managed,' Polly told him with a voice of ice.

'Er. Good. And how can I help you?' He managed to divide his attention between the two of us that time.

To make it easier for him to remember who he was actually meant to be dealing with, I turned my back while Polly told him what she needed to do. After a little while she wheeled herself off after him and I was left standing in the middle of the floor. I found an armchair and picked up one of the complimentary newspapers – though it wasn't particularly complimentary. *THE FRAUDSTER NEXT DOOR* was the headline. I expected it to be about a conman raiding some poor old couple's pensions or something, but it turned out to be some self-righteous hysteria about people claiming benefits they weren't entitled to. Personally, having seen the hassle that Polly had to go through to get the ones she *was* entitled to, I couldn't see why anybody would bother. I turned to the back page in disgust and wished I hadn't. It was mostly taken up with a picture of a tennis player with her head in her hands. *NO HOPER? NEW DOPE BAN FOR HOPE.*

After that I gave up on the paper and sat there twiddling my thumbs and composing cutting replies to the woman on the bus, in case we ever had that argument again, until Polly came out.

I got up. 'Sorted?'

'Eventually,' she said. She lowered her voice. 'Come on, let's see if we can get out the same way.'

We performed the previous manoeuvre in reverse, which was a little bit scarier because neither of us could get our heads under the top tape without Polly's front wheels first being well onto the downward slope. I had visions of her sailing off down to the street below, clotheslining herself as she went, but she was too skilful to let that happen.

'Right,' I said when we were safely back at street level. 'What a palaver. Library?'

She looked up at me, backwards, and I saw with a sudden shock that she was slumping in her chair, and her face was tense with the effort of controlling her fatigue. 'Yes,' she said. 'And that had probably better be it.'

The route to the library was blissfully free of obstacles; the ramp was long and gentle, and the doors swung open with obliging swiftness. 'This is more like it,' I said.

'Isn't it?' Polly agreed.

I wanted to get this over and done with. 'Where do you want me to take you?'

'Stick me in front of the audiobooks and go and amuse yourself for ten minutes. I'll meet you at the main desk.'

'Sounds good to me. The audiobooks are...?'

'Straight ahead almost as far as you can go, and to the left.'

'Gotcha.' I left Polly there as requested – after we'd stopped for her to explain to a little boy that she used the chair because she was ill and walking made her very tired (and to his father that he didn't need to apologise, it wasn't anything to be embarrassed about, and the earlier in life people understood that, the better) – and wandered off.

I wasn't really sure what I was looking for. I'd never been much of a reader. I didn't want to look at Sport, but that was all I knew about. Didn't have a clue where to start with Fiction. I ambled past Self-Help (*Be The Person You Dream You Could Be*, one told me, and I mentally stuck two fingers up at it) and Religion (*Forlorn Hope*, which seemed nearer the mark). Eventually I decided that I should stop worrying about what to borrow and just join the damn library. This would be what a normal person without an unspeakable past would do when he moved into a new town, wouldn't it?

My route back to the front desk took me past True Life (*Shame and Heartache*), Crime (*Gone Forever*) and Books In Foreign Languages. I picked up *Le Pur et L'Impur*, which happened to be on the end of the shelf, and flicked through it, finding to my surprise that the French was not too difficult to understand. I'd assumed that it would have evaporated from my memory now that I wasn't using it, but it seemed to have stuck there. Hardly surprising, really; it had only been a couple of months since I quit. Not that it was of any relevance now. If it came to that, I could probably still ride a bike, too.

I asked at the desk about how to join the library. 'You just need something with your name and address on it,' the attendant said. 'A utility bill, council tax statement, something like that.'

I didn't have anything like that with me, so I said I'd come back another day. Shortly afterwards, Polly wheeled herself up to the desk, a collection of CDs and DVDs in her lap. 'All sorted,' she said to me cheerfully. Then, to the attendant, 'These to go back, please, and these to come out.'

'Well,' said the woman behind Polly, 'I think you should be ashamed of yourself.'

It seemed to be aimed at me. 'Me?'

'Letting your girlfriend carry all those things by herself, and not even pushing her...!'

'She's not my girlfriend,' I said, going for the assumption that was easiest to contradict.

'You don't mean to deny it, and in front of her! Well, that's the most disgusting thing I've heard in a long while. I saw you come in together! And you're obviously not her brother!'

Polly, having sorted out her loans, wheeled herself around. 'It's quite all right,' she said. 'I'd much rather he denied it. He's not my boyfriend, as it happens.'

'Oh!' She clearly didn't know what to say to that. Polly took advantage of her confusion to wheel herself off towards the main doors. She was stifling laughter or tears, I wasn't sure which. It might even have been both. Feeling somewhat shell-shocked, I trotted after her, picking up the audiobook of *Madame Bovary* that slipped off her lap.

She stopped when we were out of the line of sight from the desk. 'Fuck, Ben, I'm so sorry about that.'

'Not your fault,' I said. 'People jump to conclusions.'

'Yeah, but you didn't deserve to have her have a go at you like that.' She *was* crying, or pretty close to it, as she buttoned her coat up.

'What do you want to do with those books?' I asked, changing the subject with more plausibility and grace than I usually managed.

'In the main pocket of my rucksack, please.' It was slung over the handles of her wheelchair. I unzipped the pocket; she handed the items to me one by one, and I put them in, pausing once to smile blandly at the officious woman as she flounced past us.

'Home?' I said.

Polly frowned. 'Do we have anything to eat at home? I'm wondering if we should grab something now...'

I wasn't sure that was a good idea. She seemed close to a proper meltdown. 'If we don't,' I said, 'I'll run out and get something from the offie.'

'But they haven't got...' She checked herself. 'OK. You're probably right.'

'Where's the nearest taxi rank?'

'Taxi...? Oh, yes, you're probably right about that, too.' She didn't like that. 'I'll pay.'

Small victories. 'Which way?'

'Bridge Street. No, Sainsbury's. Actually, no, Bridge Street.'

We made for Bridge Street. Thank God, the first cab in the queue was a Leopard, not Porter or Hammer, both of whom we were, apparently, boycotting. 'Porter were vile to Polly last time she used them, and one of the Hammer drivers forced me off the road and then called me a fucking cunt,' Vicki had explained.

Vicki boycotted an unfathomable number of companies, several of them mutually exclusive. It was only possible to get drinkable Fairtrade coffee, for example, at the supermarket that she wouldn't go to because they kept all their staff on zero hours contracts. Clearly both my own employers were anathema to her for this reason; it was just as well that she had little need of a hotel here, and none whatsoever of industrial quantities of foam rubber.

Polly had limited patience with this way of carrying on, pointing out that we'd all starve to death before we attained consumer purity, and anyway, buying anything from anybody around here was probably keeping someone in a job. She was picky about taxis, though, and I couldn't really blame her.

Fortunately, this driver was patient to a fault and had a better idea than I did about how to fold up Polly's chair to get it into the boot.

'This is the first thing we've done today that hasn't been far more difficult than it needed to be,' I told him as we drove home.

I was in the front: Polly was trying so hard, and so obviously, not to cry that I thought I'd better give her some privacy. 'Could have been worse,' she said from the back seat. 'If we'd had to take the train anywhere there's a whole new set of things to go horribly wrong.'

'Well now, trains,' the driver said. 'I was once booked to drive a lady to Liverpool because the lift was broken here and they couldn't get her to the right platform with her wheelchair.'

'I had a whole train diverted to a different platform for me once,' Polly said. 'Some people are really helpful.' She smiled, damply, at the driver via the rear view mirror, including him in *some people*. Maybe me, too?

'Yes, but you shouldn't have to rely on people being helpful, should you? There should be a system in place to make things happen whether you happen to meet the helpful people or not.'

'*Yes*,' Polly said. 'Systems are very under-rated, if you ask me.'

'Only if they actually work. Our bookings system, for example...' It got detailed. I let my attention wander until this conversation got us to River Way. I reached for my wallet. Polly saw. 'I'm getting this one, Ben.'

'Oh, yes. Sorry.'

When the cab drew up outside our house she paid the fare; I, meanwhile, got out and walked round to the back end. Unfolding the wheelchair was, I knew, easier than folding it up, but I still needed the boot opened before I could do anything useful. The driver ended up doing almost everything. Polly shuffled out of the taxi. She really did look dreadful, and I was glad we hadn't tried to take the bus both ways. I don't think either of our nerves could have stood it.

'We going in, then?' she said as she settled herself in the wheelchair.

'Oh, yes, sorry.'

'Top tip. Go and open the door first; it's much easier than trying to reach over my head with the key.'

'Roger. Wilco.' I almost managed to make her laugh with that, and I smiled to myself as I headed up the path to unlock the door. I stopped smiling when I turned back, though; from a few metres' distance it was easier to see how much she'd wilted. She must have been putting up a hell of a front for the benefit of the taxi driver (now hurtling off down the close) and now she'd stopped trying. Or she just couldn't keep it up any more, even if she wanted to.

'You said you need to eat,' I said as I wheeled her through the front door.

'You said you'd fix something,' she retorted half-heartedly.

I left her in the sitting room and went to see what there was in the fridge. 'Ham sandwich OK with you? Or cheese?'

'Ham, please. And pickle, if there is any.'

'Your lucky day,' I called back. It was possibly a mistake. I tried not to notice that she was crying again, and concentrated on making the sandwiches, and a mug of tea for each of us. I saw her point. From her perspective it must have been a lousy day.

'Thanks,' she said when I brought the plates and tea through. 'That's a bit above and beyond.'

'It's a sandwich.' I took a bite out of mine. To be fair, it was a pretty good sandwich.

'Still. On top of everything else.' She nibbled absently at the edge. 'Uncalled-for abuse from members of the public.'

I asked, 'Do people say that kind of stuff to Michael, when he's with you?'

'Not so far.' Polly grimaced. 'But give it time. Just when you think you've encountered every possible permutation of ableist bullshit, something new pops up to surprise you.'

'I thought we must have crossed everything off the list today,' I said. 'Well, not the train stuff, like you were saying in the taxi, but apart from that...'

'We're still missing "benefit cheat", "scrounger", et cetera,' she said, and sipped her tea.

I didn't tell her about the newspaper. Instead, in an effort to lighten the tone, I said, 'Just unfounded allegations of shagging dope cheats.'

Polly snorted, though I don't think either of us really found it particularly funny. 'I don't think she knew who you were.'

'Yeah, but you did.'

'*Touché.*' She giggled softly. It became a sob. 'Sorry, sorry – I'm just so *tired*... If you can force your heart and nerve and sinew to serve your turn long after they are gone – yes, but I was only trying to go to the fucking bank!' She hid her face from me and went on crying. I half-turned away from her, not entirely sure whether she wanted me there or not, and, since I was there anyway, passed her a tissue. I knew that this was about as much as I could do to help.

Because I'd been there myself. I knew what it was to be so literally exhausted that I couldn't move, to have burned all my matches and finished a stage on sheer willpower. I knew how shattered I'd felt the day after.

People talk a lot about willpower. Most of it's bullshit. Yes, you *can* use will-power to push on through; you *can* make your body do things you wouldn't believe. But it's the equivalent of putting vintage cognac in your petrol tank: not very effective, and horribly expensive. It's not sustainable.

So you learn to choose your battles. You don't go all out, all day, every day. Some days you take it easy, sit in the peloton, stop fighting, roll in with the autobus. Whatever it takes to get you to the end.

But what if every day was a battle you couldn't choose to opt out of? What if going to the bank was the equivalent of the Alpe d'Huez?

I knew what Polly was talking about. I knew about being on the edge of my body's limits, even if my limits were very different from hers. But I was only just beginning to realise how far I was going to have to adjust my frame of reference in order to *understand* what life was like for her.

And, because I couldn't tell her any of that, I just passed her another tissue.

Chapter 11

To my surprise, the first major argument wasn't between me and Polly. It was more between Vicki and... well, the rest of the world, I suppose. At any rate, Vicki started it. Over toilet roll, when it got to half past eight in the evening and we discovered that there wasn't any.

'Bugger,' Vicki said, through clenched teeth. 'I was going to get some on the way home from work. Bugger, bugger.'

'I can run out to the offie and get some now, if you like?' I offered. It was only just getting dark.

Vicki shook her head. 'They only have Andrex.' She seemed unreasonably distressed by this.

'I'll pay,' I said. 'I don't mind.'

She shook her head angrily. 'It's not that.'

If it wasn't that, I didn't know what it was.

Polly did. 'Vicki,' she said, 'please could you consider that the world might not come to an end if *just this once* we don't buy recycled bog roll? Or whatever it is you're angsting about this week?'

'Not really, no.' She glared at Polly. 'I'll get some tomorrow.'

'And what are we meant to wipe our arses with in the meantime?' Polly asked pleasantly.

Vicki started to say that she didn't care, but burst into tears halfway through. She stormed out, slamming the door behind her. A tea towel slid from the oven door to the ground with a sad little *fwoomph* noise.

Polly went on eating her cereal as if nothing had happened, though her breath was going in tiny, sharp, affronted gasps through her nose.

'What on earth was that about?' I said, after a little silence.

'She's knackered herself to the point where she just doesn't care any more. She's running on guilt. No matter what we do, or she does, at this point, it's going to be wrong.'

'You seem remarkably calm about it.'

Polly shrugged her shoulders. 'Says more about her than it does about me. Specifically, that it's time she had a break. When she's got herself together I'll see if she has any leave booked. I suspect not.'

'This is a regular occurrence, then?'

'Every couple of years. She used to get like this at uni, too.' She frowned at the puddle of discoloured milk at the bottom of the bowl. 'The trouble is, she has no idea of her own limits and she just keeps going and going until she hits a brick wall at full speed. Then someone tells her to take a holiday, but it turns out that she can't for another three weeks until they've wrapped up this urgent case or rehomed this family or whatever it is. So she limps through those three weeks completely burnt out and hating everybody.'

'You were quite robust with her,' I commented.

Polly accepted that with a little nod. 'No reason to take shit from her, even if she's got some to unload,' she said. 'Makes her feel less guilty about being a bitch after the event, anyway, than if I just sat there and took it.'

When I'd finished my own dinner, I walked down to the corner shop and got some toilet roll. Not Andrex, but still branded, and not recycled. I threw the packaging away before Vicki could see it. Nobody said anything.

Things made a little more sense the next morning, when I went downstairs and found Vicki gazing morosely into a cup of coffee. She was dressed more smartly than I'd ever seen her before, in a neat suit with a striped blouse. 'Do you have an interview?' I asked. She hadn't mentioned anything like that.

'Mm?' She looked up and saw me looking at her clothes. 'No, I always dress like this for work.' She sounded stuffy, and I saw that her eyes were watery and her nose was red. 'It's just that I usually change at the office.'

'Taking the train today, then?'

She nodded.

'You look awful,' I said.

She grimaced. 'Thanks for that.'

'Seriously. Are you sure you should be going to work?'

'Probably not.' She looked at her half-drunk coffee, grimaced again, and disentangled a bunch of keys from the bracelets and small change in the bowl on the table.

'What do you think it is?'

'Probably just a cold.' She didn't sound at all convincing, or convinced. 'Nothing worth letting people down for, anyway.'

I munched my way through my toast and wondered whether I should persuade her not to go in. I hadn't had to take a sick day myself, yet. Maybe I'd be going in for this heroic self-sacrifice, too, if I were in Vicki's situation. 'What about your colleagues?' I asked.

'What about them?'

'What will they say to your spreading your germs all over the office?'

'One of them probably gave this bug to me in the first place.' She broke off to blow her nose. 'And they are much less likely than me to be let go of if they don't come in.'

'That's not right,' I said.

She blew her nose again before answering. 'I'm being unfair on them, actually. There's nobody who doesn't put the hours in, who wouldn't turn up feeling and looking worse than I do.'

'Two wrongs don't make a right,' I said. Back in the day, if I'd shown up at the breakfast table looking like Vicki did at this moment, I'd have been rushed back to bed in ten seconds flat, partly because I'd be sod all use on the bike, but mostly so I didn't infect my team mates with my evil death plague germs. These days, of course, it was simple. If I didn't turn up I didn't get paid. Well, I'd have to see what happened when I went down with something. Which wouldn't be long, if I spent any more time in the same room as Vicki.

I don't think she could read my thoughts, but she got up, tipped the dregs of her coffee down the sink, and said, 'See you later.'

'Come home if you feel bad,' I said, for all the good it would do. She obviously already felt bad. She simply sniffed, and walked out.

A few moments later I saw her, now with a light jacket on over the suit, getting her purple bike out of the shed. She wheeled it across the lawn and disappeared from view down the side of the house.

She texted me later in the day to say that she'd been sent home ill by her boss (who clearly wasn't such a sadist as she'd made out) and could I pick Polly up on my way home. It seemed that one of Polly's church ladies was going to drop her off at the Three Bottles after some event, and Vicki was going to pick her up when she got home from work. Quite why the church lady couldn't take her all the way home I couldn't work out, but since it wasn't really any of my business I didn't ask, just texted back to say that would be no problem. And, because I had a headache, felt slightly virtuous about it.

The Three Bottles was quite lively for a week night. I eventually found Polly at a small table behind a very rowdy book group. The substitution of me for Vicki didn't seem to be a particular disappointment, so she'd evidently been warned.

She motioned me to sit down, and murmured, 'I've been eavesdropping for the last quarter of an hour. They've established that the biscuits were metaphorical, but they can't work out whether or not the incest was literal.'

'What on earth are they reading?' I kept my voice down too, though it was hardly necessary.

'I'm not sure. I haven't been able to catch sight of the book. It sounds vaguely like Ian McEwan, but I don't think it's one I've read, if so. The biscuits don't sound right. Though the whole group seems to want to stab the hero in the face, which does.'

'Right,' I said. I still hadn't put anything on my new library card, and whatever this book was, it didn't seem like a very good place to start. 'What about a drink?' I offered. Now that I was inside, in the warm, I was reluctant to go out into the rain. My headache was getting worse, though; I hoped I wasn't coming down with Vicki's cold. I told myself that it was probably just dehydration.

She smiled. 'Yeah, why not?'

'What's yours?'

'Orange juice, please.'

I went to the bar. My timing was bad: two of the women from the book club had got up just before me, and were putting in an order for their entire table. I thought I heard someone say my name, but when I looked around nobody seemed to be trying to get my attention. The place was crowded; I'd obviously been mistaken.

The barmaid cleared her throat, loudly. 'Are you being served?'

'Oh, yes,' I said. 'Sorry.'

I got an orange juice for Polly and a Coke for myself. By the time I got back, the rest of the book club had got sidetracked onto the 1924 Everest expedition, and I gave up on trying to follow it.

'Thanks,' Polly said. She looked closely at me. 'Are you all right? You look a bit pale.'

'Headache,' I said. 'That's all.'

'I've got some paracetamol, if you'd like.'

'Don't worry,' I said, 'it'll pass off in time.'

Polly looked sceptical. 'I doubt it, in here.'

Which was a good point, but I had a drink now. 'I'll survive.'

'And be miserable.'

'Yeah, well. I don't like taking drugs when I don't have to.' Then I realised what I'd just said, and added, 'These days.' Come to that, I hadn't exactly enjoyed the process when I was in the peloton.

81

'Well,' Polly said, 'you've seen the stuff I take every day. Don't think I do it for fun, any more than I eat food for fun.'

'You're actually ill, though. I've just got a headache.'

'Ben,' she said, 'stop being such a bloody martyr and take some paracetamol.'

The more we talked about it, the worse it felt. 'I'll take that as a prescription,' I said. 'You're the nearest thing to a doctor I've got.'

'God help you.' She reached backwards to pull her bag round onto her lap and scrabbled in it until she brought out a little quilted pouch full of pills. From this, she extracted a blister pack of paracetamol. 'Here you go. The longer I'm ill, the more I realise what a terrible doctor I'd have been.'

That surprised me. 'Vicki said you were doing really well on your course before you had to drop out.'

'Oh, academically, yes, I was good – but I had no empathy and no willingness to believe I might be wrong.' She laughed, and almost managed not to sound bitter. 'I think all doctors – nurses, physiotherapists, you name it – should have a stint at being ill. It broadens your horizons no end. The irony is, of course, that I don't think I'll ever be well enough now to do the hours.'

'That sucks,' I said. I knew better by now than to say, *oh no, I was sure she'd get well*.

'Doesn't it? I'd be such a good doctor now. I'd be able to tell the difference between malingering and actually needing help.' She scowled at the table. 'Do you know, when we met I'd had the wheelchair less than a year. I didn't want to admit how life-changing it was. I still half-believed I could make myself better by sheer will-power.'

'Doesn't work,' I said. 'Take it from me. If *really, really wanting* to be even a tiny bit fitter made any difference, I'd be halfway up a mountain at this moment. No.' I looked at the clock. 'I'd be flat on my face, getting the aches and pains of a day's work massaged out of me.'

'That paracetamol not kicked in yet?' Polly said drily. I don't think she much liked my drawing parallels between our situations. I couldn't blame her. *Cheat* is an unpleasant word even when you fully deserve it. Polly didn't deserve it at all, and she'd had it chucked at her often enough to resent being bracketed with a real one. 'It's odd, though,' she said. 'You and your paracetamol. Me and my wheelchair. We both know that if we only gave in and used them, we'd have hours more productive time in the day. I wouldn't be exhausted, and you wouldn't be in pain.'

'It's half past six in the evening. I have no intention of being productive.'

'Point taken. But imagine it was half past eight in the morning: you'd still be manfully soldiering on. And this time last year I'd have slogged fifty yards down the road, *with* the cane that even I couldn't pretend I could do without, slogged fifty yards back, and achieved precisely nothing for the whole of the rest of the day. And I would have told myself about *willpower* and *moral fibre* and *hauling myself up by my bootstraps*. And those things are bad enough when I'm the one telling myself: imagine if I *had* become a doctor; imagine if I was telling people as ill as me, worse than me. It doesn't bear thinking about... I used to think it was all in the mind, you know,' she said.

'What was?'

'This.' She gestured at herself. 'Before I got it myself.'

'So what is it really?' I asked.

She grimaced. 'They don't know. That's why they like writing it off as a mental illness. Now, don't get me wrong, I've got a mental illness, too, but *this* is pretty damn physical.'

'I never said it wasn't,' I said, startled.

'No.' She smiled sadly. 'I think I'm talking to my past self, if I'm talking to anybody.'

'Does she listen?'

'No.' She said, suddenly, 'Michael believes that I will get better. Which is great, because it saves me having to do it.'

I let that one lie where it fell. 'Mm,' I said.

'And he believes that I'm a human being who's worthy of respect and a bit of dignity even before I get better. Which also saves me having to believe that all the time, because very often I don't.'

I had no idea what to say. No idea at all. So I offered her another drink.

Chapter 12

I don't know whether it was due to self-delusion, high overall fitness, or a deal with the devil, but Vicki got over her cold almost before the paracetamol had dealt with my headache. She was back at work after a day in bed, and on Saturday she took her bike out for a mighty ride, the same as usual, and was back in time for lunch. I'd taken Polly into town that morning, and we'd bought cheese and a pork pie from the farmers' market as a special treat. We just beat Vicki back to the house; so it turned out that we all ate together, and spent the afternoon playing board games. Peace seemed to have been restored.

Until Vicki's phone buzzed, that is.

She glared at it, swiped the screen irritatedly, and then exclaimed, 'Oh, *really*?'

'What's up?' Polly asked.

'Nothing, really. Except Gianna P., whoever she is, has just beaten my Q.O.M. over Shepherd's Top. *Again*. Don't laugh,' she said to me.

I wasn't laughing; it had just taken me a moment to remember that Q.O.M. was the women's equivalent of K.O.M., King of the Mountains. Well, *mountain*, singular, in this case. 'You said, again?'

She tapped at the phone and handed it to me. It showed the profile of Shepherd's Top and the leaderboard of times. At the top was Gianna P. – set just now. Seven seconds behind, Vicki W. – set four hours ago. A long way down in third was a Laura F., and fourth, fifth and sixth were several minutes further back.

'You're still ahead of Paul Cunningham, though, right?' Polly asked.

'Well, yes,' Vicki said, as if that were hardly worth mentioning.

I tapped on Vicki's name, to see all her times for that climb. She'd been improving steadily over the past few months. Then I tapped back out of that and looked at Gianna P., and saw Vicki's point. Every single one of her top ten times was ever so slightly faster than Vicki's equivalent. Vicki had set her time on Saturdays; Gianna had set hers on Sundays. Except today.

'Well, you've got her running scared,' I said. 'She's changed her routine.'

'Do you think that's what it is? I was just assuming she had some engagement tomorrow and was getting her ride in early.'

'May I see?' Polly asked. I passed the phone to her. 'No,' she said after a little while, 'I think Ben's right. She's reacting to you. You went really early today; that gave her time to get out this afternoon.'

'Ha, d'you think?' Vicki was blushing. 'Perhaps I'll go out on Sunday next week. That'll show her.'

'What about the club ride?' Polly asked.

'What about it?' Vicki asked. 'They aren't going anywhere I haven't been before.'

I was working all day that next Sunday, and came out into a serene spring evening, with a calm sunset over the sea fading to a cool blue sky overhead, and the very last of the sun bathing everything in gold. I decided that it was too beautiful to run through, and walked home instead.

Polly looked disappointed to see me. 'Oh, it's you.'

'Who else would it be?' I kicked my trainers off.

'Vicki.' Polly was trying to sound unconcerned.

'She's not back?' I wasn't particularly worried. Vicki had been working more sensible hours this week; she was leaving after me and getting home before me. But of course today wasn't a work day for her.

'No, she's not,' Polly said. 'And she hasn't replied to my texts. I'm starting to get worried.'

I'd left the house before anyone else was stirring. 'When did she go out?' I asked.

'Just after lunch. She was going to ride up Shepherd's Top.'

'That's right.' I remembered now. 'Beat the mysterious Gianna. Perhaps she was there. Perhaps they got in a fight.' I couldn't really imagine Vicki getting in a fight with anyone – not a physical one, anyway – and even Polly smiled.

'She hasn't got much daylight left. I'm going to phone her,' she said.

'OK.' I went into the kitchen and turned the oven on to preheat. Through the open door I could hear Polly talking.

'Vicki? Vicki! Are you OK?... You *what*? When?... Oh, OK... Yes, it *is* that late; Ben's just got in, and he wasn't even running... Well, so long as you've got lights with you... OK, good... Fine... See you later, then... Bye...'

She tramped into the kitchen and announced triumphantly, 'She's just leaving the Fiddler's Elbow now. She didn't realise how late it was.'

'Really,' I said. 'Shall I do fishfingers for you, too?' Since the toilet roll incident, I'd taken to offering Polly food as a matter of course. I wasn't as good a cook as Vicki, but I'd got to the point where I could reliably arrange some starch, protein and vitamins on a plate and nobody would throw up. And if we were going to share Vicki's wrath, we might as well share my non-sustainable fishfingers, too.

'Please. Just a couple. And she found Gianna P.'

'Cool. Did she beat her?'

'She didn't say.' Polly was smiling to herself. I had the feeling I was missing something, but I couldn't work out what. Polly, having apparently spilled as many of the beans as she felt necessary, changed the subject and asked me about work, and I got so deeply involved in the story of Eddie and the spare grapefruit that I forgot all about Vicki and Gianna P.

It wasn't until about nine that I remembered, when Vicki came in, with her cycling shoes click-clicking on the concrete path. I was messing around upstairs, but I could hear Polly going through the motions of telling her off for giving us a fright. Then she said, in quite a different tone, 'So...?'

I couldn't hear Vicki's reply, but, after a couple of false starts, it went on a while. Then Polly said, 'So when are you seeing her again?' And then, 'Well, don't rush into anything.'

Ah, I thought. And then, *oh*.

When my alarm went off the next morning, I remembered. I jabbed at my phone until the beeping stopped, and lay in bed for a few minutes, reviewing the evidence and wondering if I was an idiot. I hadn't made an idiot of myself, I could reassure myself of *that*, at least, but... should I have seen this coming? Should I have known?

I could pretend that I'd made no assumptions, had been waiting to see if Vicki turned up with a partner before I jumped to any conclusions. In reality, the conclusions I'd jumped to without even realising it were, firstly, that she was so busy with her work that she didn't have time for a love life, and, secondly, that if she turned up with anybody, it would be a boyfriend.

After all, I'd assumed that if she and Polly lived together, and Polly was with Michael, then Vicki must be straight too... Now that I spelt it out to myself, I could see that there was no logic in there at all. Polly and Vicki were, after all, two independent human beings, with no particular influence over each other beyond what they ate for dinner. Polly could have had a whole harem of men for all the difference it would make to Vicki. But...

The peloton – well, the men's peloton – is a very heterosexual place. All that testosterone and competitiveness floating around. I suppose there must have been gay guys in there – what was that statistic? One in ten? If you extrapolated from that then the equivalent of a whole team in every race would be gay. Maybe less than that, maybe people were less likely to go into pro cycling if they weren't straight, but all the same, there'd have to be *some* in there.

It was different in the women's sport, of course. I could name several lesbian professional cyclists without even thinking about it... When I put it like that, I really felt like an idiot. Why hadn't the possibility even occurred to me?

Because she asked for your autograph, a sneering little voice in my head suggested. No. Surely not. I admitted – quite often, as it happened – to being a bit of a dickhead, but I wasn't that sort of entitled creep. I honestly hadn't thought that Vicki was interested in me. Well, I mean, I'd been ridiculously grateful that she'd chosen to think of me as a human being; maybe she did find me *interesting*, but I hadn't thought that she was *interested*. At least I couldn't possibly think that now...

Fortunately, my alarm went off again before I could tie myself up in any more logical knots. So I got up and went to work, and stopped thinking about it for most of the day.

'So,' I asked Vicki that evening when we were cooking our respective dinners, 'did you beat her?'

'Beat her?' she echoed, and blushed.

'Her time? Over Shepherd's Top?'

She gave a little self-conscious laugh. 'Do you know, I didn't actually check.'

'You didn't check?'

Her blush grew deeper. She mumbled, 'So surprised to actually meet her... didn't think to stop the ride recording until about half an hour after we'd actually finished...'

'And you didn't look at the leaderboard for the climb?' I said, wickedly.

'No,' she said, puzzled. 'Wow. Suppose I'd better look now.' She fished her phone out of her pocket. Her eyes narrowed, then a slow smile spread across her face.

'Well?' I thought I knew what the answer was going to be.

I was wrong.

'No. She beat me.' She moved to turn down the heat on a pan of boiling water.

'Oh.'

Her smile grew broader. 'That means a rematch, then.'

And I got it. She looked as if she'd be happy chasing this woman up hills every Sunday until kingdom come. I felt very lonely all of a sudden.

'I got the impression that you were going to meet her again anyway,' I ventured.

'Yes, but now I have an excuse to make it happen.'

I got the end of a packet of peas out of the freezer. Just enough for Polly and me, I thought. 'You like this girl?'

She looked down at the floor. 'I like her a lot.'

'Love at first sight?'

'Can't be. I don't believe in love at first sight.' She looked up, still grinning. 'And she still might turn out to be an axe murderer. All strangers are axe murderers. My dad says so.'

'Even axe murderers need love.' I dumped the solid block of peas into a bowl, added a dribble of water, balanced a plate on top, and shoved it in the microwave.

'Not from me, they don't.' She grew serious. 'I don't even know whether she likes women.'

'She didn't mention...?' I ventured.

'She didn't mention boyfriends, girlfriends, *anyone*, past or present.'

'You didn't ask?'

'Too shy,' she said, which wasn't like Vicki at all. 'She said she lives alone, and I'm ninety-nine per cent sure she's single.'

I tried a different approach. 'You told her you *do*...?' Pretending it wasn't news to me.

'I very carefully dropped in a mention of my ex-girlfriend. I tried to stress the *ex* and the *girl* equally. I think it pinged something, but whether she was just mentally recategorising me I don't know.'

'So you find out on Sunday?'
'I hope so.' She was smiling again. 'I really hope so.'

Chapter 13

She found out – and the answer was the one she'd been hoping for. Suddenly we were seeing even less of her than usual. She stopped doing shopping on Saturday and ordered groceries on the internet instead. She dumped the cycling club to go out with Gianna. She started spending the evenings with her too.

But she did eventually bring Gianna back to the house for dinner. It was a mighty palaver: Vicki tended to get stressed enough just cooking for herself, and, while neither Polly nor I were likely to complain about being fed, cooking for a girlfriend was a big deal. I had the idea – probably based on her name alone – that Gianna was a fantastic cook herself.

Michael was not invited, which should probably have told me something. At the time, knowing Vicki's opinion of him, I wasn't exactly surprised. So it was just Polly and me there when Vicki opened the door, chivvied herself and another person through it, and announced, 'This is Gianna! This is Polly, and this is Ben.'

Gianna was shorter and stockier than Vicki, with dark hair and eyes. She wore jeans with a shapeless maroon jumper, high-heeled leather boots, and wire-framed glasses. Her hair was tied back with a green scarf, and if I hadn't seen her record I wouldn't have guessed she was a cyclist.

'Polly. Ben. It's nice to meet you.'

I hadn't expected the Scottish accent. It threw me a little, and I couldn't work out how old she was: five years older than Vicki, perhaps? She was shy, awed equally by my notoriety and the knowledge that Polly was the best friend whose approval had to be won. *It's fine*, I wanted to tell her; *if Vicki likes you, Polly will put up with you*. But this wasn't the kind of thing you could say at a first meeting.

It was, as ever, awkward that the interest we all held in common was the one that was the most embarrassing for me. I bring my own personal elephant into every room I enter. So I led the conversation round to the women's sport, and asked whether Marianne Vos could beat Beryl Burton if you gave them both the same bike.

Vicki, predictably, said no. Gianna said probably. Polly said that it would depend what era bikes they were using, and we got sidetracked and started talking about downtube shifters while Vicki saw to the potatoes.

'They take a bit of getting used to,' Gianna said. 'I don't mind them, though.'

I admitted, 'I've never actually tried them.'

'I'd offer you a lend of my bike, but it'd be far too small for you,' Gianna said.

I was glad that Vicki's attention was on the cooking. I said, 'That's kind of you, but I don't cycle at all any more.'

Gianna nodded. 'That's fair enough,' she said. There was no censure in her voice.

'Vicki told us you aren't a member of the cycling club,' I said.

'She told *me* I wasn't missing much,' Gianna retorted, with a cautious little smile.

'That tallies with what she's told us,' Polly said. 'I wouldn't know, obviously.'

'So why *do* you stick with it, Vicki?' I asked as she put plates down in front of Gianna and Polly.

'It's not as bad as all that.' Vicki's face was flushed and slightly shiny. She'd mashed the potatoes into submission, but they'd obviously fought back. 'Everyone except the secretary is perfectly pleasant.'

'Ah, yes, the notorious Paul Cunningham,' I murmured.

'Paul Cunningham,' Gianna echoed. 'What's wrong with the guy?'

Vicki and Polly looked at each other. 'Well, he's –' Vicki began. 'Oh, he's just –'

Polly said, 'He's like – no –'

Gianna glanced at me, questioning.

'No,' I said. 'I've never met him, so I've no idea.'

'He's a smug, misogynistic git,' Polly said, 'and he can't deal with the fact that Vicki's a better cyclist.'

Gianna didn't look any less confused. 'So... how does that manifest itself?'

'Snide comments. Forgetting to update the leaderboards when I happen to be at the top of them. Always giving the *Member of the Year* trophy to his mate Steve.'

'*Member* of the year,' Polly said, and giggled.

I was probably looking a little sceptical. I was certainly thinking that they were being a bit harsh on the guy, and I was pleased when Gianna said. 'Is he really as bad as all that?'

'And more. You'll have to come on a ride one day and find out.'

I was about to protest that I'd given up cycling, had Vicki forgotten that, when I realised that she meant Gianna. Who said, 'It's no skin off my nose. I've never belonged to a cycling club anyway.'

Perhaps fortunately, Polly hit on the idea of asking Gianna what she did for a living. 'Vicki said you were an artist.' She just about managed not to sound disapproving.

'That's a bit generous,' Gianna said. 'I'm a silversmith.'

'Oh – cool,' I said. 'How did you get into that?'

She smiled properly for the first time. 'A bit like that, actually. I saw it on the list of summer school options at my college, thought it sounded interesting, and went from there.'

'And it's your full-time job?' Polly asked. Vicki winced very slightly, and I could see her point: it did feel rather like a Victorian father asking about a young man's prospects.

'And then some,' Gianna said ruefully. 'I spend half my time making stuff, and the other half selling it. Occasionally, I sleep.'

Even Polly wasn't brazen enough to ask how much she made doing this. She just said, 'Well, so long as it's keeping you going.'

'Just about,' Gianna said. 'Just about.'

Polly said, 'I'm always telling Vicki off for overworking herself.'

'There's always something that needs doing,' Vicki protested, quietly. This wasn't a proper argument; they were just going through the motions.

'Which is why you have to stop and decide you're going to do it tomorrow.' I realised then that Polly wasn't warning Gianna off. She was just warning her.

Gianna's eyes opened ever so slightly wider. 'So, Ben,' she said, 'Vicki says you work at a hotel now?'

'And a warehouse,' I said.

'Oh, right? What sort of warehouse?'

'Foam rubber,' I said. I'd discovered – mainly from talking about it at my other job – that I could raise a laugh simply by saying the words, lengthening the last consonants. *Foammmm rubberrrr*. It raised a laugh now. Then Gianna said, 'So, who buys it?' and that led us on to my inexpert overview of the rubber market. From there, we got onto Vicki's work, and, because we all three knew a little bit about it, there weren't so many landmines for anybody to put their feet in.

After dinner, I cleared the plates off the table while Vicki went up to her room to dig out the Scrabble set. Polly, meanwhile, interrogated Gianna about previous girlfriends (none) and boyfriends (also none). As far as I could make out, Gianna had made it to the age of twenty-nine without falling in love with anybody, concluded that it was just wasn't going to happen, and got on with her life. Vicki seemed to have come as a huge surprise to her – but then, I admitted to myself, Vicki *was* surprising, generally.

I couldn't imagine what it must have been like, that first encounter at the top of the climb. I knew that Vicki was well-nigh irresistible when all she wanted was an autograph: what must it be like to be chatted up by her? What if you didn't realise for the first hour or so that chatting up was going on? When did the duel become a date? It wasn't as if Vicki had set off up Shepherd's Top in search of a girlfriend: when had she realised what was going on?

Just as I was beginning to feel weird, wondering about all this, Vicki got back with the Scrabble. I'm not very good at Scrabble. Gianna, it turned out, was better than both me and Vicki. None of us were as good as Polly, who racked up her score by knowing all the silly little two-letter words and stacking them three deep, and then managed to use all seven of her tiles changing IS into PERTUSSIS. By some fluke, however, I managed to land a Z on a triple word score, which edged me up into third place, and I didn't humiliate myself completely.

Vicki didn't seem to mind losing at all.

I offered to wash up, and Polly said that she'd dry and put away.

'You're not too tired?' I asked, a bit worried that she was going to overdo things.

She smiled. 'I had a massive nap this afternoon. Trust me: I wouldn't have offered if I didn't think I could do it.'

Vicki and Gianna, looking rather self-conscious, made some grateful noises and disappeared. Probably upstairs. I turned the radio on. Polly laughed at me.

I justified it by saying, 'They don't want to hear what we're saying about them.'

'Any more than we want to hear...' She raised her eyebrows, and the volume on the radio.

'Exactly.'

'Give me a tea towel,' Polly said. She started clearing the draining board. 'Start with the glasses.'

'I know, I know,' I muttered. I ran the tap hot and wiped the glasses under the stream of water as she brought them to me. I liked the efficient way she dried them, quick and precise. I could see why she would have been a good doctor. Neither of us said anything for a little while. I don't know what was up with Polly – maybe she was just tired – but I couldn't think of anything to say that didn't sound pervy, which I didn't want to be. When I couldn't manage that, I tried to think of something to say about the song that was playing, but I didn't know it. So we just washed and dried, respectively.

'So,' Polly said, when I'd got well into the plates and cutlery stage, 'what do *you* think?'

'Think?'

She glanced meaningfully in the direction of the ceiling.

'Oh.' Vicki and Gianna. Even I could tell that Vicki was smitten. I said so.

'And what do you make of Gianna herself?' Polly grabbed a handful of knives and forks, dried them one by one, and dropped them into the drawer.

'She seems pleasant enough,' I said. 'I thought she was a bit quiet.'

'Nervous, I suppose,' Polly said neutrally. She laughed. 'She couldn't have been as quiet as all that when they first met. Even Vicki couldn't keep a conversation going single-handedly for six hours.'

'I still don't believe it was six hours,' I said.

'I like her,' Polly said, unexpectedly. 'I just can't work out whether she's noticed yet that she's one of Vicki's lame ducks.'

'Lame ducks?' I was confused.

Polly looked at me pityingly. 'Projects. People Vicki picks up off the streets. Oh, come on, Ben, you must have worked it out! You and me, we're Vicki's lame ducks.'

'She didn't pick *you* up off the street,' I objected. I was bristling slightly at Polly's assessment of my status. Mostly because I couldn't disagree with it.

'No, but I have to keep reminding her of that. And it will be interesting to see how things work out when she's head over heels in love with one of her own projects.'

98

'I don't think Gianna thinks of herself as a project,' I said. I wasn't sure that Vicki was head over heels in love with her yet, either, though things certainly seemed to be heading in that direction. 'She strikes me as very... independent.'

'Oh, I agree,' Polly said. She folded the tea towel neatly and hung it over one of the drawer handles. 'That's why it's going to be interesting.'

Chapter 14

And then Polly and Michael broke up.

I didn't realise at first; his schedule had always been erratic and, when he didn't show up in any evening over the course of a whole fortnight, I simply assumed he'd seen Polly during the day. It took me a while to add that to Polly's bad mood and various snatches of overheard conversation ('so I said, no, it means you have a *choice*, and you've chosen...'; 'you're *sure* you're all right? I don't want to make you feel bad...'; 'well, I always thought he was a bit weird...') and arrive at the correct conclusion.

From my point of view, it was very bad timing; I'd been saving up, and was hoping that he would be able to give me some advice on buying a second-hand laptop. But I had to admit that Gianna was better company, and, if it came down to a choice between the two of them – which seemed to have been the case – I couldn't fault the decision. I didn't really know what I wanted a laptop *for*, anyway. I attempted to justify it to myself by saying that I wanted to apply for jobs, but I already had two and, while they weren't exactly careers for life, either of them, I had no idea as to what I'd rather be doing. So, I told myself, I'd just have ended up looking to see if people were talking shit about me on the internet, and that never ended well. Either they were, or – as was increasingly the case these days – they weren't talking about me at all. Anyway, I could perfectly well do that on my phone.

What was I going to do with a laptop, then? Internet dating? No, there was an app for that, too. Anyway, I told myself, that wasn't a serious suggestion. Best to avoid upsetting the delicate romantic balance in the house – any more than it had already been upset these last few weeks, that is.

Eventually, I concluded that I'd done quite happily without a laptop up until now, and left well alone.

Gianna was as good as her word, and accompanied Vicki on the next convenient club ride. Not that I remembered that this was meant to be happening until after the event. I'd lost track of time again; I'd almost forgotten that it was a Sunday, and had completely forgotten that the pair of them were riding with company. I just finished my lunchtime shift at the Grand and ran home, same as any other day.

There were voices in the kitchen.

'I really am sorry.' Gianna, sounding embarrassed. More than embarrassed. Distraught.

'You can stop apologising.' Vicki's voice was light, but there was an undertone of strain. 'It's my fault: I should have warned you.'

I cleared my throat. They turned to look at me. Gianna looked as awkward as she'd sounded. Vicki blushed scarlet.

'What's up?' I asked.

'Um,' Vicki said.

'Er,' Gianna said. I waited. 'Um. I caused a bit of a stir at the cycling club.'

'Oh?' I wasn't surprised; we all knew she was good, after all.

But she didn't mean that. 'I didn't realise that Vicki hadn't ever, er...'

'Mentioned that I lived with you,' Vicki admitted. 'Because you know...'

'Because it hadn't occurred to me that you wouldn't...'

Light dawned. I'd always assumed that Vicki wouldn't mention her notorious housemate to her purist cycling comrades; Gianna, it seemed, had assumed the opposite.

'It's fine,' I said. 'I know I'm a bit of an embarrassment.'

'I don't know why I never did,' Vicki said. 'I suppose because you moved in after I joined the club.'

'And you'd mentioned it at some point in our six-hour pub marathon...' Gianna said.

'Well, how else to impress a gorgeous, sophisticated older woman who kept beating my time?'

I was oddly touched. Gianna was blushing. I suspected that I was, too. I said, 'You're not ashamed to be associated with me, then? Because I really wouldn't blame you if you were.'

Vicki laughed. 'Honestly? At this point, Ben, you're just some bloke I happen to live with.'

It was nearly the nicest thing that anyone had said about me in ages. 'Except for the purpose of picking up girls?' I said.

'Except for that, obviously.' She grinned at both of us and, while I think she was mostly aiming at Gianna, I felt a bit warm and fuzzy myself. That radiant, treacherous sense of invincibility got to me too, and I couldn't bring myself to worry too much. What difference did it make if the local club knew that this was where I'd gone to ground? I didn't cycle any more.

It lasted for just over a week. Then Polly got a letter.

She was alone when it arrived. I still feel guilty about that, though it's not as if I could say either that I'd seen it coming or that I'd have been much help if I'd been around. God knows I wasn't much use when I did get in.

She was obviously trying very hard not to cry, and also trying to explain to me what had happened, without letting me have sight of the letter. It wasn't a sustainable combination, and after about thirty seconds she gave in and just cried. 'They're stopping my allowances,' she choked out, 'pending investigation into... into...'

'Into what?'

'*Fraud.*' She turned her face away from me and sobbed into the sofa cushion.

I was horrified. 'What? What the fuck? Of course you're not a fraud.'

'I know. But how do I prove it?'

That was how the conversation went for the next hour or so. 'What the fuck,' Polly kept saying. 'What the fuck.' And then, occasionally, 'How the fuck...?'

Vicki was more practical than me. Polly – very reluctantly – let her look at the letter, and, while she said 'What the fuck?' just like the two of us, she came up with a coherent strategy to actually address the problem. She dredged up her law degree and dissected the letter; found some blogs by people who had also been falsely accused of benefit fraud; looked up how to appeal against withdrawal of benefits.

'Why didn't I think of all that?' Polly said angrily. She hated losing her composure, particularly in front of me.

'As a general rule, people don't tend to think clearly when they're under immediate and unfair pressure that potentially threatens their immediate survival,' Vicki said.

Polly looked slightly happier, but only slightly. Vicki's reframing was kinder to her, but it didn't make the situation any less desperate.

All evening she was unfocussed, distracted; when one of us spoke to her, she'd come back to earth with a bump that was almost audible. All through dinner, all through some tennis that nobody was really watching, she was gazing off into the distance, as if she was trying to see past the huge, terrifying thing in front of her nose, and failing.

At last Vicki suggested that she go to bed, and she acquiesced with that same fuzzy docility. At least, she got up from the sofa and went into her room.

When the door had shut behind her, Vicki looked meaningfully at me. 'Can you come and look at something?' she said quietly.

'Sure,' I said.

She led me upstairs, into her room, and shut the door.

'I wanted to talk about the budget,' she said. 'Let me show you.' She flipped her laptop open.

The budget was an impressive multi-tabbed spreadsheet, colour-coded and laid out in such a way that even I could see what was going out and what was coming in. (What was coming in from Vicki's salary was, I noticed, quite a lot less than I made in a good month.) I saw our three contributions to the rent, and Vicki's share of the utilities that Polly and I handled.

'Wow,' I said. 'That's pretty comprehensive.'

'Polly set it up for me,' she said. She nodded at the screen and lowered her voice. 'Take a look at it. I want to know how fucked we are if Polly's benefits get stopped permanently.'

'You think that's likely to happen?'

'*Anything* could happen, the way things are at the moment.'

'So you're thinking about the worst case scenario, if you and I had to split things fifty-fifty and pick up Polly's share between us...?'

She nodded grimly. 'How little we can ask her to pay. Yes.'

I stared at the screen with a rising sense of helplessness. I probably could afford to pay more, yes. I worked such long hours that I didn't have much time to spend what I earned. I'd somehow managed to avoid getting into drink or fags, and these days a night at the pub with the two girls counted as an extravagance. There was more money going into my bank account than there was going out. But how much more? Would it cover the column marked *Polly*? And, if so, how long for?

'I honestly don't know,' I said. 'I'd have to look at my own –'

An email notification had popped up at the bottom corner of the screen. *Your CC membership*, it said. Vicki clicked on it –

– and clicked out of it, but the computer was slow to respond, and I saw –

Dear Miss Whitaker,

I regret to inform you that your membership of the Coastal Cycle Club has been terminated with immediate effect. This is due to your action in bringing the Club into disrepute through your association with an individual who has been banned from professional cycling for the use of illicit performance-enhancing drugs –

'Fuck,' I said.

'Fuck,' Vicki agreed. Now that there was no question that I hadn't seen it, she opened it again. It didn't look any better for being read slowly.

'Vicki, I'm so sorry –'

'Not your fault.' She bit her lip.

'It is. It said so.'

There wasn't any answer to that, really.

That night I dreamed that I was back on the bike. It was an old dream, one that had recurred repeatedly over the years, and when I was in it I felt as though all the other times had been part of one long nightmare, as though I'd been on the bike for years, climbing for years.

I was on my own on a mountain stage. I couldn't tell where I was in relation to the peloton. Sometimes I thought I was out in the front, but there was none of the can't-believe-they-let-me-get-away-with-this glee that I associated with being the leader. Sometimes I thought I was way, way behind – but where was the autobus, where was the broom wagon? I was alone.

And the mountain never, ever finished. That was the thing. It was one never-ending slog uphill, and every time I woke out of this dream it left me with the nagging sense of not having done enough, not having pushed hard enough.

Sometimes motorcycles flashed past me. I could never read the times on their blackboards. Occasionally I would catch another rider. They all looked like Caprini from behind; they always wore the fluorescent orange kit that we'd had at Hirondelle when I'd first turned pro. I looked back to see who they really were: usually they were Mum, and she'd say, 'Well *done*, Ben! Keep going!' in a false, bright tone that seemed to belong to my childhood. Once or twice it was an actual cyclist, or it was Henri.

This time there were two of them, and as I passed them I realised they were Vicki and Gianna, arguing about where to stop for a picnic. I wanted to stop too, to tell them that there was no time to stop for a picnic, there was never time to stop for a picnic, but my feet kept pedalling and the words wouldn't come out. I realised that they wouldn't actually stop, though, so I knew it was OK, and I kept going.

Once again I got to what looked like the summit, with a bright patchwork of fields swimming in the haze far below me, and once again it turned out to be a hairpin bend, and still I had to climb and climb and climb.

And then Polly passed me. It was ridiculous – or would have been, if it hadn't been a dream. She was pedalling away on a little folding bike, with a cadence that put me to shame. It was exhausting her: sweat and, maybe, tears were running down her face, and her breathing was ragged and horrible.

'Ben,' she said, as she passed me, 'haven't you heard? You're allowed to stop.'

But that couldn't possibly be true, I thought. Because otherwise she would have stopped already, wouldn't she?

Chapter 15

'It's *my* fault,' Gianna said the next time I saw her. Vicki had told her about the disaster and she'd dropped round to grovel. 'I can't believe I was so stupid. I should have thought –'

'*I* should have mentioned,' Vicki said, 'that I'd never, well, mentioned the fact –'

'– that you lived with notorious doper Ben Goddard, who you'd never even have met if he hadn't doped –'

'Stop talking about yourself in the third person, Ben,' Gianna said. 'Are you a raving egomaniac or what?'

'How about, we were all idiots?' Vicki suggested. 'And since I get the consequences, I get to allocate the blame?'

'We could ask Polly to arbitrate,' I said. 'It's definitely not *her* fault.'

'We could not. She's got enough to worry about.'

And she did, too, with her appeal scheduled in just under four hours. Vicki had taken one of her precious days of annual leave to accompany her, and had helped her to assemble a massive portfolio of evidence: bank statements; letters from her doctor, from the hospital, from the DWP; her own personal journals.

'They call it an *informal interview*,' Polly had said dubiously, 'but it's the last stop before *interview under caution*, so I'm not taking any chances.'

It ought to have been an open-and-shut case, but both of them knew that they couldn't count on the interviewer having any sense, and we'd all read stories about people being judged fit for work and dying within the week. Well, Polly's condition wasn't terminal, thank God, but it was chronic and she didn't have a hope of working. Her benefits were literally all that she had to live on.

'Vicki,' I said, when Gianna had gone, 'could it be my fault?'

'Could *what* be your fault? I thought we'd established that all this cycling club crap *wasn't*.'

'Not you. Polly.'

She looked very sceptical. 'What, you mean that someone looked at the electoral register, saw that Polly Devine lives with someone called Ben Goddard, jumped to the conclusion that it must have been Ben Goddard the rather obscure ex-cyclist, and that she must therefore be claiming benefits fraudulently? For God's sake, it's completely illogical.'

'Well, if it could happen to you... Oh, my God, what if it's Cunningham himself?'

'I really don't think so. He's got no quarrel with Polly, and, while he's a bastard, he's not an *evil* bastard.'

'It might not even be the fact that I'm a cheat.' Even in that moment I was shamefully proud that I could use the word of myself without flinching. 'Maybe whoever it is thinks I'm loaded and Polly doesn't need the money.'

'You could be a millionnaire and it would have no bearing on Polly. You'd have to be married to her for that to make any difference.' She sounded unconvinced, though; I suspected that things weren't as clear-cut as all that. After a little while she said, 'I'll have to look up what they mean by *household*. But you don't have any money, so it's not really relevant.'

'Do you want my bank statements, too?'

Vicki sighed. 'I really hope not. I'm not even going to bring you up. There's a danger that if I start suggesting conspiracy theories they'll end up believing them.'

I couldn't stay and argue; Vicki had to get Polly to her appeal, and I had a shift to work. I took out some of my guilt and frustration on the foam rubber I was hauling around, though not enough to damage any of it, and came home to find Polly back from the interview, alone in her room. She was looking at Vicki's ride log online.

'Searching,' she said, 'for proof.'

'But there's not going to be any proof,' I said. 'You can't prove a negative. There isn't going to be anything to see at all.' I looked over her shoulder. The only remarkable thing about Vicki's record was how unremarkable it was – unless, of course, you counted the fact that she'd ridden the same routes often enough to provide meaningful data. 'It's stupid. She's been improving, yes, but she hasn't been improving spectacularly. Her times have got better steadily over the last three years – long before she met me. The only thing I can see that looks even remotely dodgy is this little spike *here*.'

Polly looked. 'That's when we were at uni – it's when she got her current bike.'

'There you go. I was in Spain then. For fuck's sake, *I* was clean then.'

'You don't need to convince *me*,' Polly said, irritated. 'I've known her for years – years which included intensive medical training, for that matter.'

'Of course. I'm sorry.'

She shook her head in apology. 'No. Nothing I wouldn't have said myself. But mud sticks.'

'And I'm filthy,' I observed glumly.

Polly resettled herself in her chair. 'So that was, what, your first season with Grande Fino? Didn't you get a win that year?' she asked.

'I did!' I was so touched that she'd remembered it that I only vaguely registered the blatant change of subject. 'Stanwell.'

'You were in the break,' she recalled, 'and they thought the bunch would catch you, but then you attacked...' She fell silent. I suppose she was incorporating my assertion that it was a clean win into her understanding of events. She must have had to rewrite them once already. Eventually she settled on believing me. 'It was a great win. I didn't think you'd do it until you did.'

'Mm,' I said. My own feelings were mixed. Yes, it had been a clean win; yes, I was proud of it. And yet... 'I wish it was as simple as that.'

'Rather not talk about any of it?' she asked sympathetically. 'Sorry.'

It wasn't exactly that. 'I'll explain some time,' I promised vaguely. 'Where's Vicki, anyway?'

'Gianna took her to the cinema. Said she was trying to cheer her up.'

'You didn't...?'

'Couldn't afford it. Anyway, it would feel like crashing a date.'

Polly didn't say that cheering Vicki up used to be *her* job, but I got the feeling that this formed part of her grievance.

'Oh well,' I said, 'if that's the way it is I'm going to order pizza and we can watch something here. My treat.'

Possibly it wasn't my most tactful suggestion ever, drawing attention to the fact that I could actually afford to get pizza delivered... She declined, none too politely. I ordered pizza anyway, and ate it gloomily in my room.

Polly had got me thinking about that win. It was a memorable one – well, I supposed I was bound to say that, but, objectively speaking, it was memorable by anybody's standards.

It had been a long day out in the break. Five of us, from five different teams, had worked hard to get away and stay away, and now, with about fifty kilometres to the finish, it was beginning to look possible that one of us could take the win. We had six and a half minutes; using the rough-and-ready formula that says it takes a chasing peloton ten kilometres to bring the gap down by a minute, we were just about safe. That was assuming that none of us did anything stupid, because we could only maintain that so long as we worked together. I was surreptitiously checking out my four companions, wondering who was the strongest, who would attack first, and who would fall off the back when they did. I suspect that everyone else was doing exactly the same thing.

And then Henri's voice came crackling through my earpiece. 'Ben. I need you to stop working. We're chasing.'

'Left it a bit late,' I muttered, but not so that Henri could hear me. I had mixed feelings. On the one hand – yes, I was tired, and it would be good to sit up and get dragged along by the slipstream. On the other – I'd thought I was getting the chance of a win. Apparently not.

Either way, I wasn't going to argue with Henri. I dropped obediently to the back of the group and commenced doing the bare minimum that was required to keep me from becoming unstuck.

It didn't take long for the others to notice. 'You going to do some work, Ben?' Mikey Byrne said as he slid past me at the end of his turn on the front.

'My team's chasing,' I explained.

The news made its way through the group. 'Bastards!' Delacroix said when he heard, and attacked. It wasn't a very effective attack, though, and we brought him back. I hung on. Why not?

The time checks came through every few kilometres. We had five and a half minutes on the bunch. Five minutes twenty. Five minutes twenty-five. Then a long gap, and then four and three quarters. Four forty. Four thirty-three.

'Your team expecting us all to drop dead or something?' Mikey asked me.

'Search me. I'm surprised they haven't told me to sit up and wait.'

He muttered something that probably meant that he thought I should, for all the use I was here. We pushed on. Four and a quarter. Four eight. Four five. Under the thirty kilometre arch, and the maths still didn't add up. Four one. Four precisely. Four two. By the time we went under twenty kilometres the chase had got the gap down to three minutes, and hadn't given up.

At seventeen kilometres Delacroix cracked; that early attack had worn him out. Mikey seized the moment with an attack of his own. Gruber and Hart chased him, and so did I, though every moment I was expecting to hear Henri shriek at me to stop. We caught Mikey, and fell back into the same routine: the three of them taking turns on the front (and Gruber's were getting shorter and shorter) and me tagging along on the back for a free ride.

The motorbike flashed past us. *1'23"*, said the chalkboard. Surely the call had to come soon. *Sit up and wait for Jorge.*

Sure enough, the radio buzzed a few seconds later.

But it wasn't to tell me to sit up. 'Ben. They're not going to catch you now. Attack when you think it's appropriate. We'll slow the bunch.'

I could hardly believe it. What a chance! I'd done pretty much nothing for close to thirty kilometres. My rivals had been working hard. If I went at the right moment they'd find it nigh-on impossible to catch me.

I held off for another few minutes, trying to keep my excitement from showing. I'd looked at the road book before I began this stage; I knew there was a bit that would make the ideal spot to launch an attack... yes, here it was. A slight but sudden incline around a sharp left-hand bend. I dropped back a few bike lengths, hoping that the others would think I was losing touch. Then I went for it.

I was a hundred metres clear by the time I reached the corner. It's important to get out of sight as quickly as you can, and the bend in the road let me do that. The others didn't have a hope of sticking with me. They were twice as tired as I was, and they didn't believe they could win. Henri was screaming encouragement into my ear and I was barely aware of it. There was just me and the road. A short section of sinuous lanes, and then I hit the outskirts of Stanwell. The roads straightened out. I had no idea what had happened to the rest of the break. The bunch must be chasing again, surely; it couldn't have taken them long to work out what I was up to. I tried not to think about it. Nothing I could do, except to keep going to the line.

There were spectators lined on the pavements cheering, clapping, honking airhorns. I shouldn't think any of them had a clue who I was, but I was a lone leader with the bunch after me, and that was enough for them. The closer I got to the finish, the louder they became. Into the last kilometre. I had to do it now, surely. Surely? No. I'd seen enough near misses – had had enough of my own – to know that nothing could be certain. And the bunch could see me now. I could hear them. I didn't dare look behind. My legs were burning, my throat was burning, and I could not relax even for half a second.

I almost didn't realise I'd won. I say 'almost': there's always a part of you that knows what it saw, and in that case what it saw was the line. I had time to draw one agonising, gasping breath before the rest of the field swept in around me. But I'd got there first.

I was exhausted. My legs wouldn't hold me up. It didn't matter. There were so many people around me – hugging me, shaking my hand, trying to get me to say something, wheeling me off to wherever I was meant to be now – that I couldn't have fallen over if I'd tried. I unclipped from my pedals, slithered off my bike, and just let myself be carried along.

'Good work, Ben, good work!' It was Henri, fighting his way through the throng. He beamed at me, and suddenly I was overjoyed for more reasons than the win itself. Finally, I thought, I belonged in the team; finally I'd proved myself worthy of the chance I'd been given.

I'm no fan of Grande Fino, but it was a good place to be a winner.

I've wondered ever since how much of a sneaky devious bastard Henri really was. How much did he plan? Were my team mates always meant to chase and then fall back? Or had he really changed his mind only when it had become clear that the break was too good to be caught?

My pride wanted to tell me that it was the latter. Henri didn't want to tell me anything at all. He just smiled and said, 'You stick with us, Ben, you put what you need into the team, and we'll make sure there are more wins.'

You hear what you want to hear, don't you?

You don't realise how frustrating a dysfunctional team can be until you've been part of one. Some of the guys at Grande Fino didn't realise even when they *were* part of one. But I'd been at Hirondelle.

Hirondelle was great. Hirondelle was a laugh. Oh, we worked hard, and we raced hard. We put ourselves through hell, and willingly. We got into breaks and we sprinted even for minor places. (Well, we weren't usually in the running for top placings.) Occasionally a miracle happened, but on the whole we didn't win stuff. Our sponsors understood that – they couldn't have afforded us if we had done much better, I suppose – and so long as we were reasonably active they didn't complain.

At Grande Fino, though, we were out to win. That was the only thing that anyone cared about. Most of them – OK, most of *us* – cared about it far more than was rational.

Don't get me wrong: cycle racing has always been a collaborative sport. You get better results when you work together. It is perfectly normal for seven members of a team to ride themselves into the ground so that the eighth can win the stage, or win the race overall.

But.

This is where I think the difference is. A decent team will ask for your body. It will demand that you put in every last watt of physical power. It will ask for your will to drag you on after that. It may even reward you, if a stage looks like it might suit you and your star man is safe.

But it will leave you your soul, and your pride, and your dignity.

A better man than me would have kept his soul safe and left Grande Fino. I still can't really explain why I stayed. It was miserable.

I suppose I was desperate, and when you're desperate you can't see any options beyond the one that's right in front of you.

They put EPO right in front of me.

Or did they?

That was what I could never get away from. I could never be sure that, when Henri had told me to get better, he'd meant me to do it pharmaceutically. I could never be sure that Dr Wolfsen wouldn't have found me something legal if I'd asked him to.

Was it my fault? Was it Wolfsen's? Was it Henri's?

I suppose that the answer to all those questions was 'Yes'. But mostly the fault was mine. And it was still haunting me.

I'd thought I'd finished ruining people's lives. I'd thought that ruining my own life was payment enough for the *palmarès* I'd robbed of meaning, for the team-mates I'd smeared by association. I'd done my best to disappear off the face of the earth, but it seemed that vengeance was chasing me far beyond the world of professional cycling, and punishing the innocent.

One of whom had just got in. With my window open, I could hear her footsteps on the front path, and the jangle of her keys as she fished them out of her bag.

I'd half-expected her to stay over at Gianna's. I glanced out of the window to make sure I was right, but she was there, alone. The front door opened softly. After a few seconds I heard her start to climb the stairs.

I opened my bedroom door and, when she came past, murmured, 'Vicki?'

'Hi, Ben.' She was keeping her voice low, too.

I came out onto the landing. 'How did it go?' I asked. 'Polly didn't want to talk about it.' I didn't say that we'd spent the evening discussing Vicki's cycling record instead.

She gave a little half-smile. 'About as well as I could have hoped. They're going to write.'

That was what Polly had said. 'When will they do that?'

'When they've made a decision. We don't know how long it will take them. It could be three weeks; it could be three months.' She paused. 'I asked Polly about what you said, about whether it might be your fault.'

'And?'

'She said, Tell him not to be ridiculous, of course it's not his fault, it's practically a compulsory level in this fun game we call Being Disabled In Twenty-First Century Britain.'

'And did she believe that?'

'Yes.'

Vicki is not actually a good liar. I let her think that I believed her, and went back to my room to keep on brooding about it all.

It occurred to me that if it was my fault that Polly's benefits had been withdrawn, then it must also be Vicki's fault, at least indirectly. She'd badgered Polly into living with me, after all. Therefore she had a good reason to try to convince me, and herself, that it wasn't my fault at all.

I didn't believe her.

If Cunningham could kick Vicki out of the cycling club for living with me, then why shouldn't the government withdraw Polly's benefits for the same reason? Call one of us a cheat, call two of us cheats – and if two, why not three? It didn't make any sense, but I'd seen Polly wrangling with the endless forms and interviews and appointments, when any moron could see that she just wasn't well enough to do a nine-to-five job, and I knew that just because you knew you were paranoid it wasn't safe to conclude that they weren't out to get you. I understood. I understood why Polly had been reluctant to move in with me. I understood what she was up against.

And I was furious. Here were two women who'd done nothing worse than give an idiot a second chance (on the strict understanding that he stopped being an idiot, at that) being threatened with the loss of reputation and means respectively. Worse, maybe. What if Vicki's employer – present or future – heard about it?

I didn't think that I could help Polly. Everything that could be done to help Polly, Vicki had already done. I could hardly march into the benefits office and announce 'She needs that money to *not die*: can you get that into your thick heads?' They'd only ask what business it was of mine, and they'd have a point.

But it occurred to me as I was brushing my teeth that there was something I could do for Vicki. Oh, yes, there was definitely something I could do for Vicki.

The more I thought about it, the more I liked the idea.

I was going to be every kind of manipulative lying bastard the press and the cycling world had called me. And I was going to enjoy it, which was more than I'd ever done when I *was* being a manipulative lying bastard.

Chapter 16

I'd walked past Paul Cunningham's office a hundred times; it was a converted Victorian building in the town centre, between the bank and a firm of solicitors. CUNNINGHAM & FARQUHAR was written in tasteful gold letters across the window; behind the glass, a white blind kept out the July sun and stopped me from seeing inside. The front door was painted a shiny, forbidding black.

I took a deep breath, walked up the three steps, and turned the handle. The door opened almost without resistance.

Inside, the understated elegance gave way to anonymous office furniture. It was still elegant, all pale wood and brushed steel, but it was even more understated than the exterior. Little spotlights nestled in the false ceiling. The walls were white; the carpet, grey. Four monochrome photographs of local landscapes hung over a pair of angular leather settees. A single receptionist sat behind a massive console of a desk. It was probably meant to be impressive, but it made her seem undersized.

She smiled cautiously at me. I'd dressed as smartly as I could, but even so I obviously wasn't a specimen of Cunningham & Farquhar's typical clientele. I wasn't really sure what Cunningham & Farquhar's typical clientele *was*; their website described them as a 'Consulting Agency' and listed a string of gushing endorsements, but none of that left me any the wiser as to who consulted their agents, or what they consulted them about.

Well, I knew what I'd come to consult about. I strode up to the desk.

'Can I help you, sir?' the receptionist asked.

'I'm here to see Paul Cunningham,' I said.

'Do you have an appointment?' Her smile was faltering.

'No, but he wants to see me,' I lied. 'My name's Ben Goddard.'

It didn't seem to mean anything to her. Clearly she didn't share her employer's enthusiasms. 'May I ask what it's regarding?'

'He asked me to stop by and discuss how I could help his cycling club.'

Her face clouded. 'He doesn't usually... Oh, well, I'll see if he's free.'

I held my breath as she dialled a number on the phone in front of her. 'Oh, hi Jill. Is Paul around? There's someone to see him... Ben Goddard?... I don't know, he said it was about the cycling club so I guess...' She turned to me. 'Sorry, sir, are you Ben Goddard the cyclist?'

Bingo. Jill, whoever she was, knew her cycling. I summoned up my smarmiest grin. '*Ex*-cyclist.'

She took her hand off the receiver. 'He says, yes, the ex-cyclist. Oh. OK.' She put the phone down. 'We're just finding out if Mr Cunningham is free, sir.'

'Thank you,' I said. Then I went back to holding my breath. If Paul Cunningham had any sense at all he'd refuse to speak to me. I wasn't sure that I had much sense myself. I was gambling a lot on his curiosity and my dubious celebrity.

The phone buzzed. The receptionist answered it.

'OK, thanks, Jill.' She cleared her throat. 'Mr Goddard? I'll just show you up.'

Clearly Paul Cunningham had no more sense than I did.

Cunningham's office was upstairs, in the corner of what looked like everyone else's office: a bite cut out of the room and walled off with glass. The receptionist knocked on the door and then fled before Paul Cunningham himself let me in.

The room wasn't, I noticed with mixed feelings, completely soundproof: even with the door closed, I could hear a woman talking on the phone. That must be Jill, I supposed, sorting out the next crisis after me. I suspected that she'd sort it out fast and then eavesdrop. It meant that I'd have to rewrite my script a little. Complete privacy would have been easier, in some ways, but I could see the advantage of a semi-informed witness. I'd just have to be a bit more careful about what I said.

Paul Cunningham was a shiny man: shiny bald head, shiny satin tie, shiny rimless spectacles. He nodded at me to sit down. 'Mr Goddard... this is a surprise.'

'Oh, really?' I said, pleasantly.

'Yes. It is.' He cracked a humourless smile. 'For a start, you don't have an appointment.'

'And yet you agreed to see me,' I pointed out.

'What can I say? You're...'

'A household name?' I tried to look as if I believed it.

He fell straight into the trap. 'I wouldn't have said that, no.'

'No. But you seem to know who I am.'

His smile was more pitying this time. 'You have to admit it: you've got a certain notoriety. For as long as that lasts.'

'So it seems,' I said. I kept on smiling.

He uncrossed his legs and recrossed them the other way. 'So, Mr Goddard,' he said. 'Where are we going with all this?'

'You couldn't expect me not to follow up on groundless accusations against my housemate. And yes, they are groundless, and no, she doesn't know I'm here.' I dredged up her own phrase. 'She has principles, you see. Unlike me. Or you.'

He frowned. 'What's that supposed to mean?'

I leaned forward. 'You have kicked Vicki out of the cycling club on the grounds that she lives with me, and that I am a disgraced professional who has been banned for doping. That would, I admit, be a good reason to kick *me* out of your cycling club. But it has no bearing on Vicki. She doesn't dope. She doesn't need to. Quite apart from anything else, I can't see why the fuck she'd bother. Let's be honest: the club circular to Starby isn't going to give her a place in the world rankings. If I were a cynic, I'd say the only thing she's done wrong is ride faster than you and be a bit gobby. But if we're going to play guilt by association: well, here I am, sitting in your office.'

'What's your point?'

I raised my voice. Only slightly. But I'd seen out of the corner of my eye that Jill was off her phone call and had cocked her head in our direction.

'Here I am. Ben Goddard, at your service... What can I do for you?'

He got it. 'What do you want?' he hissed.

I leaned even further forward and said, very quietly, 'A written apology to Vicki, reinstating her membership and not mentioning me.'

His jaw was tight. 'And if I don't?'

I grinned. 'There are quite a few cycling journalists around who'd be interested in a "what the hell happened to Ben Goddard, anyway?" story. Suzie Balham, for example. If she could combine that with an exposé of doping in amateur clubs... Well. She'd only have my word for it that I'm not a lying bastard any more, but maybe that wouldn't matter. I've no intention of returning to professional cycling, so I don't much care whether she paints me as reformed rake or unrepentant fraudster, but I'd imagine you might feel differently.'

'That would be libel,' he said feebly.

'Perhaps. Though if the only thing she said was that you'd talked to me – which you're doing at this exact moment, and we have witnesses – well, it's all a question of guilt by association, isn't it, and if associating with me is evidence enough – which you seem to think...'

'I really think you're overreacting,' he said.

'Oh, really?' I did my best to look surprised.

'It's just a misunderstanding. I'm not sure what's happened at the club, but I can assure you that I'll ask for the records to be checked, and for any mistakes to be corrected.'

Well, I'd been hoping for a confession and an apology, but it looked as if this was going to be the best I was going to get. It would do. I smiled. 'I'm so glad you feel that way. You'll write to Vicki to tell her? I'll be watching the letterbox.'

Chapter 17

It wasn't just a letter. It was the club newsletter, printed in full colour on shiny paper, Cunningham's face smirking blandly from the top left hand corner, right underneath the logo. The apology to Vicki was on the front page:

*Due to an administrative error, it was incorrectly reported that **Victoria Whitaker** (mem. no 1327) had been expelled from the Club for behaviour unbecoming a member. We are pleased to report that this is not the case and we apologise to Ms Whitaker for any inconvenience or embarrassment caused.*

Vicki didn't say anything, but she pinned it to the corkboard in the kitchen, and she smiled a lot. I was pleased enough with that, until Polly got hold of it – and of me.

She waited until Vicki had left the house, and then waved the newsletter at me. 'Go on, then. Spill.'

'What?'

Polly glared at me. 'You know very well what. How did you extract such a remarkable change of heart from Paul Cunningham?'

'It wasn't anything to do with me,' I said. It turned out there was still a bit of lying bastard left in me, after all.

But apparently it wasn't a very convincing bit, because Polly said, 'Like hell it wasn't. Vicki picks her battles, and she told me she wasn't fighting this one.'

'Divine revelation?' I suggested.

'Fuck off. What did you do?'

'Fine,' I said. And I told her.

Polly's eyebrows rose higher and higher as I spoke, and when I'd finished the quality of her silence told me that she wasn't impressed. 'You blackmailed him,' she said.

'Well...' I couldn't deny it.

'Or is it even blackmail when both parties know it's not true?'

'I expect Vicki would know,' I said, slightly hurt. 'She's the one with the law degree.'

'Vicki's not going to hear about it,' she said. 'For fuck's sake, Ben – I was just beginning to think you were a decent bloke in spite of everything, and then you go and do something like this!'

I'd broken my silence, and this was all the thanks I got? 'You think I should have just sat back and done nothing?'

'I think,' Polly said acidly, 'that would have been preferable to confirming that oily shithead's idea of you and making him believe the same of Vicki.'

'But I told him Vicki was clean!'

She rolled her eyes. 'God, you're so naïve! Did you even stop to think what would happen if he called your bluff? What if he went to the press before you?'

'Well, I've got nothing to lose.'

'No, but Vicki has. Cunningham knows who she works for – what if he tells her boss about your little trick? How do you think that's going to look on her reference?'

I got it. 'Oh,' I said. 'Oh, fuck.'

'Precisely.' Her face didn't change. 'Vicki loves cycling, yes, but it's not her life. Or her living.'

'Shit. I just felt so *guilty*...' I sat down at the kitchen table, shaken by the revelation that, against all odds, I'd managed to fuck things up even worse than they already had been. I put my head into my hands. 'Fuck. What do I do now?'

Polly took pity on me. She wheeled up alongside me and patted my shoulder. 'Pray,' she said. I wasn't sure if she was serious. 'Don't try to fix it, whatever you do.'

'But I... It's all my fault.' And it really was, this time.

'Ben,' she said gently, 'please try to grasp the fact that not everything is actually about you. Cunningham's never liked Vicki.'

'But he didn't have an excuse to get rid of her until I turned up.'

'He'd have found one eventually.' She measured out a smile. 'If in a couple of weeks' time there have been no repercussions, I might admit that the thought of Paul Cunningham scared shitless by a doping smear is one that pleases me immensely. I just... can't find it funny quite yet.'

Before those couple of weeks had passed, Gianna invited us all round to her flat for dinner. 'To celebrate getting away with it,' she said. I think she felt as guilty as I did about what had happened, though it was irrelevant now. Not that this stopped any of us blaming ourselves or each other, or both at once.

Whatever the reason, Polly and I were quite keen to see her flat, if only to make sense of all the little facts that Vicki had scattered in passing. We knew that Gianna drove a former post van, which she kept on the street outside. We knew that she rented two tiny rooms with a garage beneath, and that she had converted that garage into a workshop.

We didn't know how it all fitted together, until she showed us around. The workshop bristled with tools, gas canisters and a hulking pendant drill. There was a steel workbench, lit by an Anglepoise lamp; a plastic crate full of wooden and metal conical instruments; a board with nails in, from which hung hammers with leather heads, pliers, and saws with grass-thin blades; a squat fireproof safe in the corner; and display racks stacked neatly against the wall near the door.

Polly asked to see the finished product, and Gianna unlocked the safe and passed around delicate earrings, twisted bangles, intricate pendants. On a lower shelf I could see the raw materials: silver in coils of wire and sheet metal. I wondered how long it took to make the one out of the other. Polly wanted to know the same thing.

'It depends what it is,' Gianna said. 'Estimate a couple of hours for a pair of earrings – plus the design, of course – and scale up.'

'How do you know when to stop?' I asked. 'I've always thought that must be the problem with being self-employed.'

'What, when to give up for the day? When I set fire to something I didn't mean to,' she said. 'Or when I destroy a week's work in five seconds. Thank God, with silver you can usually melt it down and start again. It could get expensive otherwise.'

Her bikes – three of them; two modern racers and a lovely old Pinarello – were suspended from the roof. A second board held tools that were more familiar to me. This was a space for her hobby as much as it was for her work. Indeed, she'd clearly chosen the flat for the sake of the garage, as the rest of it wasn't much to write home about.

'I'm afraid I have *stairs*,' Gianna had told Polly, making it sound like some unpleasant disease.

'As do we,' Polly said.

'Mine are very steep and very narrow, and all my living space is at the top of them.'

'Ah,' Polly said, seeing the problem. 'Well, I dare say we'll work it out.'

In the end, she walked up them, while Vicki and I hefted the wheelchair up between us. I tried to pick the thing up by its arm, which promptly came off, letting the rest of it crash down on my toe.

'Ow! Fuck!' I hissed to Vicki, 'Couldn't we have left it in the hall?'

'I'm not having Polly sitting in any of those objects Gianna laughably describes as *chairs*. Ready?' She picked the chair up by the hand rim of the wheel; the brake was off, so the wheel stayed still and the chair rotated backwards, bashing her in the knee. 'Ow!'

'You two all right down there?' Polly called.

'Fine, thanks,' I muttered.

On the third attempt we got the chair, and ourselves, up the stairs, which gave directly onto a square room. The kitchen worktops lined one wall; the bed had been pushed back against another. I couldn't see a washing machine. Three mismatched bookcases held a collection of art and cycling books, with paperback murder mysteries on the top shelves and anthologies of diaries and letters in the middle. I saw Vicki's point about seating: there was a pair of canvas steamer chairs and that was it. Gianna had pulled the table up alongside the bed so that someone could sit on that.

The décor reminded me a lot of Vicki's bedroom, although, where Vicki had practically created a shrine to Beryl Burton, Gianna's place was a paean to Italian cycling in general. There was a framed print of a beautiful Bianchi, a poster of Fausto Coppi, and a jersey signed by Giorgia Bronzini, plus some tatty pink streamers which I supposed had come from some Giro celebration.

We'd already got the idea that Gianna was a fantastic cook, from the way that Vicki had taken to eating round at hers most of the time. What impressed me was the fact that she was managing to create something that smelled absolutely amazing (tomatoes, beef, red wine) with a two-ring hob and no sink nearer than the bathroom. Our diet had been getting steadily duller and heavier on the carbohydrates as money ran shorter and shorter. This was a treat.

It seemed like a proper artist's lifestyle; but there was really only room for one, and I could quite see that Vicki wouldn't be moving in there properly any time soon.

'By the way,' Vicki said as we sat down to eat (she and I had taken the disreputable folding chairs, Polly, of course, brought her own seating, and Gianna was balanced on a pile of cushions on the bed), 'I've thought about the wedding, and if you think your cousin really wants me there, I'd like to come.'

Confused, I glanced at Polly. Judging by her quizzical expression, this was the first that she'd heard of any wedding, too.

'Excellent,' Gianna said, beaming. 'I'd never have been forgiven otherwise. Maria said that if she had to invite her ghastly brother-in-law, then she was inviting my girlfriend.'

'Your family are OK with that idea, then?' Polly asked. She clearly wasn't ready to let her guard down where Vicki was concerned.

Gianna bit her lip. 'As far as I can tell. It's difficult to tell from this distance. I think maybe my dad has had a word with... some of them. Anyway, Maria messaged me to say explicitly that Vicki's welcome. They all seem to be curious, but I suppose they would be whoever I brought home.' She topped up all of our glasses and thought about it some more. 'I don't think anyone will be horrible. I don't know. They haven't exactly had the opportunity before.'

Vicki flushed. 'Well, if anyone's really rude to me I probably won't understand them. Which will make a change for me, at least.'

'Then at worst this will be a chance to expand your Italian vocabulary,' Gianna said drily.

I got the impression that they'd had this conversation before.

'Tell us more about this wedding?' Polly suggested. 'I assume it isn't in Edinburgh?'

'Italy,' Vicki said, looking rather daunted.

'It's a huge family gathering,' Gianna said apologetically.

'Well, you're about due a holiday,' I said.

'That's what I've been saying for months,' said Polly. She seemed so pleased that it was actually happening that she wasn't even cross about my having said it first.

'Don't get too excited,' Vicki said. 'It's not until October.'

'Yes,' Gianna said, 'but I think we should make a week of it when we do go. Maybe two weeks, if you can get the leave.'

Vicki looked dubious. 'I might just about manage it. But what about your Christmas craft fairs?'

'They won't start properly until November, and I'll make double every week until we go,' Gianna promised grandiosely. 'Anyway, I have better things to do in October.' She glanced meaningfully at her Bianchi picture.

Polly asked, 'I assume your family are into their cycling, too, Gianna?'

'Very much so. I've asked my aunt if she would be willing to lend Vicki a bike, and if the family gets a bit much – it usually gets a bit much for *me* – then we can just go out into the hills.'

'Ah,' Vicki said, 'well, if it comes to that, I'll take your family over the Coastal Cycling Club. And we've ridden Shepherd's Top to death lately.'

Vicki being Vicki, she went back to CCC for one last ride.

'It was hilarious,' Gianna reported after the event. 'Cunningham was falling over himself to be nice to her, and she rode next to him half the way round, so he had to keep the act up for ages. And of course everyone wanted to know what the apology was about, so they were trying to get that out of me, along with whether we're a couple or not, which someone's obviously running a book on. So I'm there, riding with total strangers who are queueing up to tell me how wonderful Vicki is, and I'm saying, yes, isn't she, and not volunteering any information and just letting it all be exquisitely awkward...'

Polly chortled. I was feeling pretty awkward myself, and I could see she was enjoying that.

Vicki just said, 'It was a nice ride to go out on.'

Because that was the end. But now that she had Gianna for company Vicki didn't seem to mind losing the cycling club. They went out riding together every Sunday. Where once she would have been meeting the club down on the seafront, now she went straight to Gianna's and they took it from there. They covered much of the same ground as the CCC, but took care not to take the same route on the same day.

This meant that Vicki spent more of her Saturdays at home, because she didn't need to keep them free for dates with Gianna any more.

Polly appreciated that, I knew. Forced to do without the allowance that was meant to let her get out and about, she'd effectively been confined to the house. Gianna, a bit of a loner by nature, had never really seen the point of belonging to the club and was perfectly happy just riding with Vicki. She needed her Saturdays, too; she said it was by far the best day for craft fairs.

And, very gradually, over the summer, something interesting started to happen.

They'd get a few miles into the route, Vicki explained, and there would be Sally Rivers slogging up the hill after them, and she'd ask if they minded her tagging along. Or they'd pass Anita Crews' house on the way out of town, and, what do you know, there was Anita just clipping in, off to join the club ride, except that now Vicki and Gianna were passing she thought she'd rather join them.

'I thought it was coincidence at first,' Vicki said, 'or me not being original enough, picking routes that we'd done with the club. Then Rosie came right out and asked where the ride was going on Sunday, and I realised: we've grown a rival club.'

'All the women,' Polly noted, 'sticking together.'

'Yes,' Vicki said. 'Funny, that.'

Chapter 18

Everything was booked for Gianna's cousin's wedding, the date was just over a month away, and now Vicki was panicking about what the family would make of her, what to wear at a Catholic wedding, and the fact that she didn't know any Italian.

'You know lots of Italian,' Polly said. '*Gruppetto, maglia rosa, strade bianche...*'

'*Giustizia per Marco Pantani,*' I put in.

Polly looked deeply suspicious. 'You're not really a Pantani conspiracy theorist, are you, Ben?'

'No, of course not. Marco Pantani died of a cocaine overdose. His previous six cocaine overdoses are a bit of a giveaway. Don't bring it up, though, Vicki,' I said. 'Not until you've established what the family line is.'

'I'll bear that in mind.' She didn't look any less worried.

'Hasn't Gianna taught you any Italian?' I asked.

'Probably not the sort to use to the family,' Polly observed.

Vicki blushed. 'Not yet, no.'

Polly took pity on her and changed the subject. 'And you want something with a longish skirt and not too much cleavage, for the church bit.'

'What about a hat? Do I have to wear a hat?'

This seemed to be beyond the limits of Polly's knowledge. 'Er... probably. Google it.'

Having done the appropriate research, Vicki and Gianna decided to go out shopping together. Polly, who seemed to be getting cabin fever, blew several precious pounds on a train ticket and went with them. Since I continued to have no social life of my own, and I needed some new T-shirts, I went, too, and wandered around aimlessly while they did the girly stuff.

We had arranged to meet in one of the coffee shops. They turned up with a turquoise dress for Vicki, a navy one for Gianna, and, unexpectedly, one in fuchsia pink for Polly.

'*You're* going to this wedding now?' I said. I was surprised. Polly was still waiting on a decision about her benefits, and didn't have any money coming in.

'These two cruelly forced me to buy it,' Polly said.

'No, we didn't,' Gianna said.

'Vicki said she'd buy it for me if I didn't buy it myself, and I couldn't have that. Nobody tell the DWP.'

'It was such a bargain,' Vicki said, not very apologetically.

Polly showed me a mark on the back, near the top of the skirt. 'Some dimwit obviously tried to take the security tag off in the shop, so it was basically unsellable... to anyone who wouldn't be sitting down more or less continuously throughout an event.'

'Personally,' Vicki said, 'I think you could just sew a bow over it; but you can't argue with a tenner, can you? Not when it was north of two hundred quid to start with.'

'And the skirt's just the right length,' Polly conceded. 'Long enough not to have bare legs sticking to the seat cushion. Short enough not to get caught in my wheels.'

'Sometimes things just work out really well,' Gianna said happily. I concluded that she was taking this as a good omen.

'I don't know when I'm going to wear it, mind,' Polly said.

'Yes, you do. Fran's twenty-fifth.'

'Oh, good point.' She smiled. I wondered who Fran was.

'And your blue dress wouldn't have worked with the wheelchair,' Vicki said.

Polly admitted, 'I doubt it'd fit me, these days. When did I wear it last?'

136

'Jez and Lotty's wedding.'

Gianna was looking as lost as I felt, which was some consolation. I supposed we'd slipped sideways into some university reunion.

'That's right. Who knows, maybe I'll manage more than half an hour of the next party without having to go to bed.'

'Maybe you can join in the wheelchair conga line, if that happens again.' Vicki laughed softly at the memory.

'Only reason I got a wheelchair,' Polly said. She glanced at me. 'That was a joke, Ben.'

'I thought it was,' I said, hurt. 'But a wheelchair conga line?'

'Yup. So Vicki tells me. Like I say, I'd gone to bed.'

'How does that even work?' Gianna asked, intrigued.

'Better than you'd expect,' Vicki said. She frowned, trying to remember. 'I *think* everybody had one hand on their own wheel and one on the handle or back of the chair in front.'

'It sounds lethal,' Gianna said.

'Well, with Lotty in charge it would be,' Polly observed. 'Missing it is one of my biggest regrets of my life so far.'

I didn't ask if that one was a joke. Even if it wasn't, I could kind of see her point. It sounded impressive.

'Did you buy anything interesting, Ben?' Vicki asked me.

I hadn't. Some very boring T-shirts, a pair of trainers, because mine were going through at the sole. I'd wandered around a couple of music shops and a discount book store, but nothing had grabbed my eye. I hadn't really known what I was looking for. I just didn't seem to be interested in anything any more. I went to work to fill my days, and I fell in with whatever the girls were doing, if they invited me and it wasn't cycling, and I just... didn't do anything else, didn't expect anything else, didn't *want* anything else.

I looked at Polly, laughing at her memories, stroking the satin of her new dress, and discovered that, to my shame, I was jealous of her. She might be disabled now, she might never become a doctor, but she still had the remains of that past life. She had Jez and Lotty and Fran, whoever they were; she still had occasions to wear a fuchsia-pink frock. Most importantly, she had Vicki, who'd stuck by her through everything. I'd been abandoned. I'd lost everything – fine, I'd thrown everything away – and it didn't seem to be missing me.

I'd look a right idiot in a fuchsia-pink frock, to be fair, but that wasn't the point.

A few days later, the post brought some good news – and, thank God, it was nothing to do with me this time. Polly was waiting for me when I came in from work. She greeted me with a massive grin. 'Ben! You're off the hook! So am I!'

'They've given you your allowance back?'

'*And* apologised for the inconvenience.' She grinned. 'They are very sorry, they know this must have been very distressing for me, but I will of course understand that they have to follow up reports of suspected fraud... I asked at the interview,' she said with a distinct change of tone, 'what it was that prompted the report. Just, you know, so that I could avoid doing whatever it was again.'

'Are they allowed to tell you that?'

'Probably not. Clearly they can't tell me who put the report in, in case I put a brick through that concerned citizen's front window. But the lady I talked to gave me a fairly strong hint that it was something to do with having been seen out of my wheelchair. Which would make sense, because they were very interested in the Wheelchair Services report.'

'Just ignorance, then?'

'Probably.'

'Well, thank God for that. I'd have felt awful if I'd deprived you of your means of survival. Ruining Vicki's reputation was bad enough.'

'Yes, and I'm still cross with you about that.' But her eyes were twinkling, and I think she was quite a long way towards forgiving me.

Then I looked over her shoulder at the TV and saw what she was watching.

I'd come to terms with the fact that the sport of cycling was carrying on without me. I'd missed the Giro and the spring Classics: they're easy to miss, not being on terrestrial TV. I'd even managed to avoid the Tour, between working and running, and leaving the other two to it when they huddled around Polly's laptop or went out to persuade the Vine to show it on the big screen. But the sport wasn't going to let me get away from it so easily, and here was Polly, settled on the sofa, with the Vuelta in the background. A pack of bright-coloured cyclists had followed a dusty Spanish road across a bridge over a motorway before she followed my eyes and noticed that the advert break had finished.

She was dismayed. 'Look, we don't have to watch this; I'll turn it over.'

I hadn't realised that the girls were so deliberately careful of my feelings, and I felt a bit put out that they assumed I was so sensitive. 'It's OK,' I said. 'If I can't cope, I'll go to my room. But I'm actually quite interested.'

Polly nodded. 'If you're sure. Thank you.'

I was intrigued now. 'What's going on, then?'

'Last time I looked,' she said, a little flustered, 'there was a break of four with about three and a half minutes – look.'

The footage cut to a shot of the breakaway: a wheel-to-wheel train, heads down, motorcycle buzzing along beside them. 'That won't last,' I said. 'Hicks won't do any work in the last thirty K, and the other three aren't strong enough alone.'

'Is this even a stage for a break, though?'

'Haven't a clue. Where does it finish?' I didn't recognise any of the scenery.

She rolled her eyes at me in a good-natured sort of way and passed me a magazine, folded back to the profile of today's stage. 'I can't pronounce it.'

I looked at the map. There wasn't anything too challenging – a couple of second category climbs, which the peloton seemed to have survived more or less intact, and a gentle downhill sweep to the finish. 'I'd say that could go either way. Not with Hicks in the break, though.'

'Sounds like you don't like him much.'

'The guy's got a reputation. I'm surprised they haven't tried to drop him already.'

'They almost did, over the last climb.'

'There you go, then.'

Polly looked sideways at me. 'You sure you're OK with this? I quite like having my own personal pundit, but if it's uncomfortable...'

'It's fine,' I said. 'I'd forgotten there were guys in the peloton who were more colossal arses than me... Ooh, sticky bottle!'

I ended up watching it all the way to the line, arguing with the commentators and amusing Polly hugely. It happened exactly as I'd predicted: Hicks stopped working, the others noticed, and the break collapsed with twelve kilometres to go. It came down to a bunch sprint, which was won by the star man in Hicks' team. I suspected that their *directeur sportif* had known exactly what he was doing.

'Congratulations,' Polly said, when the rest of the bunch had hauled itself over the line. 'Excellent prediction there.'

'I hope I didn't annoy you?' I realised now that I'd been a bit vocal on occasion.

She smiled, a lovely, open smile that crinkled the corners of her eyes. 'Don't worry,' she said. 'I'd have kicked you out if I'd been annoyed.'

Chapter 19

The weather turned horrible the moment Vicki and Gianna left for the wedding, and Polly and I were very envious of their catching the last little bit of Italian sun. I got soaked on the way to work and the way home from work, and the way between work and, well, work, every day. Polly didn't go out at all.

At least she had the internet, and plenty of people on it to talk to, as I discovered one evening. I was in the living room, minding my own business. Specifically, I was watching an early evening quiz show, and eating something called Hot Corn Chips. Suddenly, Polly put her head around her bedroom door, saw me, and burst out laughing.

'What?' I said.

'Nothing.' She continued to chortle quietly.

'Seriously. What's so funny? Have I got spinach in my teeth or something?'

She looked innocent. 'Can't see from here. No, it's... something on the internet.'

'What's that got to do with me?'

She giggled. 'I'd tell you not to assume that everything's about you, except this is, kind of.'

I knew better than to look at things on the internet that might be about me, but she'd piqued my curiosity. 'Go on. Tell me the worst.'

Suddenly, she was awkward. 'It's not horrible. I think, at least. I mean, not really horribly horrible.'

I peeled myself off the sofa. 'I want to see, now.'

'Come on, then.' She disappeared back into her bedroom. I followed her.

'You have to look at this first.' She had sat back in her chair, with her laptop open on one of those cushioned trays across her knees. I sat down on the bed where I could see over her shoulder. 'This is a discussion board for chronically ill people, yeah? So they were getting a bit irritated about *this*.'

This was the old photo of me as a little boy in my wheelchair, flush against a photo of me in Grande Fino kit, with the caption *You can become anything you can believe in* written across the two in flowing script.

I'd seen the meme before, and been vaguely flattered. These days, it made me cringe. I winced. 'With a healthy helping of luck, being in the right place at the right time, and not...'

'I know, right? Typical inspiration porn. That's not the funny part.' She scrolled hastily down a wall of comments, most of them harping sarcastically on the theme of *what you can believe in*. Then there were more pictures. Someone had taken the original image and superimposed a dripping syringe over the two halves. A few had changed the caption. *You can become anything you can believe in, with a little help from EPO.* That sort of thing. Then Polly let the screen stand still.

Someone had added a third panel. They'd put dates on the two original pictures – *1995* for the first, which wasn't quite right, and *2015*, which was near enough, to the second. The new panel was a large question mark above the word *NOW*.

The other commenters seemed to have run with this idea. Polly started scrolling again. The extra picture was different in each case. One of them showed a man behind bars. ('Confused, or just wishful thinking?') One seemed to suggest that I'd become a superhero. One had a still from *Follow That Camel*.

'So I came out,' Polly said, 'to make sure that you hadn't turned into Kenneth Williams and joined the French Foreign Legion, and see what you were really doing now.'

'Sprawling on the sofa eating own-brand tortilla chips,' I admitted.

'Are you going to make a meme of your own?'

'Someone had already thought of that one. Though they've got you in your underpants.'

'Not really me?' I couldn't think where someone would find a picture of me in my pants.

'Well, duh.' She looked a little bit embarrassed, though given the fact that we shared a washing line she must have known what my pants looked like by this time. She scrolled down to it.

Of course the guy in his pants wasn't me. But there was something else wrong, now I was looking properly. I snorted. 'You know what the really funny thing is?'

'What?'

'The second picture isn't me, either.'

'No!' She squinted at it. 'Are you sure?'

'Positive. It's Caprini, on my bike.'

'What, did he puncture or something?' She laughed, delighted. 'That's hilarious. Was he doping?'

'I'm fairly sure of it,' I said. I'd never known exactly what was what at Grande Fino, but most of the time I would have put good money on Caprini's being doped to the eyeballs. 'More to the point, he's never used a wheelchair that I know of.'

She scrolled back up the page to find the original. 'It's the same picture. You're right. How did I miss that?'

'I don't know. Look at the chin.' It was about all you could see of the face.

She looked at it, then at me. 'Obvious, when you look at it. Well, that gives me a *really* smug comment to make.'

I winced. 'You're not going to say that the third picture should have me sitting on your bed?'

'No: I don't want to look like a fantasist, and presumably you still don't want anybody finding you? On the off-chance they do believe me, I mean.'

'No. Thank you.' Come to think of it, I didn't think she'd want to go through all that again, either.

'Where's Ben Goddard now?' she asked rhetorically. 'Apologising profusely for the inspiration porn, and actually turning out to be quite a nice guy.'

I almost wished she'd go back to disapproving of me. 'Yeah, you're definitely making it up. Well, the second bit. God knows I don't want to make anyone feel guilty about stuff they can't do.'

Polly smiled and started typing in the comments box: *Er... has anyone noticed that the guy in the second picture isn't Goddard at all? It's his team-mate Caprini. FAIL!*

I left her to it, feeling oddly pleased.

'Fancy going out to the pub?' I asked, after I'd cooked dinner for both of us.

She looked surprised, then pleased. 'Yeah, why not? Why should Vicki and Gianna have all the fun?'

'I hope they are,' I said.

'Vicki texted me earlier,' Polly said. 'She hasn't been driven out with pitchforks and flaming torches; also, Gianna's aunt's bike is a dream and she wants to steal it.'

I nodded, considering. 'That does sound like she's having fun.'

It had, miraculously, stopped raining, and it looked like it was going to stay stopped for the evening, so we walked. Well, I walked, I mean, and pushed Polly.

'Wow, the water's high, isn't it?' she said as we trundled across the road where our close met River Way.

'I suppose it is,' I said. 'I hadn't really noticed.'

Polly laughed. 'Maybe it's crept up on you. I haven't been outside – well, apart from putting the washing out, and *that* was a waste of time – for thirteen days.'

'Bloody hell,' I said. 'I'm sorry.' It wasn't just the last week. Months had ticked past almost without my noticing. I got up; I went to one job; I went to the other job; I came home; I ate; I slept. Now that I didn't have the racing and resting seasons to mark the passage of time, it was all passing me by.

'Not your fault. You have a job to go to.'

'Yeah. Still.' I felt vaguely guilty. I knew that I hadn't anything to feel guilty *for*, that I'd signed up to be a tenant, not a companion, but I couldn't help but feel bad about Polly being stuck in the house on her own. 'I didn't realise it had been as long as that.'

'Church last Sunday,' she said.

'Right. Was Michael there?' I asked idly.

'No, thank God. I think I'd punch his stupid face if I saw him.'

I wasn't entirely certain that she was joking. 'What happened?' I ventured. 'I assumed he was a dick about Vicki and Gianna...'

'Yes,' she said shortly. 'I –'

– a bus hurtled past and I couldn't hear what she said after that –

'What was that?' I asked.

She shook her head repressively. 'Anyway, it's very nice to be out today,' she said. 'I nearly put on my new dress to celebrate going outside.'

That clearly hadn't been it at all, but I didn't push it. 'If you like,' I said instead, 'we can go back so you can change.'

'No,' she said. 'Can't be bothered. You'll just have to imagine it.'

She'd thawed a bit by the time we got into the pub. I went to the bar and got a lager for myself and one of those posh bottles of lemonade for her. 'Cheers!' I said.

We clinked glasses. 'Cheers!' Polly echoed. 'To Gianna's cousin and the bloke she's marrying! I'm sure they're both lovely.'

I raised my glass and drank to that. 'And to Vicki and Gianna!'

'Vicki and Gianna!'

'And to you,' I said.

She nodded acknowledgement. 'And to you.'

That disposed of pretty much everyone we knew, and some people we didn't. I changed the subject to the other thing we had in common. Cycling. 'So,' I said, 'what did you make of the women's Worlds?'

'You know what happened?' She tried not to look surprised, but failed.

'Looked online. From what I could make out it seemed like it must have been a good one to watch.' I didn't tell Polly that watching that stage of the Vuelta with her had gone a long way towards rekindling my interest.

'It was,' she said. 'The telly coverage didn't start until after the first climb, unfortunately, but the rest of it was great.'

'What do you think will happen tomorrow, in the men's race? Do you think Sagan can take it again?'

She looked away. I hadn't noticed before what a lovely shape her head was. 'You're the expert,' she said.

'Not really. I haven't studied the course, and I've paid no attention to anyone's form this season.' But, seeing she didn't like to offer an opinion, I dropped the subject. 'Have you had your hair cut?'

Now she looked back at me. 'You've only just noticed?'

'I'm a man,' I said. 'Give me some credit for noticing at all. When...?' It must have been fairly recent: I surely wasn't as oblivious as all that. But Polly had said that she hadn't left the house for days.

She put me out of my misery. 'One of my church ladies came round yesterday. Usually Vicki does it for me.'

This must be, I thought, another of those things like the broadband, that the girls sorted out between themselves and that I never noticed. 'I didn't know she was a secret hairdresser. I assume she doesn't talk about where you're going on holiday?'

'No. You've seen how difficult it is to get her to take a holiday. And she knows I have no money. She talks about cycling,' Polly said.

'You could combine the two. Sounds like she is, after all. A cycling holiday. Why not take a camper van up Mont Ventoux and watch the Tour go by?'

She sipped at her lemonade, then shook her head. 'The place looks like something off *Doctor Who*. Think of somewhere prettier.'

I thought. 'Mountain stage, or flat?'

'Mountain. You only see three seconds of racing sitting next the road on a flat stage.' She spoke with authority; I suspected that she'd been there and done that, and I wondered when that had been: before she got ill, or afterwards?

'I'm not really the person to ask about scenery,' I said. 'I was usually looking at the arse of the guy in front. Or the road. Or some idiot in a mankini running along beside me.'

'Inspiring,' she commented, deadpan.

'Sorry.' I had an idea. 'What about the Stelvio?' I'd never ridden it, but I'd seen enough TV coverage of that long green climb, unfolding hairpin bend after hairpin bend, the race strung out in a long chain of suffering, to know that it would be worth watching in real life.

'*Now* you're talking.' She glanced at me, with an unfamiliar expression of sympathy on her face. 'You're sure it doesn't bother you, talking about this?'

For some reason, this needled me. 'It doesn't bother *you*?' I retorted. 'I mean, there's nothing to stop me going to watch a race if I felt like it. You'd find it more difficult.'

She shrugged her shoulders. 'Perhaps. In a different way. But, you know, if you're happy to watch the sport, then you can hire that camper van and we can both go.'

I thought it unlikely that anyone would rent me a camper van, given my lack of driving experience. In any case, that surely wasn't the main objection to the idea. 'Wouldn't you get tired, though?'

'I'd work something out,' she said. 'If we had that camper, then I could nap, for a start.' She sighed. 'It's frustrating, is what it is.

147

Particularly when you look at sport. People recover from the most ridiculously horrible things, and come back, and race, and win.'

I didn't think she was being entirely fair on herself. 'Yes,' I said, 'but you don't hear about the ones who don't. They just... never come back. And you wonder how they're doing, when you remember, and you watch to see how their replacement shapes up, and before you know it half the season's gone and it's like they were never there at all.'

Polly laughed. 'You're a little ray of sunshine, aren't you?'

'I'm just saying: you only hear the feelgood stories, but it doesn't mean the others don't exist. The papers don't want to hear about how Didier Lemarc never got his right hip and leg back to normal and how he's flipping burgers now.' I watched to see if she recognised the name.

She did, almost immediately. 'Didier Lemarc... time triallist? Went down on the descent off the Galibier?'

'The nearest thing we had to a time triallist at Hirondelle,' I allowed.

'I'm impressed.'

'It was a horrible crash. But he wasn't with Hirondelle then, was he? They were never in the Tour de France.'

'No, he'd moved up in the world. For a short time.'

'But you do know what happened to him. You've just told me.'

'You didn't, though.' That was a cheap shot and I felt slightly ashamed. 'Actually,' I admitted, 'I only know because his brother got signed by Hirondelle; otherwise he'd have disappeared off the face of the earth so far as we were concerned. That was a few years back, though. I hope he's progressed up the fast food ladder since then.'

'Poor bastard,' Polly said.

'It's a bastard sport.'

'It's a bastard world.' Having taken the concept to its logical conclusion, Polly was quiet for a few seconds, then shook her head vigorously. 'No. It's not as bad as all that. It's trickier than it used to be. My friend Lotty says there are three pots: time, money, and energy. I used to have energy, and a bit of money, and now I just have time. It would be nice to have all three of them, but there we go.'

'Time, energy, money,' I echoed. 'I have the energy and some of the money – not as much as I used to have, but enough – but not the time.'

Polly nodded. 'I suppose the idea is that you can usually top up one of them from one or both of the other two. Up to a point.'

I couldn't help asking, 'And where's that point?'

'Right now, I feel like it's a long way away from here,' she said, seriously. 'I mean, look at us. We're alive, we're more or less sane, we've got food on the table and a roof over our heads. We're having a drink in a pub, like normal people do. We're OK.'

'I'll drink to that,' I said, and I did. 'It's not so bad, is it? Or is it?'

She shook her head. 'No, it's not so bad. OK, it's not what I planned, and there's lots that I'd change if I could. But life is definitely worth living.'

Chapter 20

Shortly after Vicki and Gianna got back from Italy, my parents came to visit. It was awkward. I suppose it never had a hope of being anything else. I'd gone way off-script, and they were never much good at improvising.

I'm still mildly impressed that they stayed together after my childhood illness: but there was a story that they could tell themselves in there. *Sticking together to make it through this.* Of course, it got easier as I got better, came out of hospital. *Getting back to normal.* Easier still once I got into cycling. *It's good for Ben to have a hobby, and he turns out to be so talented.* Dad drove me all over the country to compete in junior races. And once I started getting good... Well, they'd rather it had been a higher-profile sport, but even so, they liked that story a lot.

They didn't like this one. They had very little to say about it.

I made them coffee and we sat stiffly in the living room while an autumnal gale lashed at the window. They kept looking at Polly's wheelchair, which she had left in the corner by the door, expecting me to explain it. I didn't.

'We've put the house up for sale,' Mum ventured after a long silence.

'Oh, right?' If someone had told me that was what she was going to say, I'd have expected that I would have cared more. This was my childhood home, after all. But it felt like it had pretty much nothing to do with me.

'We feel it's time for a change,' she explained.

'Where are you going to go?'

'Actually,' Dad said, 'we were thinking of moving abroad. Spain, possibly.'

'But you don't speak Spanish!' Not to mention the whole Brexit thing. I didn't mention the whole Brexit thing.

'I'm sure we'll pick it up. Besides, you hardly need it, these days.'

'And we thought,' Mum said, 'that it would be good to be on the spot, if. You know. If you ever.'

'If you ever went back into cycling.'

So they were still backing the fall and redemption story. At least it was "if" and not "when". 'No chance,' I said.

'At the very least,' Dad said, trying to make a joke of it, 'the weather will be good.'

'I can't argue with that,' I said, though I could have done if I'd thought there was any point.

That was when Polly came out of her room. I made the introductions. Mum was frosty. Dad was downright rude.

'And what do you do?' he asked, though the fact that she was still in her dressing gown at midday must have given it away.

I was about to say, 'Polly's recovering from a serious illness,' but she got in first, and told him, 'I'm disabled and unemployed.'

'Oh,' Dad said. 'And do you, er, *contribute* to the household?'

'She's the only one who ever cleans the bathroom,' I said shortly.

'That isn't what your father meant, Ben,' Mum said.

'That's a pity,' I grunted. Because I didn't think I was going to like what he did mean.

'What I *meant*,' he said, 'was, do you expect my son to subsidise you?'

'Oh, the government does that,' she said tightly.

He chuckled. 'You mean taxpayers. So you mean my son. And me. Frankly, I think there are better things to spend the money on.'

'Than keeping me alive?' she said innocently.

'Let's go,' I said, before he could answer. 'I've booked a table at the Vine.'

They thought they knew the story about Polly, too.

'I'm surprised you're living with that woman, Ben,' Mum said over lunch.

'Which one of them?' I knew they meant Polly, of course, but a little devil told me to give them enough rope to hang themselves. 'You haven't met Vicki yet, of course...'

'The one we did meet.' Disapproval dripped from Mum's voice. 'Polly.'

'That's right. Her.'

Irritation twisted in me again. 'Polly.'

Mum stabbed a tomato. 'I realise things have changed, Ben, but you do need to think about who you associate with. More than ever.'

'Believe me,' I said, 'there's nothing *my friends* could do to my reputation that I haven't already done.' *To theirs*, I didn't say.

Dad left that where it lay and moved on to quizzing me about my career prospects, which I played down out of sheer contrariness. Well, yes, I *might* be promoted some day... no, I had no idea about what posts might be coming up... no, I wasn't undertaking any extra training... no, at the moment I was just trying to get back on my feet.

Well, I thought, I'd had to swallow my pride. My parents could do likewise.

I ate a mouthful of gravel-like peas and asked if they'd seen anything of Tim, my best friend from school. Yes, said Mum, she'd seen his parents in the supermarket, he was getting married next year, why didn't I get in touch with him?

What about Alex? Months away from completing a PhD.

I ran through the whole class register. It took about twenty minutes. Twenty minutes in which we weren't talking about me. Except we were, of course.

I couldn't help rubbing it in: what I'd lost, how badly I was doing, how unmentionable I was these days. Even hearing that Andrew Finch had lost his driving licence didn't quash my fervour for the comparison game. Had Finchy killed anybody? No. Seriously injured them? No. Then I was still the worst person we all knew, and Mum and Dad were going to have to put up with being the worst parents.

And until they understood that Polly was a better person than I was ever going to be, that wasn't going to change.

Chapter 21

They went back home to Stourbridge. I thought that it was very possible that I'd never go back there again. I wished I'd been brave enough to point out to them that, if things had gone only slightly differently when I was seven, I could so easily have ended up in the same position as the one Polly was in now: unable to work, dependent on benefits. That I was lucky to have got better, let alone become a professional sportsman.

The more I thought about that, the more angry I became – with myself. I'd had so much, been so lucky, and I'd thrown it all away. I didn't know how to apologise to Polly for my parents having been so vile to her. Whatever I said, it couldn't begin to address the fact that my father had flat-out told her that she didn't deserve to exist.

Meanwhile, someone else had been doing some grovelling. Michael had reappeared. Not at church – he had, Polly said, lost his faith – but on the doorstep.

Which I didn't realise until I found them in the kitchen arguing about cycling.

'No,' Polly was saying, 'it's not a case of *letting everyone ride their own race*. If they did that then no one would win. It's about teamwork.'

I caught her eye over Michael's shoulder. She blinked – it might not even have been deliberate – and looked back at him.

'Yes,' he said, 'but everybody on the team is out for himself.'

Still hovering in the doorway, I surveyed his back. I thought he'd lost a little bit of weight, but that might have been the effect of a new jacket. He'd definitely had his hair cut. There was a line of paler skin at the nape of his neck, which couldn't have had the chance to tan yet.

'Even if that's true,' Polly said, 'that usually means helping the leader to win. Or the sprinter, whatever. If they want their contract renewed.'

'Team orders,' Michael said, disapprovingly. He was, I seemed to remember, a motorsport fan.

'I suppose you could put it like that,' she said.

'But however much it's a team sport, every man is going for his own victory. It's only natural.'

'Not in cycling,' Polly said wearily.

'You're so naïve,' he told her. I could imagine his indulgent smile.

'I'm not.' She didn't look at me. 'Believe me, I'm really not.'

'Oh, you are.'

I couldn't bear it any longer. 'Everything that Polly has told you is quite correct,' I said.

He turned around. Looked suspiciously at me, then at her, then at me again. 'Oh. Fair enough, then.' And then he said, 'So, have you seen that thing they're building on the seafront?'

The sudden change of subject knocked me sideways. 'What? No. Oh. That thing. I heard it was another hotel. Is it something to do with the convention centre?' I was aware that I was babbling. I said, 'Anyway, didn't mean to interrupt you. I'm going to my room.'

I dashed up the stairs and lay down on my bed, closed my eyes and tried to make my breathing slow down. Tried to make myself think rationally.

But.

He'd just accepted what I said. As if he knew that I was an authority. So Polly must have told him that I was.

I told myself that this wasn't any different from Vicki telling Gianna. But it was.

Downstairs, Polly said something sharp to Michael. A little while later, the front door banged.

I heard Polly's footsteps on the stairs. They stopped at the door of my room.

'Ben,' she said. 'Ben, what's wrong?'

I didn't want to look at her, but I sat up. 'He didn't ask how I knew,' I said, very carefully. 'He'd argued back at you so much, and he didn't argue with me at all. Did you...?'

Something like hurt flickered across her face. 'I've never told him who you are. I thought you deserved your privacy.'

'Well, he acted like he believed me.'

'Yes,' she agreed. 'He did, didn't he?'

She sighed and turned away.

They patched things up somehow, and I kept out of Michael's way after that. I wondered sometimes why he didn't drive Polly, pessimistic and sardonic as she was, round the bend. He certainly irritated me. I couldn't work out why I suddenly disliked him so much. He had always been pleasant enough. I didn't think it could be anything to do with the church thing – it wasn't as if I was religious myself, and if his loss of faith didn't bother Polly I didn't see why it should bother me. He'd apologised to Vicki for whatever it was he had to apologise for. I'd never been told what that was, but going by the timing of the original break-up I could take a guess.

And Polly was happy with him. At least, she said she was.

An amateur psychologist might have said that Michael threatened my position as alpha male in the household, which had me cackling with laughter as soon as I thought of it. If this were a team, I'd be a domestique.

Was that what it was, then? Was I worried about upsetting the balance of the team? No. I didn't have this problem with Gianna, even though her relationship with Vicki had made much more of a change to the household dynamic.

Was I worried that he might want to move in now? It seemed like a possibility. If he was no longer regarding sex as sinful (if he ever had in the first place, and that was something that I didn't really want to think about), there was no reason why he couldn't. Except that Vicki wouldn't like that. (And nor, I thought, would I.)

I didn't begrudge Polly a love life. Did I? I'd long ago got over any surprise I might once have had at a disabled person having a boyfriend. Why on earth should that come popping up now? And the more I thought about it, the less likely it seemed. Any bloke would be lucky to have Polly: she was funny, she was clever, she was absolutely gorgeous when you looked at her properly. If anything, *he* wasn't up to *her* standards.

Although she obviously thought differently.

Perhaps, I thought, I was feeling leftover outrage on Vicki's behalf. Over breakfast, I tried, discreetly, to find out what *she* made of recent events.

'The deal,' Vicki said, 'not that it was ever a deal in so many words, was that I would put up with him so long as he wasn't actively a dick.'

'And then he was?' I guessed.

She inclined her head. 'Not directly to me. I didn't ask what he said about me to Polly, mainly because I didn't want to hear it. And now I'm glad I don't know, because I think it would be difficult to forgive, and I have to be polite to him.'

'But whatever it is, he's apologised for it?' I put a slice of bread in the toaster.

'Polly's happy,' Vicki said carefully. 'And of course now he's an atheist... Mind you, that doesn't necessarily mean anything. Look at Gianna's family: they've all been fine. I think Michael still finds it difficult to understand why not all women tremble and swoon in the heady waft of testosterone, but he has at least acknowledged that other people's relationships are none of his business.'

'You still don't sound very enthusiastic about it,' I said.

Vicki made an apologetic face. 'I'm not. I don't like him, and I never have – don't you dare tell Polly I said that – but that thing about other people's relationships cuts both ways.' She wrapped a tea towel around her hands and retrieved her porridge bowl from the microwave.

'I'm sure she knows you don't like him, after all this time.'

'Still,' she said, 'I'm not telling her so, and nor are you going to. Because she's my friend, and if I pick a fight with her over Michael then there's a risk we're not friends the next time she has to dump him.'

'You think there's going to be a next time?'

'He's not right for her,' Vicki said.

'You don't think he's good enough for her.' It was a shot in the dark, really – I knew that was my own opinion, not Vicki's. But she didn't argue.

'Michael was the first person who asked her out after she became ill. I think she should have shopped around more.' She paused. 'That sounds awful. Nevertheless.'

'She did seem happier, when she wasn't with him,' I said, though maybe what I meant was that she'd been nicer to me.

'Better to be single than in a relationship with Michael,' Vicki said. It was difficult to tell whether or not she meant that seriously.

I said, 'Well, yes, for you, obviously.'

She narrowed her eyes. 'For anyone. I think definitely for Polly, though. But she does. She sells herself short. Because...Well...' She pulled up short, then headed off down another tangent. 'I failed my first year. I was devastated. And I had all sorts of well-meaning people tell me that it was all going to be OK, that first year marks didn't count, that I could do retakes – and it was no help at all, because it came nowhere near touching the fear.'

'The fear?' I was lost.

'That I'd never be the person I was meant to be. I was going to change the world, you know. Still am. It just took me a while to work

159

out that it wasn't going to be as a lawyer.' She looked grave. 'I have no idea how Polly's coped. Or you, I suppose.'

'Sometimes I wake up and can't help but be impressed by the fact that I'm not broke or drunk,' I confessed.

'That isn't quite what I meant,' she said, chasing the last spoonful of porridge around the bowl. 'I think. Maybe it is.'

'But Polly?'

'Yes.' She got up and rinsed the bowl and spoon under the hot tap before she said, 'You know she was going to be a doctor. That's an understatement. *Of course* she was going to be a doctor. Nobody doubted that she was going to be a doctor. When you said "Polly", you meant, "Polly-who's-going-to-be-a-doctor". It's weird even having to explain this to you. It was so much a part of who she was. And now she isn't. Not for a very long time, probably never. No wonder it's taken a hell of a lot of getting used to.'

I could see her point, but she seemed to be missing something obvious. 'But it hasn't stopped her being Polly.'

Vicki turned around to look cynically at me. 'And you're still Ben, are you?'

This was all very deep for this early in the morning. 'I guess so. I've had to be.'

'Was Ben a cyclist, then? I mean, if you cut him in half, you'd find gear cables running through him? Or was he Ben?'

'He was a mess,' I said frankly. 'But he didn't have to be a mess as a cyclist. He'd have been a mess whatever. It was more... *he was someone who kept getting better.*' I drew a breath. I didn't realise until I'd said it that it wasn't necessarily true. 'Polly doesn't get better and better, does she?' I said slowly. 'But she's still Polly. Michael or no Michael.'

'Yes, and the essential Pollyness of her doesn't go away, doctor or no doctor,' Vicki said. 'I don't disagree with you; I was just trying to show what a huge thing it was to come to terms with.'

I wasn't really listening. 'So I don't actually *have* to get better and better.'

'It's a biological impossibility,' Vicki agreed. She didn't quite seem to grasp the momentousness of this revelation.

'It's what I've been doing all my life. Up until I quit.'

'Maybe you're getting better in other ways,' she said with a lascivious wink.

'Chance would be a fine thing,' I said.

Vicki laughed gently and went off to the shed to get her bike out. I finished my toast alone at the kitchen table, washed it down with coffee, laced up my trainers, and set off to work at a gentle jog. I had things to think about.

Life goes on. I hadn't been getting better, and life had still gone on, without my noticing it. Well, I'd got better at some things – remembering breakfast orders, for example – but it wasn't the martyred slog towards physical supremacy that I'd been inflicting upon myself since the age of seven.

I wondered, now, what on earth Mum would have done if I'd died. It was possible, I supposed, that I was finding out – from a very safe distance. I'd given up all hope of *getting better*, and given it up in spectacular fashion.

Well, they talk about professional suicide, don't they?

You'd think it would have stopped when I got the all clear. I remember a party, a huge card, a cake, all my family, Grandma too, all there to celebrate the fact that I was officially one hundred per cent better.

Well, of course that was only half the story. Those long months in bed had left me very weak; such muscles as I had once had wasted away. While my peers had been getting fitter and taller and stronger, I'd been lying in a hospital bed, concentrating on not dying.

I had some catching up to do. And I did it. Not that it ever made any difference. Mum never got out of the habit of saying, 'But you're going

161

to *get better*, Ben,' even when I was twenty-two and winning professional bike races. Dad, meanwhile, was very keen on my being just a normal boy, able to do all the things that normal boys did. He always looked slightly disappointed if he found me reading a book or playing a computer game, and sent me outside to play football with my mates. Assuming I could find any of them, that was. I suppose that was a good thing, really: it forced me back into the gang. They'd all been a bit shy and stand-offish when I was in hospital, so of course when I got out I worked twice as hard to prove I was just the same as them, that the experience hadn't changed me.

Mum would have liked to have been over-protective, I can see that now, but Dad never gave her the chance. And even then I could tell at some level that she was worried, so I always went out of my way to prove that I was OK. Dad didn't believe in wrapping kids in cotton wool, he said, none of this health and safety b... balderdash, what was the point of my getting through the last year if I couldn't have a normal childhood?

He bought me my first bike.

Actually, it was my second bike. I never got to ride the first one. I never saw it. Dad bought it a month before my birthday and locked it in the shed. Ten days before my birthday I was taken into hospital. By the time anybody thought of my riding a bike again... well, I'd grown, and it was time for a bigger one.

Dad didn't believe in stabilisers, either. I just had to perch myself on the saddle and throw myself down the path until I stopped falling off. It resulted in quite a lot of bruises. Mum hated it.

'Stop telling him to be *careful*, Sue,' Dad used to say. 'He'll never learn if he's careful.'

I'd had enough of being told not to do things, anyway. I kept getting back on again.

'That's the spirit,' Dad told me. 'Keep trying. You can do anything if you try hard enough.'

162

Once I got the knack, it turned out that I was actually quite good. I was pleased about this, because it was becoming obvious that there was precious little else that I was good at. I was moved down a year at school when they decided that there was no hope of my ever catching up with the rest of my class. I interpreted this as meaning that there was no hope of my ever doing anything, and stopped bothering. I wasn't much good at football, either. It turned out that my aim was dreadful and I got breathless with all the running.

But I could beat anybody on a bike. Even Minnsy, who was twice my size.

Dad did a bit of research. Signed me up to a junior club. Took out a loan for a really nice bike for me. Encouraged me vigorously to enter competitions. And all this despite that fact that road bike racing was an unknown quantity for him. He didn't really approve of all the leg-shaving (not that I had to worry about that for a couple of years, anyway) or the weight-watching (he'd have liked me to have had some visible muscles in my arms) but the culture of stoicism made up for that. I think he was confirmed in his certainty that cycling was the sport for me when one of the older lads broke his collarbone and didn't even cry.

Mum worried constantly, but, so far as Dad was concerned, the harder I raced, the better it proved I was. In every sense.

Chapter 22

'This woman called for you earlier, Ben,' Polly said when I got in, one evening in late October.

I finished undoing my trainers and looked up at her. 'For me? Did she leave a number?'

'No, literally, rang the front doorbell.' She looked keenly at me, half-amused by my confusion.

'How weird. I don't think I know any women. Apart from you two, obviously. And work. But why would they come to the door?'

She shrugged her shoulders. 'Well, you'll find out. She said she'd come back. I don't think it was anyone from your work, though – she didn't seem to be local. I even wondered –'

'What?'

'I wondered if she was someone from your cycling days.' She dropped the suggestion in with care, and paused briefly to see how I took it. 'An ex-girlfriend, or something.'

I couldn't imagine either of my ex-girlfriends turning up on the doorstep. Kennedy would have turned straight round and gone home when she saw my less than palatial quarters, and Lola... well, if Lola wanted to see me again I'd be very worried about why. We hadn't parted on good terms. 'Italian?' I asked. 'American?'

Polly shook her head. 'French, if anything.'

'Not an ex-girlfriend. But that doesn't really narrow it down. What I want to know is, where did she get my address?'

Polly glanced towards the kitchen, where Vicki was boiling an egg, and lowered her voice. 'Maybe Cunningham's blown your cover.'

'Shit – I hope not.' We were all paranoid these days. 'It's the least I deserve, I suppose. But I don't know what anyone would be chasing me for now. I'm clear with the UCI and Wada.'

'She didn't look old enough to be any sort of official,' Polly said, doubtfully. 'Might be a journalist.'

'Maybe. *We asked has-been doper Ben Goddard for his opinion...*' I sighed. 'Well, whatever she is, I'd better go and have a shower. No need to be *stinking* has-been doper Ben Goddard.'

'I'll keep her talking if she comes when you're in there,' Polly promised. It wasn't exactly reassuring. Perplexed, I went upstairs.

I was showered, changed, and prodding at a pan of baked beans when the doorbell finally went.

It wasn't an ex-girlfriend. It wasn't an official. It wasn't a journalist. 'Hello, Ben,' said Mélanie.

I didn't recognise her at first. Part of it was the fact that for once she wasn't wearing a polo shirt and tracksuit bottoms, her face wasn't flushed and her hair was tidy. More than tidy. Immaculate. But mostly it was that she was the last person on earth I'd expected to see here.

'Mélanie,' I said, helplessly. 'How... why...?'

'I came to talk to you,' she said. 'Your friend said you would be here.'

My friend. She meant Polly. 'As indeed I am. But *why* do you want to talk to me?'

'It will be just like old times,' she said, with a heavy helping of sarcasm.

'I can't see that that's an attractive proposition for either of us.' I was conscious of Vicki and Polly a little distance behind me, out of sight round the corner of the sitting room.

Mélanie's face cracked into a smile. 'I think you understand my point.'

The point that I'd got to was the one where I had to choose between hearing her out and shutting the door in her face. And I was intrigued. 'Come in for a moment,' I said, 'while I grab a jacket. Then we can find somewhere quiet and catch up.'

I hadn't seen her – had barely thought of her – since I had left the team. Like me, Mélanie had been thoroughly chewed up by the Grande Fino machine. I'd seen her come in as an idealistic nineteen-year-old, fresh from her massage courses and sports science exams, and awed by the prospect of serving the giants of a discipline she loved. I'd seen her become a jaded dogsbody, forced to do the dirty work, cleaning up the evidence. My evidence, among others'.

The question was, had she been spat out as well as chewed up? And if not, why on earth was she here?

Rather than have my housemates gape at us while we talked through whatever it was she wanted from me, I took Mélanie to the pub. I bought the drinks, in a probably futile attempt to regain some sense of control over what was going on.

She looked wildly out of place amid the dark varnish and orange paint of the Vine. Her face was perfectly made up, her hair sleek and sculpted into an elegant pleat; her clothes couldn't have looked more French if she'd tried. Maybe she had.

It took me a little while to realise that she was intensely nervous.

'How did you get my address?' I asked. This was both the point where I was most confident of having the moral high ground and the one that worried me the most.

'Your parents are listed as your emergency contact in the team's records,' she said. Her colour rose slightly. 'That should have been destroyed after you left, but it wasn't.'

'You shouldn't have been looking,' I said. 'You'll get fired if they find out.'

'Too late. I left last week.'

I raised my glass to her. 'Wow. Do you have another job lined up?'

'Yes. I don't tell you which team it is with. I have three weeks' break first, however.'

'Congratulations.' I clinked my glass against hers. 'I'll have to have words with my parents, then. What did you say to them?'

'I spoke to your mother. She thinks that I am going to persuade you to return to the sport.'

'*Does* she. And I bet *she* told *you* that, not the other way around.' Mélanie giggled. 'She was very helpful to me.'

'I'm sure she was. I assume that's not why you're really here.'

'No – though it hasn't been the same since you left.' She sipped at her vodka-and-orange. 'I want to expose Grande Fino,' she said.

I said, very cautiously, 'Expose – how? What do you mean?'

'What I say. Show those parasites at the top of the team for the corrupt unscrupulous bullies they are. Get the anti-doping agencies to bring a case against them, if possible.'

'Wow,' I said. 'You're brave.'

She shrugged her shoulders; she couldn't deny it, could she? 'Will you help me?'

I drew a deep breath. 'What sort of help do you want from me?'

'I don't know, yet.' She glanced away as she said it, which made me think that actually she did know; she just wanted to get a handle on my feelings before she showed any cards.

'Who have you got on board so far?' I was careful not to say, *who else*. Not yet.

'You are the first I've spoken to. I think Liebowitz, Starr, will be sympathetic. The other soigneurs, perhaps, but they are so vulnerable. You are the first link in my chain.'

No wonder she was nervous. I took a long pull at my drink before answering. 'Aren't *you* the first link in your chain?'

'Yes, of course – and don't think I ask you to do anything that I won't do myself. But if I go to the authorities now, they just say, Mélanie Lopez, who the fuck is she, and nothing happens.'

'You think they'd listen to me instead? I was only a cog in the machine.' I'd blustered convincingly enough to scare Paul Cunningham, but what Mélanie was talking about would call for a far heavier burden of proof.

'Not alone. But I have to start somewhere.'

'So here you are.'

'Here I am.'

Neither of us spoke for the best part of a minute. Mélanie stirred her drink with the straw. I chased a beermat around the table with a finger. 'What do you want to know?' I asked at last. 'Whether I'm in?'

'Yes. If in a month, six months, a year, five years, I come to you and ask you to tell what you know to a lawyer, a prosecutor, you will do that.'

I wanted to shake her by the hand and say *yes*. But I found that there was a strong undertow of resistance. For months I'd been dealing with the cycling world on my own terms – which was to say, not at all. And now I wanted to throw myself head-first into the febrile scheme of a disgruntled soigneur? Could I face publicity, God knew what sort of legal shenanigans, the loss of what little reputation I had here? I'd got off relatively lightly – why throw all that away now?

But there was another note, battling to be heard over all those arguments: the siren song of justice, the chance, perhaps, to tell my story, to show the world I wasn't the spineless cheat they'd written me off as. That it hadn't *all* been my fault.

'Let me think about it,' I said. 'How long are you here for?'

'I leave the day after tomorrow. Tomorrow I go to Liverpool, to speak to...' She didn't finish the sentence. 'Tomorrow I go to Liverpool, but I come back in the evening. After *that* I'm going to London next, to find Danielle, if I can.'

'Have dinner with me tomorrow night, then,' I said. 'I'll have an answer for you.'

I wasn't on duty at the Grand the next morning, but I got up at my usual time. I wanted Vicki's opinion, and this was by far the best time of the day to catch her. While she ate her breakfast, I told her who Mélanie was and what she'd said to me.

169

'But what does she actually want you to *do*?' Vicki asked between mouthfuls of porridge.

'Well, er...' I hadn't been sure last night, and I wasn't sure now. 'Be ready to testify, I think.'

'Testify what? To whom? Where? Under what circumstances? If you want my advice – for which I will charge by expecting you to do the washing up – it sounds dodgy as hell.'

'I think it's my washing up anyway,' I admitted.

'The burned-on baked beans certainly are,' she said.

'Oh. Sorry.'

She looked at me sharply. 'Do you two have history?'

It took me a moment to understand what she meant. 'Only professional. Comrades in arms on the same miserable team at the same miserable time.'

Vicki swallowed the last of her coffee. 'Well, find out exactly what she plans to do and what she wants you to do for her. And even then I'd probably tell you to stay out of it. But then I'm biased, and it's your life.' She bent in her chair to fasten her shoes, then looked up, smiling. 'Any further questions, or can I go?'

'No. Thank you. That's helpful.'

I watched her absently as she left the room. I hadn't entirely meant that. It was good advice, I realised that, but I wasn't sure it was helpful. It wasn't the advice I wanted. I wanted either an enthusiastic yes or an unequivocal no, not lawyerly caution. I wanted someone else to make the decision.

I made some coffee for myself and thought about it some more. I sat there at the kitchen table all morning, making myself a list of pros and cons, asking myself what I'd have done if I'd been clean, if this had been my first team, if I'd been a multiple Grand Tour winner. I kept coming back to Vicki's point – that I was seriously short on data – but fundamentally I felt that the detail shouldn't matter, that it should come down to the basic principle of telling the truth or not telling the truth. Except my truth wasn't as simple as all that...

When Polly got up, I asked her what she thought. She was no more help. She just said, 'Well, which would make you feel better about yourself?' – and then tried to tell me she wasn't being bitchy.

I didn't argue. I booked a restaurant table for that evening; then I got changed and walked down to the warehouse for my noon-to-six shift. It was mercifully hectic and for most of the afternoon I managed not to think about the question at all. There was only just time to run home for a shower before I met Mélanie. Granted, if I hadn't run I could have got away without the shower, but I also didn't want my colleagues grilling me about a date, which would have been inevitable if I'd brought a change of clothes to work. It would have been far too complicated to explain.

Besides, running clears my head.

I looked in on Polly before I left. 'I'm going out for the evening. Will you be OK?'

'Sure, sure. If I get lonely, I'll text Michael.' She looked me up and down. 'You do brush up nicely. I won't wait up.'

'It's not a date,' I said.

'Never said it was.' She grinned mischievously. 'I'm just assuming you have a lot to catch up on.'

Mélanie was waiting for me outside the restaurant. She'd dressed up again, and was wearing a mermaidy green dress.

'You look fantastic,' I said.

'Thank you. You, too.'

I think we both looked better by comparison with our Grande Fino personas. After all, Mélanie had usually seen me stark naked, sweaty, and probably covered with mud or blood to boot. She was fidgeting with something, turning it over and over in her hands. A notebook of some sort, I thought. 'Shall we?'

Mélanie dithered over the menu, less, I thought, because she couldn't make up her mind than because she didn't really care. I picked a prawn starter and a slow-cooked lamb dish, and got her to choose the wine. 'I may never eat out with a Frenchwoman again,' I said.

'We aren't all wine nerds, you know,' she said, but the one she picked tasted good enough to me.

It didn't feel like a date – still less when Mélanie put her notebook out on the table in front of her – but that didn't stop the staff of Ultima Thule ostentatiously giving us our privacy. Which was no bad thing, given what we were actually there for. We exchanged anodyne gossip about other teams while we ate; the subject of Mélanie's mission squatted in the corner like the proverbial elephant.

'So,' I said, when we'd finished our mains and I'd braced myself with a swig of wine, 'I've decided.'

Mélanie pushed her plate to one side and reached for her little notebook. 'Yes?'

'I will tell you what I know, and then you can decide whether it's of any use to you.'

She uncapped a pen. 'Go on.'

'I was clean for the first year with Grande Fino. And everything before that. If anybody had ever doped at Hirondelle, I didn't know about it. When I moved to Grande Fino...' I hesitated. I'd promised myself I'd stick to facts, and *it just felt different* wasn't really a fact. 'When Henri first took me on, when I signed the contract, he said, "We expect a lot from our riders. I trust that you will not be afraid of that." I didn't think, at the time, that he meant anything beyond very hard work.'

'It was Marcelle who interviewed me,' Mélanie said when she'd finished writing. 'She said that I should be prepared for some unpleasant tasks.'

172

'Maybe she meant Liebowitz's saddle sores,' I suggested.

She looked severely at me. 'The time Gilbert got food poisoning was the worst in that respect. But anyway, Henri implied that he would ask you to dope?'

'That might have been what he meant,' I said. 'But at this distance I'm really not sure.'

She clicked her tongue, unconvinced. 'So what happened next?'

'Nothing much, for my first season. I got a stage win. Henri was pleased. I kept training, throwing everything I could at it.' The words were spilling from my mouth. It was such a relief to talk to someone who'd been there, somebody who already knew the worst. 'Then we came back after the winter break, we went out to training camp, and suddenly Caprini was a whole lot better than me.'

Mélanie wrote it down. *Tonio Caprini.*

'You can write down Luiz and Adrien as well,' I said. 'They're the two I'm sure of.'

'I didn't know about Adrien... Did they speak about it to you? Had Henri instructed them...?'

'Luiz mentioned it to me, once, quite openly, a little while after I'd started myself. Someone must have tipped him off. I wouldn't like to bet on who that was.' *Might not have been Henri*, was what I was trying to say. 'Who else do you know about? You mentioned Starr, Liebowitz, Danielle...?'

She shook her head. 'I want to hear your story first.'

'Adrien, I wouldn't have guessed either. But I caught him with a pill bottle one day, and he just looked guilty as hell. Maybe it was vitamins, you know?' Of course she knew. There was plenty of legal stuff that we could – and did – take in the hope that it would give us a bit of an edge, and Mélanie had often organised it for me. 'But I doubt it.'

'And you?'

I drew a long breath. 'Me. OK, then. Caprini got better, and that worried me. He'd always been the one I measured myself against. He was exactly my height, and a month younger than me. We'd had a kind of rivalry going on in our first season – nothing stupid, nothing that would have upset the balance in the team, but, you know. I only got that stage win because he'd got one the week before and I was extra motivated. He was the one whose times I tried to match, whose weight I tried to match. And now he was doing better than me all the time – sometimes by whole minutes. It was bloody ridiculous. It was bloody depressing.'

'Did he ever admit to you that he was doping?' she asked urgently.

'We never talked about it. On the one hand, we didn't need to, because it was obvious. On the other, I didn't want to know. If it turned out that it was true, I'd lose all respect for him. If it wasn't... well, what did that say about me? Was I completely deluding myself, that I could hold my own in a decent team?'

'Not decent at all,' Mélanie said, with a touch of censure.

'A team that won things, then.'

'They do that, it's true,' she said. 'Go on.'

'I panicked. I pushed myself to my absolute limits all the time. I never let myself recover. My results got worse and worse. Do you remember Nancy?'

She frowned. 'Nancy? – oh, the town. Your pronunciation needs some work. Yes. You couldn't stay with the lead group. Karl had punctured, and there was no lead-out for Jorge. Henri was not happy.'

'That's putting it mildly,' I said, with feeling. 'Well, after he bollocked me in front of all of you, he left it a couple of days and then called me to see him. He apologised for shouting at me, for humiliating me – it left me feeling worse than the original yelling. He told me that he was worried about me, that my results had been deteriorating. Which was true.'

Mélanie reached across the table to take my hand. 'The manipulative bastard.'

'He said that if he let me go, he didn't think another team would take me. He said that he thought I might be ill. He recommended that I go and consult Dr Wolfsen.'

Mélanie's fingers tightened on mine.

'And he said he'd give me the rest of the season, but if I wasn't back up – *back* up! – to Caprini's standard by then, he'd have to sack me.'

'And?'

'And I went to see Dr Wolfsen.' I took another big gulp of wine. 'I knew he had a reputation, but I also knew that nothing had ever been proved against him, and that some guys who, I was almost certain, were clean had consulted him.'

'Tell me about that,' she prompted.

'Well, he had two practices, if you like. He was first and foremost a sports doctor, he had some really good physiotherapists working for him, and if somebody went to him after an injury then nobody batted an eyelid. But he also ran an anti-ageing clinic, and that was where the interesting stuff happened.'

Mélanie winced at the word *interesting*. 'Was that all Henri said, go and talk to Dr Wolfsen?'

'At the time, yes. He didn't say I should do anything particular beyond see what Wolfsen had to say.' I looked her in the eye. 'You want me to tell you he told me to dope. I can't. He didn't. I could give you Wolfsen tied up with a pretty satin bow, but I haven't anything that looks remotely like proof against Henri. He never asked. He only cared that we won. Which I did. Twice. I've thought about it – long before you came knocking at my door. I could put everything I know on the table, and Henri could still turn round and say he'd no idea what Wolfsen was getting riders to do.'

Mélanie let go of my hand to make a note. I felt suddenly bereft. 'I see,' she said. She'd tried to cover her disappointment by looking down at her book, but her voice gave her away.

'I'm sorry,' I said. I turned my hand palm-up, offering all the nothing I had. 'Everything I know, I'll tell you. But I don't think it's going to be enough.'

She put the cap back on the pen and closed the notebook. 'Thank you,' she said. She placed her hand very gently on top of mine, so the tips of her fingers lay on the cords of my wrist. 'I think you're right, but thank you for being honest.'

For a moment, we were absolutely still. Then she moved a fraction – or I did – and her third finger was hovering over the pulse point and my blood wanted to jump up to reach her. Slowly, questioningly, she brushed the inside of my wrist.

My mouth was dry. I looked up to meet her gaze. Raised my eyebrows.

She nodded, half-smiling, as if to reassure one or both of us.

'Wow,' I murmured.

'I know. This was not part of the plan.'

A thousand bad jokes about *flexibility* and *adapting to changing race circumstances* came to my mind. I didn't tell any of them. Instead, I called the waiter over and asked for the bill.

'Where are you staying?' I said to Mélanie, while we waited.

'The Grand, on the beach,' she said.

'Oh.' I began to laugh. I couldn't help it.

'What's so funny? It's nicer than many places we've stayed.'

'I work there.'

'Oh.' The corners of her mouth twitched deliciously. She'd seen the joke as well. We'd avoided breaking the taboo on intra-team relations by means of both leaving the team, but I was pretty sure there'd be something in my contract with the Grand about not shagging guests on the premises. Which I was pretty sure I was about to do. Right then, I didn't care.

Mélanie asked, 'Should we go to your house, then?'

176

I thought of my unmade bed and my week's worth of sweaty running gear spilling out of the laundry bin. I thought of Polly, either canoodling with Michael, which would be awkward, or greeting us on her own, which would be more awkward. I thought of the long, long walk in the chilly fog.

'You'll have to sneak me in,' I said. 'We can speak French to throw them off the scent.' It gave an extra little thrill to proceedings, and I wondered why I'd never thought of Mélanie like this before.

'*D'accord*,' she said, with a slow, devastating smile, and nudged my foot with hers.

God knows the two of us had been in plenty of hotel rooms in our time, but never like this. And it wasn't just the fact that both of us were naked this time. We had always been cyclist and soigneur, doper and assistant. Conspirators, not lovers. And even now the team was there in the room with us, a history that neither of us could escape from.

'You've changed,' she murmured.

'I have?' Mélanie had always taken a professional interest in my body, of course, and I was worried at first that she'd see a marked deterioration. Inevitably, I'd put on weight. My arms must have doubled in size since I'd started working at Benson's.

But she chuckled softly. 'Of course,' she said. 'You've stopped shaving your legs.'

After that she stopped laughing, and became grimly serious, flinging herself against me as if I was both cause and cure of all her problems. I caught her mood, and the whole thing became a reciprocal exercise in getting our frustrations out. She wanted something from me that I couldn't give her. I was furious with her for dragging me back into a world I'd been glad to see the back of. She was all blighted idealism and avenging angel; I was trust betrayed and a body that was never going to do what I wanted of it. Everything we'd been complicit in and hated in ourselves and in each other, everything we'd dreamed and desired and despised, we laid it out there.

I felt better afterwards. So, I think, did she.

'It wasn't your fault,' she murmured. 'You have to remember that.'

But it wasn't quite as simple as that, no matter how much she wanted it to be, and I lay awake for quite a while after she'd drifted off to sleep, wondering what had really happened, and what on earth was going to happen next.

Chapter 23

I woke several times in the night, paranoid that I'd oversleep and miss my shift. At least twice I dreamed that I had. At last, at a quarter past five in the morning, I gave up and crept out of bed. Mélanie rolled over but didn't wake. She looked very peaceful in the half-light, the fire of justice banked up and invisible for the moment. I dressed swiftly and quietly and leaned over to kiss her on the cheek. Her eyelashes quivered and she smiled very gently in her sleep. Then I slipped out of the room and down the stairs.

I had to go via reception. My staff pass wouldn't have let me through the fire door at the bottom of the stairs, certainly not from the bedroom side. Fortunately there was no one at the desk, and if I showed up on CCTV as a non-resident making his escape after a one-night stand, well, that was exactly what I was, and probably the picture would be too fuzzy to identify me.

I went for a brisk walk along the sea wall, beyond the reach of the street lights, and then turned and headed back into town. Sunrise was a way off, and the sea was still inky black, but there was a hint of a paler blue above the hills in the east. I didn't have time to go home for my uniform, but I knew where the spares were kept, and, so long as I put anything I borrowed back washed and ironed, nothing would be said.

I wasn't even the first one in the kitchen. Eddie was there, firing up the cookers, and Agnieszka had started the coffee machines. 'Morning, Ben,' she said. 'You are all right?'

'Not bad, thanks,' I said. 'You?'

It was just like any other morning.

Callum was on the welcome desk when Mélanie came down to breakfast. I pretended not to see her, clearing a just-vacated table while Agnieszka took the coffee order. Then I had a group of my own to issue with hot beverages. But I made sure that my path back to the kitchen took me past Mélanie's table.

She made the most of the opportunity. 'Excuse me,' she said, leaning heavily on her accent, 'is there anyone here who speak French?'

'Je parle un peu de français, madame,' I responded.

'Ah, super! Pouvez-vous m'éxpliquer, qu'est-ce que c'est "kedgeree"?'

'Bien sûr.' Though I wasn't sure that I could explain kedgeree at all. *'C'est un plat au poisson, riz, et oeufs – comment dit-on "hard-boiled"? Boulli?'* I glanced around. None of my colleagues was eavesdropping; it was safe to ask what she really wanted to say. *'Et qu'est-ce que c'est que tu as vraiment voulu dire?'*

'Je voudrais savoir si tu n'as pas rappelé rien d'autre, ou si tu penses encore comme hier.' Had I remembered anything else, or did I still think the same as yesterday? She winked. *'Non, je ne mange pas du poisson au matin.'*

'It's the same menu as yesterday, madame,' I said gravely. 'Unless you'd like to suggest something different yourself?'

She laughed. 'As I thought. I will take a mushroom omelette, please.'

'Aux champignons, madame? À quelle heure devez-vous partir?' Was she going to rush off? I wanted to talk to her properly.

'Le train part à onze heures trente-cinq.'

'D'accord. Attendez-moi à l'arrêt de bus à onze heures; je marche avec vous à la gare.'

She nodded, and tipped me a five euro note with her phone number and email address written on it. *'On ne sait jamais,'* she said.

At the end of my shift I got out as quickly as I could, leaving with my borrowed uniform bundled up under my arm. Mélanie was waiting at the bus stop, as promised.

'Surely,' she said, 'it doesn't take thirty-five minutes to walk to the station.'

'No,' I said. 'I'll get you a coffee before your train.'

She smiled. 'It used to be my job to get coffee for you.' She hoisted her holdall over her shoulder. 'Which way?'

'This way. Are you OK with that bag?'

'I think,' she said, 'you have your own burden to carry.' She made it sound like she didn't mean the flapping legs of my work trousers. 'You haven't remembered anything else, I take it?'

'You didn't think I'd change my mind because we...?' I couldn't quite believe we *had*: teasing me about coffee, her hair blowing in the sea breeze, she was the Mélanie I'd first met, worlds away from the furious, tormented soul I'd known last night.

'No, of course not. I wouldn't ask you to lie. Besides, I'm glad we did.' She was blushing.

'I enjoyed it myself,' I said. 'Are you going to report back to my parents that you couldn't persuade me back into competing?' File that under *things they didn't want to know*, I thought.

'I think I'll let them draw their own conclusions,' she said drily. 'Or you can tell them.'

'I'll tell them you turned out to be a debt collector chasing my unpaid fines. That'll teach them.' Fucking Dad and his fucking *contribute* and *subsidise*.

'Do you *have* unpaid fines?'

'No.'

'Then don't be too hard on them,' Mélanie said. 'They don't know what it was like.'

'*Don't* they?' But I wasn't going to get into that. I moved onto slightly steadier ground. 'Do *you* think I should race again? What would everyone else say?'

'Are you unhappy now, not racing?'

I thought about that. 'Not really,' I said. It was still true. It wasn't just that I wasn't unhappy. I was actually, actively, happy.

Mélanie went on, 'If I were you, if I had got out and had found something else to do, I wouldn't go back.'

'If I were *you*, if I'd got a job on a decent team, I wouldn't leave.' Again I wondered which team she was bound for, and if they knew about her amateur detective efforts.

'It sounds like we're both in the right place, then,' she said, pleased.

'Or both in the wrong one.'

Mélanie swapped her bag onto her other shoulder. 'You ask me what will people say. You know perfectly well: it will depend on the person. Some will be glad to see you back. Some will say, fucking doper, kick him out.'

It was true. I already knew all that, and it didn't help. 'I'd be more convincing on your story if I came back.'

'Ah, then you should definitely come back, in that case.' She grinned, either to show that it was a joke or to show that it wasn't. I regretted saying it; it raised the ghost of the disappointment that had haunted last night.

'So you're off to London now. To see...'

'Danielle. She is a physiotherapist now, at one of the big hospitals.'

I tried to picture Danielle, and succeeded in summoning a memory of brown hair and a Geordie accent. 'Give her my regards.'

'Of course.'

We walked into the station; there was half an hour left before Mélanie's train departed. I bought the coffee, as I'd promised; meanwhile, she cleared the detritus off a table and sat down as I joined her.

'So,' I said, 'good luck.'

'Thank you.'

'You'll let me know if anything happens?' I'd almost said *if anything ever happens*.

'You've got my number,' she said. 'Give me yours.'

I scrabbled in my pocket for the crumpled banknote. 'I'd better put it somewhere safer than that,' I said, and got out my phone.

There was a message from Polly.

Received about nine hours ago.

Ben – assuming A you have been persuaded to return to pro cycling or B it was a date after all. If B please come home when convenient as we have been burgled. P

'Fuck,' I said, and pressed the *Call* button.

It rang several times before Polly picked up. 'Ben! You're alive!' She was talking too high and too fast. 'We were beginning to think that Mélanie was going to turn out to be a contract killer!'

'What?' I said, bewildered. 'Me? Never mind me: are *you* OK?'

Even through the phone I heard her draw breath. 'A bit freaked out. Otherwise unharmed.'

'Thank God for that. Are you at the house? On your own?'

'Yes, I am, and no, not yet. Michael's been here, but he's – gone. Vicki's here now but she's going to have to go into work soon.'

'I'll come as quick as I can.' I ended the call, and only remembered when I saw the banknote what I'd got the phone out for.

Mélanie was smiling patiently. 'Emergency?'

'House was burgled; Polly's OK but I should get back.'

She looked concerned. 'She was on her own?'

'I assume so. She said that her boyfriend had been over, but it sounded like that was this morning.'

'I didn't realise she had a boyfriend,' Mélanie said. It seemed like an odd detail to pick up on, and it irritated me bizarrely. 'It was good of him to stay with her.'

'But he hasn't stayed with her,' I said. 'That's the point. He's fucked off, so I've got to get home before our other housemate has to leave.'

'No, I didn't mean that. It was good of him to stay in a relationship with her after – what was it? An accident?'

'*Oh...*' I said. 'No.' I wished she hadn't said that. 'She hadn't even met him before she got ill. And she dumped him a while ago, and then they got back together. The man's a dickhead, but he's not a dickhead about her being disabled.'

'Oh.' Mélanie flushed. 'I'm sorry.'

'I didn't mean –' But I had, kind of.

'You'd better go,' she said reluctantly. She took out her little notebook one final time. 'Give me your contact details, and I'll let you know what happens.'

I wrote down my phone number, complete with international dialling code, and email address. 'And you know my postal address, of course. Though if we have to move because of this shit... well, my email will still work, obviously.'

'Thank you.' She tucked the book away in her holdall. We smiled awkwardly at each other.

'It's been very good to see you,' I said. I meant that. Now that I'd had to think about it, I'd realised that there were a few people from Grande Fino I'd be happy to encounter again, and Mélanie was definitely on that list.

'You, too. Last night...' She tailed off, blushing.

'Unexpected, but enjoyable,' I said.

'Yes.' She nodded. 'If things were different...'

'Different how?' I asked.

She shrugged her shoulders. 'I don't know. Never mind.'

I looked ruefully at my cooling coffee and stood up. 'Well. Goodbye, then. And good luck.'

She stood up too. 'Goodbye. And thank you.'

We settled for a Gallic kiss-on-both-cheeks thing, and I left her there, sipping her coffee, while I went home to see what chaos had developed in the real world.

Vicki was there, dressed for work and hopping impatiently from one foot to the other. Gianna was there, rattling the keys to the van. They left almost as soon as I'd crossed the threshold.

The police were there, taking statements. Mine was brief, irrelevant, and embarrassing. I had to admit that I'd been at work when I shouldn't have been and that work wouldn't or shouldn't know about it, and give them Mélanie's number so that she could corroborate my story.

'Nothing to worry about, sir,' the officer reassured me. 'Miss Devine tells us that she got a sight of the intruder and she's satisfied it wasn't you.'

'Too tall and too wide,' Polly said. She turned serious. 'Which is just as well, because one of the things he took was my prescription.'

'If it wasn't EPO, I'm not interested,' I said. Nobody laughed. I turned to the policewoman who was writing things down. 'Not funny, sorry. I used to be a professional cyclist. I was banned last year for using performance-enhancing drugs. But I've never been interested in anything Polly takes, and if I was I'd just get it out of the medicine cabinet.'

'We'll have to follow up on that one,' the officer said doubtfully.

I tried to ignore the feeling of apprehension creeping down my spine. 'Which prescription was it, anyway?'

'Anti-depressants,' Polly said. 'I can't see that they'd be much use to anybody, if I'm honest.'

'Maybe someone just grabbing them on the off-chance they were saleable...' one of the policemen suggested. 'You surprised him before he could get hold of anything valuable.'

'I thought it *was* you, Ben,' Polly explained. 'I was just getting off to sleep, and I heard someone messing with the front door lock. And then there was this crash, the broken glass, and my head wasn't quite with it so I put on my dressing gown and came out to ask you what the fuck it was you thought you were doing.'

'Nasty surprise,' I observed.

'For me and the burglar. Obviously, he didn't have time to get much, and I *think* it's just the stuff that was on the coffee table – Vicki's laptop, and my pills, which is a bloody nuisance, and my jewellery, which I really am annoyed about, because that was my grandma's.'

'Oh, Polly, I'm sorry,' I said. I meant it, but it probably sounded insincere.

'Can we go through all that again, sorry?' the policewoman asked me. She was looking suspiciously at Polly as well as at me. That worried me.

'All...?'

'Your movements last night, sir. With times, if you can remember them.'

I was feeling steadily more uncomfortable. 'Right. OK. Well, I left here at about ten to seven – what do you think, Polly? – to get to the restaurant.'

The policewoman glanced at Polly, and I regretted asking for her confirmation. 'And the restaurant was?'

'Ultima Thule.'

'On Broad Street?'

'That's right,' I said, grateful that we could agree on one thing at least. 'They'll have a record of my booking. Seven forty-five.'

'And how did you get there?'

'I walked. I met Mélanie – my ex-colleague – there. We had dinner –' I was *not* going to say what we talked about; let them think it was a date if they wanted to – 'and decided to go to the Grand, where Mélanie was staying. We must have left the restaurant at half past nine or so – they'd remember; it wasn't very busy – and went straight to the hotel. Well...'

'Yes?'

'Stopped at a chemist on the way.' That didn't sound great, either.
'For?'

I wished Polly wasn't in the room. 'Condoms,' I admitted.

The policewoman's face was professionally blank. 'Which chemist?'

'The one on the corner of Lion Row. Is it a Lloyd's? It's directly on the way from Broad Street to the seafront.'

She nodded. 'So you got there... when?'

'I didn't check the time.' I'd had other things on my mind. 'But we went straight there.'

'Would any of your colleagues have seen you going in?'

'We made sure they didn't,' I said ruefully. 'We would show up on the CCTV, though, assuming it hasn't been wiped yet.' Suddenly I was hoping that I was recognisable, after all.

'And you left...?'

'I left at five-thirty this morning. Went for a walk, then back to the Grand for my breakfast shift.' As I said it, I realised how dodgy it sounded.

'I see. Would you give us the lady's contact details? Just a formality, you understand.'

And that, I suspected, meant that they might ask Mélanie, but they wouldn't believe her.

We worked our way through some other things that were also, we were told, nothing more than formalities; then the police left and the landlord arrived with some plywood to block up the broken pane of glass. I made sandwiches for myself and Polly; then, satisfied that she was not too worried, got changed and left for my shift at Benson's.

Myself, I was very worried indeed.

Chapter 24

I got home from the warehouse just after eight and found a minor piss-up going on at the kitchen table. Vicki and Gianna were most of the way through a bottle of red wine. Polly was drinking something very bright red indeed.

'What's that?' I asked.

'Cherryade,' she said. 'I'm trying to compensate for not having the alcohol that I'm not allowed to fucking drink on these fucking pills that I do not fucking have because some wanker has fucking *nicked* them.'

'Hang on,' I said. It had been a long and trying day, but I didn't think that made sense under any circumstances. 'If you don't have your medication, doesn't that mean you *can* drink?'

'It would be a very bad idea,' Polly said. 'Which is not to say I'm not tempted.'

Vicki and Gianna glanced worriedly at each other. 'Have a drink, Ben,' Gianna said. 'We'll open another bottle.'

I sat down.

'How many E-numbers are there in two litres of cherryade, do you think?' Polly asked. She topped up her glass; it foamed pinkly, almost over the brim.

'Quite enough,' Vicki said dourly. She tipped her chair backwards to get another tumbler from the draining board, poured the last of the wine into it, and handed it to me.

'Thanks,' I said. 'Bloody hell, what a day.'

'You don't know the half of it,' Vicki told me.

I flinched. 'Go on. What don't I know?'

'I've dumped Michael,' Polly said. She glared at me, daring me to argue, perhaps.

'OK,' I said. I hadn't been expecting that. 'Any particular reason?'

'Oh, God. Where do I start?'

'Your meds got nicked,' Vicki prompted her.

'I was aware of *that*,' I said, not bothering to disguise any bitterness that might have got into my voice.

'My meds got nicked,' Polly echoed. 'That was my whole supply. I'm not a happy person after a day or so without them, so I phoned to see if I could get a doctor's appointment this afternoon, to get a replacement prescription.'

'OK,' I said, again. I didn't see what this had to do with Michael, but people were giving me wine, so I wasn't complaining.

'Miracle of miracles, I could. Except it was really short notice. I couldn't get a taxi. Vicki was at work. You were at work. Gianna was still in Lingholme after dropping Vicki off. So I called Michael. It's his afternoon off; he could have got round here in ten minutes.'

'And...?'

'He refused.'

'He was doing something else?'

'No. He thought this was a brilliant opportunity for me to come off antidepressants.'

'He what?' I'm no expert, but this sounded like a very bad idea to me.

'So I told him to stick his brilliant opportunity where the sun don't shine.'

'Well,' I said feebly, 'that sounds reasonable enough, but why on earth does he...?'

'Let's just say,' Polly said icily, 'that we had radically different ideas on the power of prayer. And, while faith may move mountains, I'm not sufficiently faithful to come off the pills that keep me sane.'

'Not sufficiently *stupid*,' Vicki muttered. Her face had flushed a dull scarlet all over.

'I thought the guy was an atheist now?' I said.

'He may be an atheist,' Polly said, 'but he's still a fully paid-up member of the Positive Thinking Church of the All In Your Head Woowoo.'

'Tell me more?' I prompted, knowing that I was going to hear it anyway.

'He is convinced that anti-depressants are pure placebo and that I should stop taking them immediately. I should replace them with fresh air and seeing more people. To do him justice, he did offer to provide both the fresh air and the company, but even so, I am not taking him up on his offer.'

'I assume he *is* wrong?' I ventured.

'Demonstrated by experiment,' Polly said bitterly. 'Accidental experiment, but convincing nonetheless. I ran out of them about eighteen months ago, and didn't get round to getting the prescription refilled. The results were – not good.'

'No?'

'No.' Her mouth shut like a trap.

'Did you tell Michael that?'

'Yes, but he has his own bullshit theories about why my brain melted.'

'It's a bit weird, though,' Vicki said. 'It's almost as if his thought processes are exactly the same as they were before, he just doesn't believe in God any more.'

'It's not really *weird*,' Polly said. 'In my experience people's beliefs – their deep-down beliefs, I mean – don't change. Not without a lot of navel-gazing, preferably accompanied by a very big shock.' She glanced at me. 'He's always been hung up on willpower. He used to talk a lot about not acting in one's own strength, but what he usually meant was that you weren't trying hard enough.'

'He sounds a real charmer,' I said.

'You needn't tell me that now.' She glanced suspiciously from me to Vicki to Gianna. 'God. I wish I was drunk.'

I wished I was. I was luckier than Polly: I could act on that wish. Though it probably wasn't a good idea. I was going to have to talk to the big boss tomorrow – before the police did it.

I slept badly and fidgeted my way through the breakfast shift. When at last we were all washed up I went off to the offices and tapped on Andy's door.

'Hello? … Oh, Ben. Is everything all right?'

I liked Andy. He was a big bloke: quiet, but you sensed you didn't want to get on the wrong side of him.

I shifted from foot to foot. 'Andy. I've got something to tell you.'

He raised his eyebrows. 'New job?'

'That depends on your reaction to what I'm about to tell you.'

'Go on. Do you need to shut the door?'

I wasn't sure if I *needed* to, but I did. 'I'm not sure if it's sackable or not,' I said.

His eyebrows went even higher. 'Sounds like you should sit down. Come on, out with it.'

But I was way too much of a wuss to do it in any other way than tiptoeing around the edges. 'A couple of days ago, someone I used to work with came looking for me. She wanted –' no, this wasn't relevant, '– well, the night before last I took her out to dinner to find out what she wanted, and...'

'One thing led to another?' He said it with a gentle irony that told me that I could assume nothing.

'Yes. But the thing is, she was staying here...'

'So one thing led to another *here*?' His face grew grave.

'Yes.'

'And you're telling me all this why?'

I took a deep breath. 'Because my house got burgled the same night and it's possible that the police will want to know where I was at the time. I've told them I was here, but they might want to look at the CCTV from reception.'

He looked sceptical. 'Why would you burgle your own house?'

I gulped. 'Whoever it was took my housemate's prescription drugs. And I was stupid enough to mention my doping history when I gave my statement.'

'Would these have been drugs that would have been used for doping?'

'Well, no. I don't think that they would give anyone any advantage.' I swallowed. It was beginning to dawn on me that I might just have made a huge mistake.

'So I repeat, why would you burgle your own house?'

I shook my head. 'I suppose I wouldn't.'

Andy sighed. 'You don't have much luck, do you, Ben?'

That sounded ominous. 'I've been fairly lucky since I left cycling. On the whole. But I've also been stupid.'

'This woman was someone from your cycling days?'

'Yes.'

He was silent for a long moment, tapping his pen on his desk. Meanwhile, I tried not to think about the possibility that I'd overreacted hugely, the fact that *drugs plus police* didn't necessarily equal *big trouble for Ben* any more than *two plus two* made *three hundred and fifty million,* and what felt like the increasing likelihood that I'd just thrown away my job for nothing.

'OK,' Andy said at last. 'Two things I need to know. You had sex here – was it consensual?'

'God, yes,' I said, shocked. 'I can give you Mélanie's phone number if you want to hear it from her.'

He nodded. 'And I think I do need to know what you were meeting her about.'

'Long story. But she basically wants to expose the doping culture in our old team. You can check that with her, too.'

193

'Mm,' he said. 'I think I will. Would you give me her number?'

I handed my phone over, grateful that I'd copied the details across. The five-euro note wouldn't have helped my cause at all.

'They'll have her details in the system, of course,' he said as he dialled the number from his desk phone.

'I suppose they will.' I hadn't thought of that. I prayed that Mélanie had given it when she checked in.

'Hello? Hello – is that Mélanie Lopez?... This is Andy Royston; I'm calling from the Grand Hotel.' He motioned at me to leave the room. I did, making sure to shut the door properly behind me. I wanted desperately to know what Andy was saying to Mélanie – and vice versa – but I was glad of the chance to regain my composure. I leaned against the wall and breathed as deeply as I could manage.

After about a million years Andy opened the door. 'Come back in. Sit down.'

I sat down, none too gracefully.

His face was stern. 'You are absolutely right,' he said. 'We take any sort of... inappropriate relationship between our staff and our guests very seriously. It's for staff's protection – particularly female staff – as much as guests'. Not to mention the hotel's reputation. And I have dismissed staff for it in the past. *However –*'

'Yes?' I said eagerly Perhaps he'd give me a decent reference, I thought.

'However, having talked to the lady – and don't think it wasn't very awkward for both of us – I do recognise that there were exceptional circumstances. Namely, that you knew each other before. And so I'm not going to sack you.'

'Thank you,' I said. I wiped my hands on my trousers. 'I'm incredibly grateful.'

Andy nodded. 'If she finds herself back in these parts, I'd recommend that she stays at – oh, the Bellevue. Anywhere else, really.'

'I'll suggest that, if I hear from her that she's coming back this way,' I said. I was doing my best to imply that it wasn't very likely.

'And if the police ask, which to be frank I think is unlikely, I'll tell them that I've no reason to doubt what the two of you have just told me. I'll ask Dave not to wipe the CCTV just yet.'

'Thank you. I really do appreciate your putting yourself out for me...'

Andy smiled wearily. 'Just don't make me do it again.'

'I won't.' I felt able to make that promise without reservations.

'Hm.' It didn't seem like a dismissal, so I stayed where I was. 'One other thing,' Andy said at last.

'Yes?'

'Agnieszka said she heard you talking very good French to a lady at breakfast the other day. Knowing what I know now, I assume that was...'

'Mélanie. Yes.'

'I was going to make – a suggestion? an offer? – and, having thought about it a bit, I still am.'

'Oh?' Now I was really at sea.

'My daughter's at college at the moment. Sixth form.' He smiled. His tone had changed completely. 'She wants to study French and Spanish at uni. She's good – been getting excellent results – but she's not confident. She's really worried about the interviews.'

'I didn't go to uni,' I said. I'd no idea what an entrance interview might be like.

Andy said, 'Yes, but you'd be someone she doesn't know who could speak French to her.'

I was very cautious. 'What exactly were you thinking of?'

'You'd come round our house and just talk French with her. An hour, once a week or so until she's through the process. Twenty quid a time.'

'Wow,' I said. 'After everything I've just told you?' If I were a father, I didn't think I'd trust me with my daughter.

'Well, I'd really recommend that you watch your step,' he said drily.

'I'm not great on the grammar and all that,' I said, concerned that Agnieszka had talked me up beyond my actual abilities.

'Not worried about that. Sarah's got the sort of brain that picks up that kind of stuff. I literally just want you to talk to her.'

'Wow,' I said again. 'How could I refuse?' I'd have found it difficult to refuse if he'd offered me a job wrestling crocodiles in a vat of slurry and expected me to pay him for the privilege of doing it.

He laughed. 'You'd say, thanks Andy, but I'm not interested.'

'But I won't,' I said. I couldn't believe my good luck. 'I might be stupid, but I'm not that stupid.'

Chapter 25

When Andy said that Sarah was shy, he wasn't joking. Even in English we were only talking in words of one syllable as Andy introduced us.

She obviously wasn't keen on the idea. I supposed she was going along with it to please her parents. Or maybe she really did think it would give her the confidence to get into wherever she was trying to get into, and was just gritting her teeth and forcing herself through it until the confidence turned up. I couldn't argue: that was pretty much how I'd approached my career.

For propriety's sake, we did our French practice at the kitchen table while family life went on around us. We stumbled our way through conversation that Sarah must have learned years ago, establishing that her hair was brown (*cheveux bruns*) and so were my eyes (*les yeux bruns*), that she had a little brother (*un petit frère*) and that I was an only child (*fils unique*), before she muttered, '*C'est vrai, donc, ce que mon père m'a dit?*'

What had her father told her? '*Ça dépend,*' I said, caught off guard. '*Qu'est-ce que c'est que ton père t'a dit?*'

She'd been using *vous* all the time, as befitted my relative age, my celebrity, or, more likely, the fact that we were strangers. Now she switched to *tu*. '*Il m'a dit que tu étais cycliste, avant de... faire de dopage.*'

I'd been a cyclist, before doping. I couldn't deny it. '*Oui, c'est vrai, ça. Tu ne l'a pas vu sur l'internet?*' Hadn't she looked me up online?' I'd have looked me up online.

'*Non – selon l'internet, tout le monde est... dopeur.*'

I admitted that yes, the internet tended towards a fairly jaded view of most sportspeople, and cyclists in particular. I said, '*Tu aimes le sport, toi-même?*' I thought, the moment I'd said it, that we were going to lapse back into the *j'ai dix-sept ans* script, it was such a cliché of a question. Did she like sport?

But she said, '*Jouer, ou regarder?*' and, without waiting for an answer, she was off, telling me about her football team – or, rather, teams: Lingholme United, which she supported, and the school one she played in.

'*Moi, j'étais nul à football,*' I said.

She smiled sympathetically and disbelievingly, but it was true. I'd never been good at football. I started explaining, and suddenly we were comparing our sporting histories in surprisingly competent French. Somehow, I didn't mind at all.

Mélanie rang me one foggy evening about a month before Christmas. I answered with caution. 'Hello?'

'Hi, Ben! I have made some progress!'

I sat down on the edge of my bed, thinking back to what she had told me of her plans. 'Liebowitz? Danielle?'

'No.' The tone of her voice fell a little. 'But I have found someone who wants to talk to you.' It was almost a question.

'To me?' I did not let my guard down one little bit.

'His name is Russell Simpkins. He is a TV producer.'

I didn't like the sound of that. 'We didn't say anything about TV.'

She became defensive. 'Well, no, but this is a great opportunity! He would want to make a documentary. You would be the focus of it; you would have the chance to tell your side of the story.'

I didn't even have to think about it. 'No,' I said. 'Absolutely not.'

'But why?' she asked.

'Because, as I said before, my side of the story is a crap story.' I had to fight hard to keep my voice down. 'It doesn't tell anyone anything they didn't know already. Henri will sue the pants off me, and my pants are about all I have left now. And it won't do anything to clean things up, will it? I have no hard evidence against Henri, and to be quite frank I've got no desire to expose myself as a cheating git on national or international television just when everyone's forgotten about me. And that's what my side of the story is.'

'Oh.' She sounded crushed. 'He really wants to meet you. He's finishing a project and then he'll be in London in three weeks' time.'

'Forget it. I'm not going to fucking London.'

'Oh.' She sounded bleaker than ever.

A sudden suspicion struck me. 'How did you find him, anyway? Or how did he find you? I thought you were looking for a legal case, not publicity.'

'Suzie Balham passed him on to me,' she said miserably.

That was a name I'd never forgotten. 'Suzie Balham the journalist? Suzie Balham who broke the news about my dope test in the first place?'

There was silence at the other end of the line.

'Well?' I demanded. 'That Suzie Balham?'

'Yes. That Suzie Balham.'

'How does she know you?'

'There are a *few* people in the media who realise it's worth talking to the soigneurs,' she muttered.

'*I* bet. So were you the one who let her know I'd tested positive, by any chance?'

She didn't answer. She didn't need to.

'And were you ever going to tell me that?' I hissed. 'Saving it up as a nice surprise for when I'd spilled everything to this Simpkins guy, were you?'

'It wasn't like that!' she protested.

'So what was it like? And if you're thinking about not telling me until I agree to speak to your Simpkins, then forget it. I don't care that much.'

'She said she'd heard that there'd been a positive test on the team. After that it was just a process of elimination, she said.'

'God, you're lucky Henri never found out.' I was furious. What gave her the right to betray my business, the team's confidence...? I realised with horror that I was siding with Henri. And that couldn't be right. It made me even angrier with Mélanie.

'I'm lucky. I know,' she said. Her voice changed. 'And so are you, but you don't seem to want to make much of it.'

'I... what? Mélanie, I told you what I would and wouldn't do, and you haven't given me any option I'm prepared to act on.'

'Fine,' she said, sulkily.

I sighed. My anger was ebbing away now; I felt cold and ashamed. 'Look: what we said before, that still stands. If you can find enough other witnesses to make a case, I'll be the first on the stand. But I'm not doing any self-pitying chat-show crap. I'm sorry if I didn't make that clear before.'

'It's OK, it's OK,' she said. 'I understand. I will tell Russell it's no good.'

First-name terms, eh? I didn't comment on that, didn't want to look jealous. I just said, 'Yes, please do.' That sounded a bit cold. I added, 'It's good to hear from you, Mélanie.'

She thawed a bit. 'Yes; you too.'

'I hope you're keeping well? How's the new team?'

She made a non-committal noise and said, 'I'm settling down.' That could have meant either that it was just like Grande Fino, or that it was nothing like it. 'You?'

'Oh, same old, same old.'

A bubble of laughter grew in her voice. 'You are still working at the hotel? Is everything OK there?'

'It's fine.' I smiled, remembering. 'Thank you for being such a good sport about... well, Andy, and the police, and everything.'

'Don't mention it.'

We exchanged a few more pleasantries and then she rang off, the bridge between us not reduced entirely to smoking ashes, after all.

I thought about the conversation for a long while, gazing out of the window at the orange mist. Then I decided I needed coffee in order to think about it properly, so I went downstairs to make some. There was an insistent little voice in my head that told me that I'd just wussed out of my chance to right some wrongs. That any publicity was useful publicity. That even if all the Simpkins documentary did was make it clear that riders were still vulnerable, it was worth doing. I stirred hot water into instant coffee with such violence that I sloshed half of it over the side of the mug. For fuck's sake, what right did Mélanie have even to discuss something like that with some hyena journalist?

I hesitated a moment, then went and tapped at Polly's door.

'Come in!' she called. 'Oh, hi, Ben. What's up?'

'I need a sanity check,' I said.

Polly looked intrigued. 'Sit down and tell me about it.'

I put my coffee down on her bedside table and sat down on the edge of the bed. Polly closed her laptop and wiggled the wheelchair around so that she faced me.

'Mélanie just called me.' I explained what she'd said, her proposal to go to the media rather than the courts, and what my response had been.

Polly listened with grave attention, waiting until I'd finished the whole story before she gave her verdict. Which came in the form of a question: 'What do you think she's trying to achieve?'

'She's trying to bring down Grande Fino.'

Polly shook her head. 'I don't think so. From what you say, it sounds like she's given up on that idea.'

'Go on, then. What do *you* think she's doing?' I'd had enough of trying to read Mélanie's mind for one evening.

'I think she's trying to expose a general culture of doping in cycling.'

'She's a bit late to the party, then,' I said. 'Someone's done that at least once every year since 1998.'

201

'I know that. If you hadn't noticed, I'm a fan.' Polly smiled ruefully. 'Nevertheless, you're a good story. You can be honest – you don't want to go back to the sport, you're not fishing for a ride.'

'Yes, but the story she wants to hear isn't the one that I want to tell.'

'Has she ever believed that, though?' Polly murmured and, without waiting for an answer, went on, 'You want people to hear the story where you're a grown-up, don't you? You want to show that you've taken responsibility for your actions, even when they were the actions of a complete... muppet.'

I didn't ask what word she'd originally been thinking of. 'You're saying that's a bad thing?'

'No, not at all... It's just not what Mélanie is ever going to want to hear. So far as I can judge from an acquaintance of five minutes plus what you've told me about her, of course,' she added.

I thought she was being overly forgiving. I probably deserved a lot more vilification. I wouldn't get it from Mélanie or her friend Russell Simpkins. The irony was, if I could have been confident of being torn to shreds, I'd probably have agreed to do the thing. I sighed. 'If you were me, what would you have done?'

'Asked for the guy's phone number to find out first-hand what he actually wants to do.'

'But then he'd have your phone number,' I pointed out.

'True. There's something to be said for not opening the can of worms in the first place.' She thought about it. 'OK. Assuming you're right about what would happen and why, I think I would ask myself: who have I hurt, and how? And will my doing this heal the hurt?'

I squirmed a little: *hurt* seemed like a very physical term for a non-physical crime. Well, I supposed it had been physical for me, but for everyone else the effects could only have been mental, ideological, emotional, spiritual. 'Who have I hurt? Clean cyclists in the peloton. And cycling fans. Family and friends who trusted me. And –' I was wrong; I'd caused hurt on the material level, hadn't I? 'And you and Vicki.'

She waved an impatient hand. 'File Vicki under "cycling fans". Me, too.'

'No, but the Paul Cunningham thing...'

'Well, file that under "clean cyclists". And it wasn't you who kicked off all that benefits shit, so discount that. Go on.'

'How have I hurt them? I have thrown suspicion on riders who aren't in fact doping. I have... Well, you're a fan. You tell me. What did you feel about it, before you met me?'

She looked faintly embarrassed. 'I can hardly remember. Disappointed, mostly, I suppose. I –' She hesitated. 'It's always *innocent until proven guilty*, but that still implies that a crime has been committed somewhere, by someone, doesn't it? It's like a country house murder mystery, where you don't know whodunnit but you know damn well that one of these people here gathered did. *Innocent until proven guilty*. Not just you. Everyone. And not just cycling: all sports. You have to believe that everyone you're watching is clean, otherwise why would you bother watching? And when it transpires that somebody wasn't – well, you can't be surprised, after all these other cases, but you can be disappointed. And after that it all depends on how they handle it.'

'That's what I'm asking about,' I pointed out. 'How *do* I handle this?'

Polly nodded. 'If I'd never met you...' She trailed off.

'Yes?' I needed to know, badly.

'If I'd never met you,' she began again, but I got the feeling she was following a different train of thought this time, 'I think I'd have been... impressed. No, that's not quite the right word. But you made it very easy for the fan on the sofa. Until I met you, I knew what to think about you. A clear-cut contravention of the rules. No missed tests or doctor's certificates or anything. You took EPO, you got caught, you admitted it. Then you left the sport. I haven't had to watch you this season and *wonder.*'

'A fan's ideal doper, am I?' I commented.

She acknowledged the irony with a quick smile. 'If I'd never met you... I'd probably have forgotten about you by now.'

'And would you want to be reminded?' Because that was what Mélanie had been asking me to do, wasn't it?

She took a long time to answer that. At last she said, 'I think I would think less of you. After all, it's not as if we haven't heard that story before.'

'From considerably more distinguished sportsmen, at that,' I agreed. 'You mean you'd assume I was doing it for the attention?'

'Probably,' she allowed. 'Yes. No. For the *approval.* I'd think you wanted someone to tell you that you hadn't done anything wrong. I mean, knowing you now, I don't think that would be true, but if I were your average cycling fan – or even your average telly viewer – yes, I think I would.'

'Hm.' I thought about that. It stung, but I couldn't deny that it seemed reasonable. 'And is that sufficient reason not to do it? I mean, what if that's just something I have to live with for the sake of the greater good?'

'From what you're saying, the greater good wouldn't be much affected one way or the other,' Polly said impatiently. 'Like I said, it's not really adding much we didn't already know.'

'I sort of feel obliged...' I said. 'Like it's my duty, like it's a trick question.'

'But do you actually want to?' she asked.

'No,' I said, with feeling.

'There you go, then.' As if it was as simple as that.

'But...'

'Do you believe in your heart that it will make any difference?'

I didn't, not really, but I said, 'It might. There's a chance.'

'But do you *believe* it will?' she asked again.

I took a deep breath before I answered. 'No,' I said.

'Then don't do it. Keep your powder dry for the legal case. It might happen. You're allowed to move on, you know.'

'Bloody hell,' I said. 'Can I get that in writing?'

'I...' Whatever she had been going to say, she didn't. She tried again. 'Ben, you didn't think...' That didn't seem to be going anywhere, either. Finally, she settled for, 'Yes.' She grabbed a piece of paper from the printer tray and wrote on it,

BEN GODDARD IS ALLOWED TO MOVE ON.

Then she signed it. *P. D. DEVINE.* And handed it to me.

'Thank you,' I said. I laid it on my knee.

'You're welcome,' she said. 'Although really you should write it for yourself. It's not me who's stopping you, you know.'

'I can't write my own doctor's notes!' I said, scandalised.

'Why not? I do it all the time.'

'You're... much closer to being a doctor than I ever will be.'

'I'm not sure there's much to choose between us, these days. But it's irrelevant. It's got nothing to do with qualifications. It works much better if you write your own. Look.' She reached under her bed and pulled out a red-painted metal cash box. It wasn't locked. She took out a piece of paper, unfolded it, and gave it to me.

POLLY DEVINE IS ALLOWED TO STOP DOING THINGS BEFORE THEY'RE FINISHED IF SHE'S FEELING TIRED.

Later, in a different pen, she'd added, *OR EVEN IF SHE ISN'T TIRED.*

'Cheesy as hell,' she commented, 'but it works. My counsellor taught me this trick.'

'Well, yes, but... you're a proper patient. I'm just a cheat.'

Polly rolled her eyes, picked up the note that said *BEN GODDARD IS ALLOWED TO MOVE ON,* and held it up in front of her face.

'OK, OK, I get it. But what I mean is, it's surely a doctor-patient thing.'

'All a patient is,' Polly said, 'is someone who suffers. It's from Latin; it comes from the same root as the word "passion". So all these people talking about things they're "passionate" about, they mean, things they love so much it hurts. Or just that they're prepared to suffer for them.'

'As a cyclist,' I said, 'that doesn't exactly surprise me.'

Polly laughed. 'Well, cycling is its own special breed of masochism, isn't it? One big cult of suffering.' Then, more seriously, 'It can't be healthy.'

'And yet you still watch it,' I said, stung.

'I do wonder, sometimes,' she said, 'if we're any better than the crowds who watched the gladiators.'

'I never began a race expecting to die,' I pointed out. Though it was always a possibility. If a support motorbike got too close, if you misjudged the edge of the road on a descent, if you hit your head on a wall or a tree... Add in doping, and there were a whole lot more ways to die. When I was at Hirondelle there was a horror story going round the peloton about a blood doping mix-up. In one version the guy had ended up with AIDS. In another it had just been the wrong blood type and he'd died there on the bed. None of us really believed that it had actually happened – the story was always suspiciously short on details – but that wasn't the point. It was plausible, and there was a first time for everything.

'But the thing with sport,' Polly said, 'is that you have to care a huge amount about something that doesn't really matter at all. No wonder you all have a warped sense of reality.' Her smile took the sting out of it. 'And you're all fit, but you're not healthy. People pontificate about the health risks of drug use, but really, is it any healthier to ride so long and so hard that you vomit?'

'Now who's pontificating?' I asked, wondering if I was about to be forgiven.

'And then tennis fucks up your wrists, and running fucks up your knees, and gymnasts get eating disorders, and ice skaters get eating disorders *and* fucked up knees, and fame just ruins your life generally, and we watch it all and pretend none of that is happening...'

'You're a model of optimism today,' I said. 'What's up?'

She laughed. 'Sorry. I got into a very stupid argument on the internet about the theology of the body. No,' she went on, 'we don't expect you to die. But we expect you to win, to get better, to push yourselves further than you can possibly go. We expect you to do it without drugs, we expect you to beat the guys who are using drugs, and we know that's probably impossible. So what we really want is never to find out. We don't want to be made to feel guilty for letting you destroy yourselves for our entertainment.'

I didn't realise until quite a long time afterwards that this was an apology. At the time, I just said, 'I don't really know what to say to that.'

She shook herself. 'Don't tell Vicki about this conversation. Please. I could do without her feeling guilty about her one remaining uncomplicated pleasure.'

'You're not feeling guilty yourself, then?'

'If people want to put themselves through physical and psychological hell against a backdrop of the most beautiful scenery in the world, it would be churlish of me to turn down the opportunity to fill six hours of my empty meaningless life watching it,' she said acidly.

'Wait,' I said, 'you don't actually believe that, do you?'

'What, about my empty meaningless life? No, but I've met plenty of people who do. You, at one point, I believe.'

'I never said that,' I said, devoutly hoping it was true.

She looked at me severely. 'Don't tell me you never thought it.'

'Guilty. Probably. But it was before I got to know you.'

'Oh, well, that's all right, then. I have nothing to fear from people who don't know me,' she said, deadpan. 'Never mind, anyway. We weren't talking about my empty life. We were talking about *your* empty life. Empty of everything except suffering.'

'Are you trying to tell me I'm better off here than I was two years ago? Because I'm not sure you're going the right way about it.' It was true, even so.

She sighed, suddenly deflated. 'I don't know. I'm probably using humour as a coping mechanism and taking it too far. I often do.'

'I'm sorry you feel you have to cope with me,' I said, trying and failing not to sound huffy.

'Force of habit,' she said. 'And it's not *coping with you*, anyway.'

I was already regretting snapping at her. 'This is another example of me making it all about me, right?'

'Yes, and it's an example of me being touchy when I know your intentions are basically good,' she said ruefully. 'I'm sorry. Force of habit. Not that that's an excuse.'

I held my hand out. 'Truce?'

She took it. 'Truce.' Then she loosed her grip and pressed the permission slip into my hand. 'Let's move on.'

We'd wandered so far off track that I'd almost forgotten what I'd come in to talk to her about. I only remembered when I got up to go and she said, 'Don't forget your coffee.'

'Right.' I took a swig. 'So, to recap, you think I'm right not to do this interview.'

'I think it's up to you,' Polly said. 'But I certainly haven't lost any respect for you since you decided against doing it.'

I couldn't help saying, 'That implies you had some respect for me in the first place.'

She looked pained. 'Don't fish. What have we been saying all evening about moving on?'

'Fine, fine!' I moved on out of her room, but I put my head back around the door and said, 'Thank you, by the way.'

She looked up, with a smile that was almost gentle, and said, 'You're welcome. Oh, and one last thing?'

'Yes?'

'Just because option A feels more difficult than option B doesn't necessarily mean that it's the morally right thing to do.'

I shook my head and left her.

I went to bed feeling better, but woke just as troubled as I'd felt yesterday. Polly had given me permission to do what I really wanted to do – which was nothing. This worried me. It couldn't, I thought, be as easy as that. I wanted a second opinion. So when I went to work I set off an hour early, walking, rather than running, to the warehouse, and looked in at Gianna's on the way.

She opened the door wearing a thick grey linen apron. Her fingers were grubby.

'I hope I'm not disturbing your work,' I said.

'Don't worry,' she told me. 'I was just stopping for a break. I wouldn't have opened the door if you had been disturbing me. For a start, I can't hear the bell from the workshop.'

I wondered how many deliveries she missed that way, and then decided it was none of my business. 'Can I talk to you?'

She looked surprised, but said, 'Of course. Come in. Tea? Coffee?' She led the way up the narrow stairs, taking them two at a time.

'Coffee, please,' I said.

'Grab a seat.' She took her apron off and scrubbed her hands under the tap, then bustled around her tiny galley of a kitchen, doing impressive things with a moka pot and a milk frother. The smell was divine. I wondered why I hadn't got myself a moka pot.

'So,' she said as she handed me my mug. 'What's up?'

I said, 'I'm doing a survey of all the cycling fans I know.'

'About?'

'My tragic life story.' *Using humour as a coping mechanism*, Polly had said. I couldn't seem to stop doing it.

'I have no idea what you're talking about,' Gianna said.

I could see her point. I outlined Mélanie's scheme, my indecision, and Polly's opinion.

Gianna was decisive. 'Don't do it, Ben. Nobody wants to see that. The world puked when it was Lance on Oprah... OK, maybe that was *because* it was Lance on Oprah, but even so.'

'You reckon?'

'Polly's right. You've got respect at the moment because you've not tried to pass the buck. We like a man who can own his mistakes.' I concluded that the Pirettis were probably not Pantani conspiracy theorists, after all.

'You see,' I said, 'I kind of know all that. I just feel that, if the world wants to puke on me, then maybe I should let it.'

'Oh, I see. You're not feeling terrible enough, is that it? You need everyone to hate you?'

It was closer to the truth than I liked to think. 'That might be it,' I admitted.

'I'd go and read some cycling forums, then,' she advised. 'It'll save everybody a whole lot of time and money and you'll feel just as bad as if you'd done the public shaming.'

And to think that I used to go to Polly for tough love. Or tough something. 'Polly said I was allowed to get over it,' I said.

'Sounds like a very good idea,' said Gianna. 'I don't think a documentary is going to help, however. You don't confess by telling the priest what he wants to hear.'

'OK, then.' I drained my coffee, feeling a bit stunned.

'On a completely different subject,' Gianna said, 'can you keep a secret?'

'Sure – what is it?'

'Come down to the workshop.'

We went downstairs to the garage. Gianna switched the lights on.

'Vicki's birthday present.' She took a pair of plastic tongs and fished something out of a tub. A faintly acid smell wafted up. She dabbled the thing in another tub and handed it to me; it was an irregular zigzag of dull white metal with a little ring at each end.

I opened my hand out as flat as it would go, afraid both of dropping the thing and of crushing it. A little dribble of water ran off it into the hollow of my palm. 'Is that silver?' I asked.

'Yes – that's what it looks like before you polish it. Do you see what it is?'

I turned the thing over. The shape was very familiar – if I hadn't seen this particular one before, I'd seen thousands like it. But never in silver. 'A mountain profile.'

She beamed. 'Yes. Shepherd's Top.'

'You soppy thing. What's it going to be, a necklace?'

'Yes – I'll join a length of chain to each of these rings. It took me ages to get them in the right place for it to hang right. Do you think she'll like it?'

'She'll love it,' I said, and wondered why I felt so envious.

Chapter 26

Vicki was indeed delighted with the necklace. Gianna had polished the silver until it gleamed, and, as she'd told me she was going to, attached a length of fine chain to each end. Vicki was wearing it when the two of them showed up at the house before we went out to the pub for dinner.

She was more dubious about her brother's present, which Polly had signed for earlier in the day.

'It's a message,' Vicki said darkly, when Gianna was out of the room.

'It looks like a slow cooker to me,' Polly observed.

'No, it's definitely a message. It's a Whitaker family tradition to give slow cookers as wedding presents, you see.'

'How many uncles and aunts do you have?' I pictured some unfortunate Whitaker cousin walled up behind sixteen boxed slow cookers.

Vicki laughed. 'Only my lot do it. Auntie Sandra does kettles and teabags. But my point is, a slow cooker from my little brother is definitely a message of some sort. Either he means that he's resigned himself to the idea that I'm never getting married and he's got sole responsibility for continuing the family line, or that he thinks I should hurry up and propose to Gianna, or that I'm effectively married to you two...'

'What a terrifying thought,' I said.

Polly said, 'It still looks like a slow cooker to me.'

'Whatever. I'm putting it in the kitchen for general use. Though considering how little any of us cook, I'll be impressed if it gets any use at all.'

'Maybe that's the message,' I said.

Vicki put it in the kitchen, where it became part of the scenery and, except for when I knocked it with my elbow when I was filling the kettle, I forgot about it.

So when, a week later, I got in from work to find the house smelling unexpectedly delicious, my first thought was that Vicki had beaten me home and had treated herself to something in a box. In my head, I ran through the contents of the freezer and didn't think much of any of it. But when I closed the front door Polly called, 'Ben? Is that you?'

'Last time I checked.'

She laughed more enthusiastically than that deserved. 'Can you cook some rice? I've made dinner.'

'You've *what*?' I went a few steps into the lounge. I wasn't sure I'd heard properly. Polly never cooked. Wandering somewhere between tact and awkwardness, I'd never asked why that was. I'd concluded, without ever consciously thinking about it, that Polly either didn't trust herself with hot surfaces, or that the whole process was just too much to handle without assistance from one of us. And if she had to get one of us to help, then it would be quicker just to let us do it, I supposed.

She looked over the back of the sofa at me. 'Don't get too excited. I'm quitting while I'm ahead and I'm not going to risk messing around with boiling water when I'm knackered.'

'But still. It smells gorgeous.'

She smiled as if that was the nicest thing anyone had ever said to her. 'Thanks.'

I was very intrigued; but I'd just run home from work. 'Let me have a shower and I'll do the rice. Vicki might be back by then, too.'

She was; she followed me into the kitchen to admire Polly's concoction. It was a rich, red curry, bubbling discreetly in the slow cooker and suffusing the room with a spicy, gingery aroma.

We looked at each other.

'I know I'm hungry,' I said in an undertone as I measured the rice out, 'but damn, that smells good.'

'I'd be impressed,' Vicki said, even lower, 'even if my mouth wasn't watering. As it is...'

'I know,' I said.

'Well, that and the fact that Polly never cooked even before she was ill. I think her mum didn't trust her: she used to show up at the beginning of each term with three months' worth of meals in Tupperware. This is zero to hero stuff.'

'I'm a bit worried now,' I said. 'Still smells good, though.' I poured boiling water over the rice and set the timer. 'You've got twelve minutes to shower.'

She was back in ten and a half. Polly, looking tired now, but still quite pleased with herself, was laying the table. Vicki, hair dripping water onto her shoulders, sat down and looked expectant. I drained the rice and ladled it out onto three plates, following it up with a generous portion of Polly's curry for each of us.

It tasted as good as it smelt. 'Polly,' I said, 'this is gorgeous. How did you do it?'

'I followed the recipe,' she said, as if it was obvious. 'Looked it up online. Found something that looked manageable. Ordered a supermarket delivery yesterday. It came this morning. Followed the instructions. Asked you to cook rice. Done.'

'You're being modest,' I said.

'Not really,' Polly said. 'Most of it's the slow cooker. It's brilliant. I can do all the complicated chopping up and sautéing in the late morning when my brain's working, and the thing minds its own business until half past seven, when I can bribe one of you two to cook some starch.'

'And by "bribe" you mean "threaten to withhold food"?' Vicki guessed.

'You got a problem with that?' Polly glared at her, in a good-natured sort of way.

215

'Oh, I'm not complaining,' Vicki said hurriedly. 'You've probably caught us just in time to spare us a horrible death from scurvy.'

'Well, you're all right,' Polly said, 'because Gianna feeds you. I do worry about Ben, though.'

'Me?' I echoed, surprised. 'I'm fine.'

She looked at me thoughtfully. 'Perhaps you are,' she said.

Carol caught me as I was leaving work at the end of the breakfast shift the next morning. 'Ben – are you free this evening? Martina's on holiday and Callum's phoned to say he's sick. I'll cover breakfast tomorrow, but I could do with an extra pair of hands on the bar.'

'Yes,' I said, 'but I've never worked behind a bar before.'

She brushed that away like a speck of dust. 'You'll pick it up, clever lad like you. Come at half four and I'll show you the system.'

I wasn't very impressed with having to be back at four-thirty, because Polly was clearly on a roll and had got something equally fragrant going in the slow cooker. I made do with a portion of yesterday's curry – which was almost as good reheated – as a late lunch, and left earlier so that I didn't have to run.

It was a quiet evening in the bar. I suspected that most evenings were quiet. As a general rule, guests would go out and drink elsewhere. The prices at the Grand are about what you'd expect of a hotel, and there are plenty of pubs within walking distance. We had the odd few drinkers, though. People who'd just got in and couldn't face going out again. Residents who had done the round of the nearby watering holes and came back for a nightcap. And, as it turned out, a few locals. Well, one. The person I least wanted to see. Paul Cunningham, smug and shiny as ever.

He tried to conceal a double-take when he saw me. 'Mr Goddard. What a surprise.'

'Mr Cunningham. Likewise.' I tried to match his cool tone. I could feel Carol's eyes boring into the back of my neck. 'What can I get you?'

'Dry white wine for the wife,' he said, enjoying the cliché. 'And a vodka tonic for me. Don't spit in it.'

'I wouldn't do a thing like that.' I didn't say that I thought *he* was perfectly capable of it, but maybe it came out in my voice. Anyway, I poured his drink, and I didn't spit in it, and I didn't overcharge him – not any more than the Grand was already, anyway.

'What on earth was that about?' Carol muttered when Cunningham had gone to join his wife. 'How do you know him?'

I glanced around the bar. It was pretty much dead. 'Long story. He tried to stitch up my... a friend of mine. Assumed things about her that weren't true, because he'd heard she knew me.'

Carol looked interested. 'Lass in the wheelchair?'

'No, the other one.' I wondered where she'd seen Polly, and how she'd connected her with me.

'Don't think I've seen that one,' Carol said. She sounded worried, somehow. 'Oh, look, he's called Andy over.'

'Probably telling him what an untrustworthy crook I am,' I said bitterly.

Carol looked very hard at me. 'That's not true, and you know it. Andy's very pleased with you. What's going on here?'

I took a deep breath. I wasn't entirely sure what I meant to say, but what came out was, 'I used to be a cyclist.' And I told her the whole story. Not in detail. I only touched lightly on my life in the peloton. I skimmed over Henri and Dr Wolfsen and his '*régime*'. But Carol was a good listener: throwing in an interested 'Oh, yes?' or a sympathetic 'Go on', but otherwise leaving the space for me. And, despite myself, I filled it.

I told her about the end. I told her about how I'd tried to disappear, cutting myself off from all my friends and family, changing my phone number, deleting my social media accounts. How I'd dropped everything and started a new life in a town where I knew nobody.

In a town where it turned out that somebody knew me.

I told her how two girls had recognised me and, knowing who and what I was, had become the best friends I could ever have hoped to meet.

How one of them had been deprived of her only means of support. How I'd thought that was my fault. How frightened she'd been.

How the other had been presumed guilty of the crime that I'd been trying to escape. How that *was* my fault.

'What happened, then?' Carol asked.

I told her about my meeting with Paul Cunningham. She chuckled softly, and glanced around the bar to see if he was still around. He was, slumped in one of the big armchairs, glaring at his vodka tonic and not listening to his wife. Andy was nowhere to be seen. I wondered whether Cunningham had told him about my blackmail attempt, and a little chill ran up the back of my spine.

I told Carol how Polly had told me off about it, and she said she sympathised. 'But what about Polly?' she asked. 'What happened to her benefits? How are you managing?'

'She appealed,' I said, 'and she got all the letters from the hospital saying, yes, she can do more with a wheelchair than she can without one, but she still can't do much, and they reinstated everything.'

'Oh, *good*,' Carol said.

'Yes,' I said, 'and I think she feels she overreacted; but she still gets a bit jumpy every time we get post.'

'Hm,' Carol said. 'I'll have a word with my brother.'

'Your brother?' I was mystified.

'Meddling little bastard.'

I was still confused. I nodded in the direction of Paul Cunningham. '*He's* not your brother?'

She made a face. 'No, but –' At that moment a gaggle of drunken conference delegates burst out of the lift and staggered towards us. 'Incoming,' Carol said.

When we'd sorted them out with more lager than seemed sensible, given the fact that I knew they had a nine o'clock start in the morning, Carol said, 'You told Andy, when he gave you the job?'

'Yes, of course.'

'You'll be fine, then. I can see why you kept it quiet with everyone else, but you've more than proved your worth, Ben. Andy's fair. Don't worry.' She patted my shoulder reassuringly.

God knows what time she must have got her brother out of bed. Whether it was after the bar closed or on her way in for the breakfast shift I don't know. But she came in and said, with satisfaction, 'I gave him hell for you, Ben.'

'That's great,' I said, 'but why?'

The story came out in segments, in between pots of tea and coffee, pans of beans, and trays of fried eggs. 'Well, I see a lot of my brother, and every now and again we go out for a drink or a meal. And we were at the Three Bottles one evening and we saw you. And you were with this girl in a wheelchair.'

'Polly,' I said. 'Was there anyone else there?'

'No, just the two of you. And I said, oh look, that's our Ben, from the Grand; didn't realise he had a girlfriend; well, isn't that sweet of him, sticking with her after the accident.'

'Twenty-two!' Eddie called, which was a relief. It gave me time to compose my reply while I took out a plate of kippers.

'She's not my girlfriend,' I said when I returned to the kitchen. 'And there wasn't an accident.'

'Well, no, I know that *now*,' Carol said as she filled a coffee pot from the filter machine, 'but when we saw her at the pub with you it seemed the obvious conclusion. You went to the bar. You had to wait a while –

there were a couple of women in front of you, with a big order, talking about some book, I think –'

'Oh, it was *that* time! I remember now – but I didn't see you.'

'Twenty-four!'

'Did you not?' Carol said. 'Excuse me a moment.'

While she dealt with order twenty-four, I ducked out into the restaurant to see what was going on and to regain my composure. I had to remove some smouldering toast from the machine. Then I had to top up the grapefruit. When I got back into the kitchen Carol was clearing soggy cornflakes into the slop bucket.

'And while you were at the bar,' she said, picking up where she had left off, 'your friend got up out of her wheelchair and walked to the toilets.'

'That threw me the first time, too,' I said. 'But it's not that she –'

'It's not that she uses it because she can't walk. I know that now, too. But we didn't then. Anyway, Joe jumped to conclusions. Long story short, he wrote to the benefits people.'

'Oh,' I said, to buy myself time. It was all making sense, quicker than I could get my head around it. 'Oh.'

Carol nodded. 'Like I said: I gave him hell for you.'

There were several obvious questions. I asked the first of them. 'But how on earth did he know who she was? You know my name, fair enough, but you couldn't possibly have known Polly's.'

'Ben, love,' Carol said, 'he's your postman.'

I ran home. I mean, I always ran home, but this time I sprinted. I got a stitch, stopped for an agonising minute until it passed off, and then ran the rest of the way at an only slightly more sedate pace. I couldn't wait to tell Polly.

It was only when I burst through the front door, kicking a pile of junk mail out of the way, that it occurred to me that she might not actually want to know.

I compromised. I knocked on her bedroom door, and when she opened it, with an irritated, '*What?*', I took a deep breath before replying.

'Polly,' I said, 'I have, honestly completely accidentally, discovered who it was that tried to dob you in and get your welfare stopped. Do you want to know who it was?'

'Oh,' she said, very quietly. She thought about it, head on one side. 'Do I know them?' she asked.

'Yes. Sort of.'

'They're someone I have to talk to?'

'Occasionally.'

She nodded, slowly. 'Then I don't want to know. Thank you for asking.'

I was surprised, but I tried not to show it. 'No problem,' I said. 'If it's useful to know, they've had a proper bollocking from... someone I wouldn't care to get a bollocking from.'

Polly laughed – a sudden, carefree, gleeful exclamation of a laugh. I hadn't realised until then how much the suspicion must have been getting to her. 'Stop! Don't tell me any more! I mean it, I really, truly, honestly don't want to know.'

'OK, then,' I said.

'Thank you,' she said again, and she smiled. And I couldn't help smiling back.

Chapter 27

I know that Mum was assuming I'd go home for Christmas. The truth was, I just couldn't face it. I couldn't face seeing all my school friends and hearing about their perfect lives. I couldn't face being polite to Dad after what he'd said to Polly.

And I'd much rather have spent the time with Polly and Vicki. Well, that wasn't going to happen. They'd made the house vaguely festive with a few strings of tinsel and an artificial tree that Polly had liberated from a skip in their first year at university, but they weren't going to be around for Christmas itself. Vicki was going to take Gianna home to Sheffield the weekend before – well, technically, Gianna was going to take Vicki, because they were going in the van – and Polly's brother was going to drive up to collect her on Christmas Eve.

I still preferred the thought of an empty house to the crushing weight of my parents' expectations. Come to think of it, I'd already turned down better offers. Though I suspected that if I called Mélanie and told her I'd changed my mind she'd still be happy to set me up with Russell Simpkins.

I preferred the thought of an empty house to that, too. I'd work Christmas morning and get double time. After that, I figured I'd get myself a pizza, a crate of beer, and some DVDs. What more could a man want?

Having said all that, it looked as if I was in for a miserable Christmas. It rained pretty much continuously from the eighteenth of December onwards. It went on raining, and when it stopped it was only to take a break for an hour or so, after which it went on raining some more.

It was still raining when Gianna came to pick Vicki up on the twenty-first.

'We're in for a real battering,' Polly said. 'You be careful on the roads. Don't take chances.'

'I'm always careful,' Gianna said. 'At least,' she amended, 'I am on the roads.'

'The coast road will flood,' Vicki said. 'It always does.'

Gianna seemed to find this partly endearing and partly infuriating. 'I've lived here for five years, my love. And if you hadn't noticed, we're headed east.'

'I know. Sorry.' She turned her attention to me and Polly. 'You two look after yourselves, OK? Keep an eye out for the flood warnings. Ben, Skype me if you get lonely. Polly, for goodness' sake make sure your brother drives safely.'

'Really, Vic,' Polly said. 'Did either of us die when you two went to Italy? Well, then.'

Vicki didn't seem to have an answer to that. She turned her attention to hefting several bags of presents out of the house and into the van.

'There's still time to take a bike if you want to,' Gianna said. 'Time and space.'

Vicki glanced back in the general direction of the shed. 'No. I've done it before – on the train, for my sins – and it's pointless, because I never get round to taking it out. OK. I'm done. Happy Christmas, Polly and Ben, and I'll see you on Boxing Day.'

'Happy Christmas,' we said. 'Happy Christmas, Gianna.'

We shut the front door and watched through the front window as they drove off into the rain, probably still bickering.

'It's coming down like nobody's business,' Polly said, grudgingly impressed.

Vicki's mention of the coast road had got me thinking. 'What if we get flooded?'

'We shouldn't,' Polly said. But she looked worried.

On the twenty-second, things looked worse. It was raining when I set out for work, and it was raining when I got back in the afternoon. Great grey clouds kept sweeping in from the sea, and the roads were slick with water. I'd seen hardly anybody in town; only the hardiest or the most desperate of Christmas shoppers had ventured out into the awful weather. At work, people had been talking about nothing else. Agnieszka said that she'd heard that houses in the lowest-lying areas had been issued with sandbags. Things were so slow at the warehouse that Gary sent us all home.

'Is this where we start worrying?' I asked Polly. She was sitting by the front window, watching the rain. For all I knew, she'd been there all day.

She didn't answer directly, just said, 'I got a taxi into town this morning and did a bit of a shop. Stocked up on tea. Cereal. A couple of tins.'

'So you *are* worrying.'

She wrinkled her nose. 'You never know,' she said. 'What's it like now?'

'I don't like the look of the storm drain at the bottom of the close,' I said. 'If that goes, we'll be swimming.'

'Number one and number twenty-five will be swimming,' Polly corrected me.

'Yeah, but if we want to leave the close... Anyway,' I said, 'I'm going to have a shower.'

While I was replacing cold wet rainwater with warm wet shower water, I did a bit of thinking. Polly was right: we were on slightly higher ground than the bottom of the close. But not much. Not more than a metre. It wasn't just the storm drain; there was a little stream that ran behind the houses on the north side of the close to join the river a few hundred yards downstream. And then there was the nature reserve, which was swampy at the best of times. I wasn't sure what that would do if all that flooded. I hoped we weren't going to find out.

When I went downstairs to the living room again, Polly wasn't there. I found her in her bedroom.

'I've been looking up the history,' she said. 'This house has never flooded.'

'*This* house?' I thought she was being very carefully specific.

She nodded and pointed to her laptop screen. It showed an aerial photograph of the town, much of it under water. 'This was the year before last. Look: that's us.'

'It was close, then,' I said.

'This time it might be worse.'

'Do you think we should retreat upstairs?'

She frowned. 'It feels like overreacting. At the same time – well, we won't have much time if it does happen, will we?'

I nodded. 'I have to say that I'd rather get stuff out of danger now, than have to cart it all upstairs in the middle of the night. And I'd worry about you.'

'I think I'd probably wake up before I drowned in my bed,' she said wryly. 'But you have a point.'

'I'm sure Vicki wouldn't mind you sleeping in her room for tonight. OK. Tell me what to do.'

'I think I'd start,' she said, 'by taking the TV up to your room.'

I did most of the lifting and carrying – piles of books, armfuls of clothes, climbing up and down the stairs until all Polly's valuables were safely stacked on the landing. There were a couple of things, though, that needed both of us to lift, more because they were awkward than because they were heavy, and the effort showed on Polly. She ended up curled in a ball on Vicki's bed, and pretended not to be crying when I looked to see where she'd gone.

Thinking I'd better leave her to it, I went out in the rain to check the shed. I rescued Vicki's bikes and found a stack of breeze-blocks that must have been left over from the kitchen extension. These I brought in one by one and used to raise the sofa and armchair a couple of inches off the floor. Assuming that we were only moderately unlucky, as opposed to extremely unlucky, that would be enough to keep them from damage. I balanced the coffee table on the sofa, and the Christmas tree on the coffee table.

I went into the kitchen to see if it was worth doing the same with anything in there. Polly seemed to be feeling better: she was sitting cross-legged on the floor taking everything out of the cupboards. 'I think we just put it all on the worktops,' she said. 'If the water gets higher than that then we'll have to abandon ship, and I dare say paddling won't kill us in the meantime.'

I nodded. 'Maybe take some of it upstairs, to tide us over if we just get a little flood.'

'Good idea. Can we do anything about the fridge?'

'I can put it on breeze-blocks,' I said. 'We can't get it upstairs.'

'OK. Let's do that. The rest of it will just have to take its chances.'

I shoved the can opener into my back pocket, gathered up some tins of peaches in my arms, and took them upstairs.

When I got back down again, I found Polly sitting with her back hard against the fridge-freezer, looking at nothing in particular. 'Shit,' she was saying. 'Shit, shit, shit, shit, shit.'

Something seemed to have gone very wrong very quickly.

'What's up?' I asked.

'I've just remembered what I didn't do in town today.' She held out a flimsy paper form. 'I didn't pick up my prescription.'

I looked at it. I couldn't make much sense of it, beyond the fact that it would win you a game of Scrabble. 'How bad is it?'

'I took my last one the day before yesterday.'

That didn't seem to be the whole truth. 'Tell me the worst-case scenario.'

She drew a deep breath. 'Worst-case scenario is: the water rises, we're cut off, I can't get more meds, the withdrawal symptoms are as bad as they were last time I tried to come off it, *plus* the depression that it treats is going untreated, and I'm suicidal inside a week. Sorry,' she said. 'You did ask for the worst-case scenario.'

'Fuck,' I said. 'That would be a very bad case.' I looked hard at her. 'On a scale of one to ten, how likely do you think that is to happen?'

She wouldn't answer.

'Ten, then. Or maybe a nine?'

'If it happens, it'll be awful,' she admitted. 'The question is, how likely is it to actually happen? What do you think the water's doing?'

I glanced out of the window. 'Well, the rain isn't stopping. Polly. What do you think is actually going to happen?'

She bit her lip. 'The most likely scenario – eighty per cent, maybe – is that I'm objectively OK, but knocked off-balance. Possibly for a good two months.'

That was a less terrifying prospect, but it still didn't sound great. I grabbed my raincoat from the back of the door. 'I'm going down the end of the road,' I said. 'See what it looks like.'

It didn't look good. The rain had not slackened, and the gutters were two swift muddy rivers. I jogged back. We needed to be fast now.

'When the storm drain goes,' I reported, 'the whole close will be cut off. I don't know what's going on elsewhere in town. I can't imagine it's going to be any better.'

'*When* it goes?' She eyed me suspiciously.

'I'm no engineer,' I said. 'I reckon it's got about half an hour, but that's a guess.' This was no time for false optimism.

'Fuck,' she said, 'I was going to call a cab to take me out to big Tesco, but they won't come if they think they're going to get stuck.'

'I could go,' I said. 'I could walk it.'

Hope flashed across her face, but it was swiftly replaced by scepticism. 'Yes, but you won't get there and back in half an hour. And like you said, who knows what it's like elsewhere?'

'Run it, then,' I said.

'Oh, Ben, don't be an idiot. It's not worth it.' But her face said otherwise. She was desperately frightened.

There was another option. It was staring me in the face – which was my fault, because I'd brought it into the house.

I took a deep breath. 'What would Vicki think about my using one of her bikes?'

Polly jumped straight to the practicalities. 'You couldn't take the road bike; it's got cleated pedals and there's no way her cycling shoes will fit you.'

I wished she would stop trying to dissuade me. I was worried that she'd succeed. 'What about the other one? I have honestly no idea how she'd feel about me borrowing her bike. Would it be like borrowing a pen or borrowing her toothbrush?'

I hadn't been on a bike since the testers had come knocking, in a different life. I hadn't wanted to. I didn't really want to now. But this was serious.

'She loves that bike,' Polly said helplessly. 'It was the first one she bought with her own money.'

'But if I said, Vicki, you aren't here, Polly needs – yes, *needs* – her prescription, and there's no other safe way to get it...?' As I spoke the words, I knew what the answer would be.

So did Polly. 'She'd say, take it.'

'Right. Tell me what I need to bring.'

Polly sorted out her prescription and scribbled a covering letter to authorise me to pick it up. My heart was pattering. I tried to calm myself as I wheeled the Dutch bike through the house to the front door. What was I so scared of? Being recognised, I suppose – though surely

Ben Goddard in jeans and sweater, waterproof zipped up to the neck, riding a woman's purple-painted town bike through a Lancashire downpour, wouldn't look much like Ben Goddard the doper, wearing Lycra and mounted on carbon fibre. Surely there were much more important things to worry about.

I was still feeling tight-chested and slightly sick, for all that.

Polly held the front door open for me. 'Ben?'

'Yes?'

'Be careful.'

I had half-thought she would try to stop me, even now. I knew she hadn't thought much of my previous attempt to be a hero. But she'd tried to be one herself, just now. I was almost certain that we were going to be flooded. Based on what she'd told me, I thought it was odds-on that we'd be cut off for long enough for a lack of medication to cause serious problems. I couldn't bear the thought of it.

Maybe they'd be able to take her off in an air ambulance. But perhaps that was only if there was immediate danger to life and limb. Under normal circumstances we'd have been best stocking up (thank God she'd already bought the groceries!) and sitting tight.

They say you never forget how to ride a bike. Certainly it would have been embarrassing if I had forgotten. All the same, there was a moment when I found that I didn't believe that the thing would stay upright if I took both feet off the ground, and I had to take a couple of deep breaths.

Once I was going, it was easy. This bike was nothing like the things I'd been riding a year ago – compare an elephant to a racehorse, and you're beginning to get a sense of the difference – but it did the job, and Vicki had kept it in beautiful condition. (I realised, slightly shamefacedly, that Vicki probably knew far more about cycle maintenance than I did. I'd never done much of it myself, and I hoped I wasn't going to have to today. A mechanical was the last thing I needed.) It trundled happily down towards the end of the close. I turned onto River Way and almost immediately struck left up the narrow, boggy, path that ran around the edge of the nature reserve. Hauling a steel-framed bike along that in the pouring rain wasn't much fun at all. I knew that I must be heavier than I used to be, too. At the very least, my muscles would have rearranged themselves. I'd have more in the arms, less in the thighs. This was a pointless train of thought, but a harmless one. It occurred to me that the pharmacy might be closed. Well, I thought, I'd cross that bridge when I came to it. I would be able to get a cab from Tesco, if nothing else.

It was a gloomy return to two wheels, as these things went, but I was too worried to think much about that. What if I couldn't make it back home before the close flooded? I didn't want to think about leaving Polly alone without her medication. I gritted my teeth and pedalled harder.

I couldn't help laughing at myself. *Who's this woman*, I thought, *that she's got you back on a bike when you swore you'd never ride again, that's sent you out for drugs with a reputation like yours?*

I think you'll find, I told myself, *that this is a valid case for a Therapeutic Use Exemption.*

I thought, *I'd do it for anybody.*

Which was true – or, at least, I liked to think it was – but it wasn't entirely relevant. Because I was doing it for Polly.

It was at that moment that I realised.

Put me back on the bike, said Tom Simpson. Well, actually he probably didn't, but it's a good story. Win at any cost – dignity and life not excluded.

Well, I didn't mind sacrificing my dignity if it could save Polly's life. And, the more I thought about her quiet, troubled face, the less I thought that was an over-dramatic way of putting it.

The way I was feeling at the moment, if Polly had asked me to go to the moon and get a rock for her I'd have done it. Except she'd never have asked me, would she? She'd either figure out a way to get to the moon herself, or convinced herself that she didn't really need a moon rock.

That was why I'd have done it. Because that was *Polly*.

I asked myself how I could have been such a self-centred idiot as to fail to see what a remarkable person she was. How lucky I'd been, to have her be the one to find me when I'd crashed and burned. Someone who wouldn't try to downplay the severity of what I'd done, but who was willing to move past her preconceptions and take a chance on me.

Not like that.

I wished she would, though.

I was going to tell her. The moment I got back, with –

I couldn't possibly tell her.

What was I even going to tell her?

Not that any of it would matter if I didn't get back –

I clicked up into the highest gear. The bike didn't like it.

'Polly,' I said. Out loud. There was nobody to hear me, after all.

I threaded my way through a housing estate, crossed over another little brook and the deserted main road, and hurtled across the Tesco car park. By the clock, it had taken me twenty minutes to get there. It had felt like three, driven as I was by that potent adrenal mix of fear and – whatever else was going on.

It was all driven out of my mind by a very unpleasant realisation.

I didn't have a lock for the bike.

Vicki used a D-lock and a cable lock with a combination. I didn't have a key to the one and I didn't know the combination of the other. And they were both in the shed back at home.

Well, I thought, it was just going to have to take its chances in the supermarket bike park. The racks were empty, apart from a couple of sad abandoned carcases missing wheels and saddles. Vicki's proud purple machine stood out like the proverbial sore thumb.

That said, the car park was pretty empty, too. Even the panic buyers had better places to be. Safe at home, probably.

I left the bike to its fate and sloshed into the supermarket. The shelves were packed with turkeys and empty of bread. Chilly air from the refrigerated cabinets swirled around me and made me shiver. I noticed it more now that I was out of the rain. But that wasn't the only reason I quickened my stride.

My fingers trembled as I handed over the prescription. That wasn't just the cold, either. There were two possibilities that worried me. Either it would turn out that Polly had forgotten to give me some vital certificate or piece of ID, or (less realistically, I had to admit) the pharmacist would recognise me for who I was and refuse to issue me with the drugs.

Neither of these things happened. The pharmacist just took the script, looked me up and down, smiled reassuringly, and told me to sit down and wait.

'Will it take long?' I asked.

'I'll be as quick as I can.'

I didn't know if that meant a minute or an hour. I thought about going outside to check on the bike, but I was terrified that if Polly's name was called and I wasn't there then they wouldn't give it to me when I came back. The pharmacist had disappeared into some back room, so I couldn't tell her what I wanted to do. So I didn't do it.

I couldn't have been waiting much more than ten minutes, really. It was agonising. I was freezing. Rainwater gathered at the hem of my jeans and dripped into my trainers. And I had nothing to do now except worry. I pictured the water rising up out of the ditches and rivers, seeping out of the edges of the storm drain, pouring along the roads. I pictured the house cut off, and Polly, alone, trapped – oh, God – for days, maybe, if I didn't make it back through the floods.

I was just going to have to.

'Polly Devine.'

I sprang to my feet.

The pharmacist looked at me narrowly, and my heart pounded. But she only asked me to confirm the address, and then handed over a paper bag, sealed with a printed label. I checked it carefully – Polly's name and date of birth were correct, and the name of the drug looked about right – and stowed it in the inside pocket of my rain jacket. I assumed that the packaging would be waterproof, but I didn't want to take unnecessary risks.

I thanked the pharmacist profusely and hurried back out.

The bike was gone. I found that I wasn't even surprised. Angry, yes; grudgingly admiring of the kind of little scrote who'd come out to nick stuff in weather like this; worried sick; but not surprised. I'd sort of known it all along.

Vicki would understand. Wouldn't she?

At that moment, I didn't care. There was only one thing I could do now. I ran.

To stop myself thinking about Polly, I tried to work out how long it was going to take me. The outward journey had taken me twenty minutes on a bike; but the bike was heavy and I was out of condition. It couldn't be as far as all that, therefore. I was in better running trim than I was cycling, but I was hardly wearing appropriate clothing. I couldn't reduce it to minutes and kilometres: there were too many variables. And the floods didn't deal in minutes or kilometres, either.

I had time, or I didn't. That was all there was to it.

I'd found a rhythm, of sorts. My soles slapped on the wet tarmac, my jacket rustled, my jeans rubbed agonisingly with each stride.

I had time. I had to have time. The alternative didn't bear thinking about.

The rain poured down. The wind whipped my hood back off my face. I let it stay there, the water running down my neck.

How long before Polly started worrying where I'd got to? Twenty minutes more than my original estimate? More?

She wouldn't do anything stupid. Would she?

I thought about ringing her, but I couldn't see what the point would be. She'd only worry. Besides, if I stopped, I wasn't sure I'd be able to get going again.

The little brook I'd crossed on the way up had risen a good six inches. Water swirled around clumps of grass, swept up towards the path. The main road was still empty, except for a solitary estate car crawling through an expanse of water at the junction.

I quickened my stride.

I knew better than to try to go back through the nature reserve: it had slowed me up on the way out, and it would be worse now. Instead, I went the long way, all the way through the next estate to ours, and tried not to notice that in some places the water was already ankle-deep.

Michael wouldn't do this for her, I thought, and found it less satisfying than I'd expected. Michael wouldn't do this for anybody, out of principle. And 'less of a dick than Michael' was a low bar.

Even if she never saw me as anything more than a slightly corrupt housemate, I was glad she was shot of Michael.

But I had to *do* this, I had to complete it, or my willingness wouldn't mean anything. This wasn't a game.

Chapter 28

The drain had gone. Long ago – except I hadn't been gone that long. I couldn't believe how quickly the water had risen. The road had become a river: it was a fast-flowing, foul-smelling torrent, cutting off the whole of the close. And I was on the wrong side of it. I pitied numbers 1 and 25, whose carpets must have already been a good couple of inches underwater.

Well, there was only one way. Through it. I took a deep breath, and immediately wished I hadn't. Praying not to fall over, I stepped into the disgusting stream.

It was all right at first, but it got deep, and the swift current tugged at my ankles. It couldn't have been more than seven feet wide, but it was the longest seven feet of my life. Finally free of the water, I pelted up the close as if I had wings on my feet, not stinking, sopping trainers.

Polly was waiting at the door for me; she had it open the moment I set foot on the garden path. There was naked relief on her face, and I was stupidly happy to see it, even though I knew that all it meant was that she'd been worried about me, as a friend, as a human being, nothing more.

Kicking my shoes off – there was no way they were coming into the house with me – I unzipped the pocket of my waterproof and handed her the paper bag with her prescription in it. Then I stepped over the threshold.

She made as if to hug me, but thought better of it. I couldn't blame her, the way I smelt. 'Thank you, Ben,' she said, softly. 'Thank you so much.'

And thank God, this time the thing in my head that should have said *no, don't do this, very bad idea* to all my stupid decisions in the past was switched on, or I was tuned into it, or something – So I just said, 'Any time,' and smiled.

It must have been awkward for her. But at least there was an obvious subject that she could move on to. 'The bike?' she asked.

'Nicked,' I confessed. 'I forgot about a lock.'

'Oh.' Polly looked dismayed. I didn't know what to say. 'She'll understand. I think she will, anyway. I'll tell her, if you like.'

I wasn't sure. I didn't answer. We just stood there looking at each other.

'You should change out of those jeans,' she said. 'You'll catch your death.'

'I know. And they stink.'

'I didn't like to say that.' She looked at me with a half-smile. 'Seriously, I am incredibly grateful.'

I couldn't quite cope with *serious*. 'I wouldn't mind a cup of tea, if the power's still on.'

She raised her eyebrows. 'It's your lucky day.'

Oh, Polly, I thought as she turned from me to go into the kitchen. If only you knew.

No: I couldn't tell her tonight. And there was no way of telling what would happen tomorrow. I hoped that no further heroics would be called for, but so long as there was any possibility of Polly being physically dependent on me I couldn't put her in a position where she might think it was unwise to say no. I supposed I should wait until Vicki got back. Or until the floods went down. Or both.

I dashed upstairs to the bathroom, trying to drip on the carpet as little as possible, stripped, and showered. We still had clean, hot water, and I was very grateful for it.

Eventually I got out. Wrapped in a towel, I went to my room and changed into clean clothes, then returned to the bathroom, where my jeans were festering in a corner. I took them out into the garden and chucked them over the washing line to take their chances in the rain and wind, and went back inside.

'It feels like far less than you deserve,' Polly said as she handed me the tea.

'I don't know how I'm going to tell Vicki about her bike,' I said. It felt like a safer subject than *what I deserved*.

'That's a problem for another day,' Polly said. 'What shall we have for dinner?'

'Whatever's in the fridge that needs eating, I guess.'

I went and had a look. There was the end of a packet of bacon, some minced beef, half a red pepper. Everything else looked as if it would keep. What if Polly was stuck here over Christmas? We could hardly manage turkey with all the trimmings. But that was a question for another day – the day after tomorrow, specifically.

I opened a tin of tomatoes and made a feeble attempt at spaghetti bolognese, rather glad that Gianna wasn't there to see it. We didn't have any onions, but a good squeeze of garlic purée made up for that. I thought about opening a bottle of wine, but concluded that it wouldn't be a good idea to be anything other than sober if there was a chance of our having to leave the house in a hurry, and it wasn't fair on Polly anyway. Not to mention the fact that I didn't want to let anything slip. I had resolved to keep my mouth shut, and it was going to be difficult enough as it was. I didn't want alcohol dismantling my defences.

'Penny for them,' Polly said.

'Mm?' I looked up. She was smiling. 'Oh, just wondering how long we'll be cut off.'

Well, it was half true.

It was a funny sort of meal: frugal, yet festive, the appliances and tins piled high on the worktops around us, both of us forced to remember how good it was to be alive and eating, and neither of us wanting to talk about that. Polly, grateful to me and resenting having to be; me, scarcely daring to look at her. I pushed my food around my plate and satisfied myself with glimpses of her warm, relieved face. We were both waiting for something, even if it was just for the ability to leave the house.

She said, suddenly, 'Was it OK? Being on a bike?'

I winced, but it was only because the bike was gone. 'Better than I expected. I didn't think about it much, after the first minute or so.'

She nodded. 'Has it changed your mind about going back to the sport?'

I hadn't been expecting that question, but the answer came easily. 'No. I don't care enough about it any more.' I risked some mild levity. 'A guy gets tired of putting himself through hell, you know? And –' I stopped myself. I couldn't go any further with that sentence. I'd wanted to say, *I wouldn't leave you*, but she'd have found that weird.

'And?'

Just in time, I found a diversion. 'And here I am. Not in London, doing Mélanie's interview. I'd have to do something like that, if I was going to go back.'

'I'm very glad you're here,' she said fervently.

'So am I.' I stared very hard at my plate in case she could read my eyes. 'But it's not like –' I ground to a halt again, worried this time that I was about to tread on a touchy subject.

'Not like...?'

'Well.' I couldn't think of a way out of this one. 'Not like you, and doctoring. I'm not sure that cycling was ever *my* dream, really.'

'You must have been fairly motivated to get as far as you did,' she observed.

I hadn't ever thought of it like that; I'd always been comparing myself to the guys who did better than me, not to where I'd come from. 'Well, you do, don't you? You just keep going and going because nobody ever tells you it's OK, you're allowed to stop.'

She nodded, recognising the picture I described. 'You work till you drop,' she said. 'Except you never actually believe you're going to drop, you think you'll just be able to keep on and on pushing through, and you never stop to think what happens after you have dropped. I suppose I assumed that it was all or nothing. Work or die. And now I can't work and I'm not dead and I don't know what to do with myself.'

That reminded me of something else. 'A while ago,' I said, 'when they first got together, you said you wondered how long it would take Gianna to realise she was one of Vicki's projects.'

Polly smiled. 'It hasn't happened, has it? I think Vicki's realised that Gianna actually has her life together, far more than she does herself.'

'Gianna lives in two rooms over a garage.'

'Your point being?'

'I didn't have a *point*,' I said hurriedly. 'Gianna's got her life more together than I have, if it comes to that.'

'Yes,' Polly mused, not really in answer to me, 'I think it's the other way round. Gianna's sorting Vicki out.'

'Does she *know*?'

'Which?'

I thought about that. 'Either of them, I suppose.'

Polly laughed. 'Who knows? I'm certainly not going to point it out to them if they don't. But we weren't talking about Vicki just now. We were talking about you.'

Actually, we'd been talking about Polly herself, but it was close enough. 'You put everything you have into it,' I said, 'and it still isn't enough. Because it's never enough. Because even when you've achieved the thing you set out to achieve your mind tells you that's not enough, you've got to do more. You do X, your brain tells you that it doesn't mean anything, that really you have to do Y. And sooner or later something cracks. Morally, in my case. Physically, in yours.'

'I never even got to X,' Polly said, but she didn't look offended, which I'd been a bit worried about when I said that. 'But hey, we're still here.'

I raised my glass to her, never mind the fact that all it had in it was water. 'And long may it last.'

Chapter 29

I looked out of the window. The water had risen overnight, and the gardens at the bottom end of the close were squares of sinister water. A car parked ten feet from the junction was almost submerged. I didn't want to guess at the depth of the water, but it was clear that I wasn't getting to work today. Further away, the odd play of light on the buildings suggested that other streets had also suffered. But it had stopped raining, and the morning light was turning even the floods golden.

And we were safe. We were dry. I went downstairs just to make sure that the water hadn't come in and then gone away again during the night; but everything was as I'd left it, the furniture looking faintly silly on its breeze-block stilts. I tried the light switch. The electricity was still on. I made myself a coffee and, not really knowing what else to do, went back to my room. I turned on my little electric fan heater, and got back under the covers.

I texted Gary and Agnieszka to let them know that the chances of my making it into work were minimal. Gary texted back to say that the warehouse was completely cut off, so not to worry. Agnieszka texted back to say that they had some unexpected guests who had been flooded out of their own homes, but she was sure they'd manage and she was glad I was safe.

After that I had nothing to do but smile at the ceiling and think about Polly, and wonder how on earth I was going to tell her.

And in the end it was Polly who told me.

She knocked at my door about an hour after I'd woken up. It startled me, which felt unlikely; she was so much in my thoughts that I'd thought I couldn't help but hear the tiniest move she made. And yet here she was.

'Hi!' she said. She looked faintly, adorably, awkward in her orange pyjamas, shifting from foot to foot in my doorway.

I leapt out of bed, unable to stop myself smiling. 'Hello. Sleep OK?'

'Not badly,' she said, and yawned. 'Sorry.'

I laughed. 'Not used to Vicki's bed?'

'Mm? Oh, no, it was fine. I was just... thinking.'

'Thinking?'

She glanced away. 'If the water keeps rising...'

'I doubt it will,' I said, thinking she was worried about her prescription running out. 'It's stopped raining.'

She shook her head urgently. 'But if it did...' she said. 'If we're cut off...'

'I don't think you're getting home for Christmas, I'm afraid,' I said.

'No – I've already texted my brother to say we're flooded in, But I mean, if Vicki can't get back...'

I couldn't work out what was worrying her so much. 'Her job? She's got leave until the twenty-eighth. And I don't think anyone's going to sack her for being flooded out.'

'You never know,' she said, in quite a different tone. Then, lapsing back into that strange, suppressed emotion, 'But if it's just you and me here, for three days, a week, if nobody else...' At last she looked me straight in the eye, and a wild hope leapt in my chest.

She couldn't mean that. Could she?

Losing my nerve, I said, 'At the worst, we've got enough rice to keep us going for weeks.'

'*Rice*?' She looked distinctly unimpressed.

'I know it's not exactly thrilling, but it'll keep it alive.'

'Ben,' she said. 'I don't want to talk about rice.' She folded her arms across her chest and took a tiny step backwards.

'Go on, then. What do you want to talk about?'

She smiled and shook her head. 'Never mind.'

She'd gone as far as she was going to. I was going to have to do the rest of it. 'If, for the next three days... I was the last man on earth...?' I ventured, praying I hadn't misread her.

The corners of her mouth turned up. 'If I were the last woman...?'

'If you were the last woman on earth?' I held out my arms and she came in to me. 'More like the first woman on earth – no, that's not what I mean. If *all* the women on earth were floating outside the window in inflatable dinghies and clamouring for me to let them in, I wouldn't give a toss.'

'We'd have one hell of a humanitarian crisis on our hands,' Polly grinned.

I held her tighter. 'I wouldn't give a toss about that, either. Can I kiss you now?'

She inhaled sharply. '*Yes*.'

I did.

She was warm and slightly minty, her skin deliciously smooth next to the cotton of her pyjamas.

Her fingers were creeping up under my T-shirt, cool and electric. I could feel each separate fingertip. If she got much further the T-shirt was going to have to go, and I couldn't say I was going to miss it. 'Would you...?' she murmured.

'Yes. Even if you weren't the last woman on earth...' I gave up and pulled my top off myself.

She waited for me to emerge and then said, deadpan, 'So what are we talking about?'

I started undoing her pyjama top as if I wasn't really interested. 'I don't know. Do you really...? Are you sure...?' I paused between buttons.

She nodded. 'Very.' Then she laughed, and said, 'And if it turns out to be a complete disaster... well, nobody has to know.'

'It won't,' I said. 'Probably. At least, I'm willing to risk it.'

'Me too.' She shivered. It wasn't because she was cold: she was kicking her pyjama bottoms off. 'You've been... this isn't a new idea for you, is it? I thought perhaps...'

'It's like a puzzle,' I said, inadequately. My pyjama bottoms were going the same way as Polly's and I was impressed that I was making any sense at all. 'I only put all the pieces together yesterday. But I've had them for a very long time.'

That seemed to satisfy her. She said, 'I'm glad it's not a surprise.'

'It is,' I said. 'But it's a good one. I just didn't think you could ever think of me that way. Not after everything I've done.'

She looked up at me. 'Ben,' she said, 'yesterday you risked your life for – my wellbeing.'

'Don't be ridiculous,' I protested, because I wasn't having the stakes so uneven. 'I wasn't in any danger.'

'You don't know that.'

'I would have done it anyway,' I said, 'even if I didn't... even if I didn't like you very much.'

'I know you would,' she said, seriously. 'That's why I like you. And this isn't just because of that. Or just because of anything.'

'Oh. Right. OK, then.'

That all having been cleared up, we could move forward.

'Do you have a condom?' she asked.

'Hang on.' I'd left my last box in Mélanie's room at the Grand. It had been a while since the time before that. I was pretty sure, though, that I had a box of them in the carrier bag of stuff I'd hung on to in case it turned out to be useful some day.

Some day before the use-by date. Which, when I dug them out of the bag in question, turned out to have been in August.

'Not that we can use,' I said. I chucked the useless box at the waste-paper basket. It bounced off the rim.

Polly laughed. 'Pity you didn't think to pick some up at Tesco.'

246

'I wasn't expecting...'

'I know.' She kissed me, slow and deep, which rather drew attention to the frustration of the current situation. 'I'll see if Vicki has one I can borrow.'

'Poor Vicki. First I get her bike nicked, then you sleep in her bed and steal her condoms... hang on,' I said as my brain caught up, '*Vicki*? Was she a Scout or something? Be prepared?'

Polly grinned. 'She doesn't *just* like women, you know. Though yes, I believe she was a Girl Guide.'

She went off to look, while I flopped onto my back on the bed and tried to persuade myself that since to the best of my knowledge, Vicki had, over the year I'd known her, been sleeping with a) nobody; b) Gianna; there wasn't much hope of her condoms being in date, either.

Polly looked lovely when she came back in, her face a mixture of glee and relief. She laid herself gently down on top of me and I almost thought it couldn't get better than that, running my hands up and down her sides and feeling her breath soft against the side of my neck. But I was wrong.

Chapter 30

'Polly,' I said, a little while afterwards, 'you're sure about this?'

She chuckled so gently that I felt it rather than heard it. 'Isn't it a bit late to be asking that?'

'Not that. *This*. If there is a this.'

'There could be,' she said. 'I'd like there to be.'

'You deserve better than me. You deserve more than I've got to offer you.'

'Ben,' she said, 'you are enough, and you always have been, and the minute you stop believing that you're not you'll...'

'What? Stop screwing my life up? And everyone else's?'

'Look at yourself. You *have* stopped screwing your life up. As for mine...' She broke off when my phone buzzed. Reluctantly, I stretched out a hand for it. Polly raised herself up on her elbow to free my other arm.

It was Vicki. 'Ben, are you guys OK? I saw the floods on TV. Where's Polly? She's not picking up her phone.'

'Polly's fine,' I said. 'At least, I think she is. She's right here.'

Polly was definitely fine. She had rolled onto her back and was smiling up at me, a wide, contented grin. Still, Vicki couldn't see that.

'We're above water,' I told her. 'The close is flooded at the bottom, but we're stocked up for the next few days and we're just going to wait it out. The electricity's still on. I haven't checked yet to see what else is working and what isn't.'

'The landline isn't, I'll tell you that much.'

'Isn't it? Oh, well. The main thing is, we're not going to drown and we're not going to starve.'

'So you're basically happy?'

'Never been happier.' It was true. I grinned back at Polly. 'There is one thing that I should tell you.'

'Oh?'

I wasn't looking forward to this part, but I was going to have to do it sooner or later. 'Polly forgot to pick up her prescription for... the anti-depressant I can't pronounce – so I borrowed your bike to go out and get it before we got flooded in. But somebody nicked it.'

A horrified gasp. 'They *what*? Again? What the fuck? Who would do something like that?'

'I know,' I said. 'I'm really sorry.'

Vicki's voice rose to a squeak. 'Ben, this is serious. You need to call 999.'

'999?' I was confused. Surely that was only if a theft was currently taking place.

'Get an ambulance – or an air ambulance – or *something*. The last time Polly ran out of that one she tried to kill herself.'

'*What*? Oh, no. Not the prescription. Your bike got nicked.'

There was dead silence at the other end of the line. Then Vicki laughed. 'My bike? Thank God for that.'

'Do you want to talk to Polly?' I asked. I wasn't sure I could keep it together much longer.

Polly took the phone and rolled onto her side. I pulled the duvet up around both of us, slung my arm around her, pressed my face against her back so I could hear her beating heart.

'Vic, no, really, I'm fine... Yes, well, you can tell Ben off for risking life and limb, too... No, he really did... Yes, I know, I'm a complete idiot and next time there's a flood warning I'll check everything... Don't be silly, we're both adults and we're more or less capable of looking after ourselves... OK, then... I'll see you next week.' She rang off and wriggled back round to face me.

I didn't say anything, just kissed her.

'She told you,' Polly said. 'I heard her tell you.'

I stroked the back of her neck, very gently. 'Was she exaggerating?'

'Not really.' Polly's voice was very small.

'I'm sorry,' I said.

'Maybe I should have told you.'

'It wouldn't have made any difference,' I said. I held her close. Then something occurred to me. I laughed.

'What?'

'You didn't tell her you stole her condom,' I said.

Polly raised her eyebrows. 'I wasn't sure that you'd want her to know.'

'Well, not the gory details, obviously. But I... at least, I assume... *are* we telling her?'

'Depends. If we're planning on doing this again – which, for the record, I am fully in favour of – then we should. Because otherwise the chances of her finding out some other way become increasingly high, and that gets embarrassing.'

A thought occurred to me. 'Out of interest, did she have any others?'

'A few. If the flood lasts more than a day or so we'll have to find other things to do.'

'We could do that anyway.'

'We could,' Polly agreed. 'We could.'

Quite a long time later, she said, 'Hang on a minute. You didn't know that Vicki liked men?'

'Hm?' I had not been thinking about Vicki. 'I didn't realise she liked women, until she got together with Gianna. Why do you ask?'

'Don't fish.' Polly prodded me gently in the ribs until I got what she meant. *Vicki.*

'Oh. No. If Vicki was in one of those inflatable dinghies she'd stay out there, too.' I generously equipped all the imaginary boats with imaginary food packs and blankets, and nudged Vicki's boat towards Gianna's – though I suspected that Gianna probably hadn't even realised that she had a boat. Either that, or she'd been quite happily fishing for lobsters over the side of it.

Polly sighed in a contented sort of way that made me wish the flood would last for a month, at least. She said, 'What I'll do is, I'll phone Vicki and tell her.'

'You'll phone her?'

'Yes,' she said. 'Later.'

Then she kissed me again.

Epilogue

Well, the floods went down in the end.

I'd like to say that Polly made a miraculous recovery and went back to medical school. Failing that, I'd like to say that there was never any more hassle about her benefits. I'd like to say that my parents apologised to her for being so disgustingly rude. I'd like to say that Mélanie rounded up enough of us repentant sinners to bring Henri down, and the whole rotten edifice of Grande Fino with him. I'd like to say that Vicki learned how to stop before she reached burnout stage. I'd like to say that I found a way back into the peloton.

None of that happened. Polly's allowance was withdrawn again because she missed an appointment when we were flooded, and Vicki had to write a letter in her best lawyer language to accompany the appeal. I haven't spoken to my father in months. Vicki got so horribly stressed in January that she was signed off sick for three weeks, and didn't appear to have learned anything from the experience when she went back again. And I am still alternating shifts at Benson's and the Grand.

But I've been promoted to a supervisor role at the hotel, and I've started going to college on Monday evenings, studying French, trying to get my reading and writing skills up to the level of my speaking and listening, and thinking about taking the A-level in a year or so. After that – who knows? And I'm cycling again. I've borrowed a bike from Vicki's brother until such time as I've found the money and the guts to buy my own.

I don't know where Mélanie's got to with her grand project, but I caught a glimpse of her on TV the other day, standing in a feed zone holding out a musette, and she looked happy enough.

Vicki has been promoted to a role that pays her proper money. Some of it she's saving, and the rest has been going on a power meter and a new groupset and things like that. Gianna has been getting more and more commissions through the internet, and she scored an exhibition at the local art gallery, too. The two of them are disgustingly happy despite everything. Sometimes I go out cycling with them, and I'm learning again why I loved it in the first place.

And now that Polly's stopped trying to push herself so hard, she's getting better. She's started volunteering, one morning a week, at the Citizens' Advice Bureau, and she's begun an Open University degree. She's amazing – well, I would think that, but seriously, she is. I love her.

And we got Vicki's bike back. Whoever took it, the effort of dragging it home through the floods was clearly too much for them, and they chucked it over the hedge into an old lady's back garden. I went round all the newsagents and corner shops with a 'Stolen – Reward' notice, and this Mrs Sanders saw one of them, recognised the bike as the piece of litter that had been dumped on her, and called me.

It was a mess, of course; it was coated with a thin but disgusting layer of mud, and the front wheel was a tangle of buckled spokes. I spent a month's worth of days off cleaning it up and replacing everything that needed replacing and you wouldn't know, now, what it had been through.

No, perhaps you would. But you wouldn't know what to look for, if you didn't know the story.

Also by Kathleen Jowitt

Speak Its Name

A new year at the University of Stancester, and Lydia Hawkins is trying to balance the demands of her studies with her responsibilities as an officer for the Christian Fellowship. Her mission: to make sure all the Christians in her hall stay on the straight and narrow, and to convert the remaining residents if possible. To pass her second year. And to ensure a certain secret stays very secret indeed.

When she encounters the eccentric, ecumenical student household at 27 Alma Road, Lydia is forced to expand her assumptions about who's a Christian to include radical Quaker activist Becky, bells-and-smells bus-spotter Peter, and out (bisexual) and proud (Methodist) Colette. As the year unfolds, Lydia discovers that there are more ways to be Christian – and more ways to be herself – than she had ever imagined.

Then a disgruntled member of the Catholic Society starts asking whether the Christian Fellowship is really as Christian as it claims to be, and Lydia finds herself at the centre of a row that will reach far beyond the campus. *Speak Its Name* explores what happens when faith, love and politics mix and explode.

www.kathleenjowitt.com